THE
ROCKS
OF
SCARR

JOHN A. WATSON

FT
Pbk

Matador
5 Weir Road
Kibworth Beauchamp
Leicester LE8 0LQ, UK
Tel: (+44) 116 279 2299
Fax: (+44) 116 279 2277
Email: books@troubador.co.uk
Web: www.troubador.co.uk/matador

ISBN 978 1848764 002

British Library Cataloguing in Publication Data.
A catalogue record for this book is available from the British Library.

Typeset in 11pt Sabon MT by Troubador Publishing Ltd, Leicester, UK

Printed in Great Britain by the MPG Books Group, Bodmin and King's Lynn

Matador is an imprint of Troubador Publishing Ltd

This book is dedicated to the memory of Lenny Watson, a brother who invariably put other people's interests before his own

DISCLAIMER

If there is a village called Scarr, I have never heard of it. The village in this book has sprung in its entirety from my imagination, as have the people. Any similarities between characters in the book and real individuals are entirely coincidental.

John Watson
August 2010

CHAPTER ONE

One Saturday Evening in October

(Somewhere in Southern Spain):

The short, middle-aged man drained his glass quickly. The bartender could see that it wasn't his first this evening. He'd appeared flustered when he came in, panting as if from exertion and with perspiration glistening on his dark skin, but he was starting to breathe more easily now. Paying scant attention to the pop-video booming out from the television monitor on its high shelf, the man looked around frequently as if waiting for something to happen. His first time in Spain? Yes; probably. The bartender had seen it often.

The stranger wore a good quality lounge suit and that marked him out as somewhat different from the ordinary tourist. The bulge over his left inside-pocket suggested a thick wad of banknotes. From time to time the man consulted an English-Spanish phrase-book below the level of the counter. The accent when he spoke was slight but hinted at English West Country origins.

'Yes,' the barman replied in Spanish to the man's comment, 'It *is* quiet this evening but it will be busy later on'. The man, uncomprehending, ordered another drink.

The effects of the alcohol were creeping over him but he didn't care. In two gulps he finished his third, (or was it fourth?), vino tinto since leaving the hostal and held out the glass for another. Christ, he must be careful not to let anything slip at the

Department about his experiences earlier this evening. They'd all laugh of course, but the Brass would use the information to pass him over for promotion once again. The bastards would make coded additions to his personal file marking him out as perverted, maybe even insane. They'd knock his reliability rating down to zero. An unreliable, insane pervert! He smiled.

The barman noticed it. What was going through the fool's alcohol-sodden brain? Better keep an eye on him.

*

Meanwhile, the man's memory was revisiting recent events:

He turns towards the waterfront – to see the real Spain, he tells himself. The large denomination banknote that he produces to pay for the drink makes an immediate impact. The man behind the bar speaks loudly towards the corner of the room and flourishes the money in that direction before bringing change from the till. The tourist, (that's how they'll have labelled him), doesn't understand the words but the voice inflexions say a lot. He takes the drink over to a games machine near the open door and turns to survey the scene. Two men are standing at the bar; another half-dozen sit at tables in the shadows playing some kind of card game. He can see bottles and glasses glinting even in the poor light. No holidaymakers over there.

He waits to see what's going to happen, a slight surge of adrenalin sharpening his perceptions, outwardly calm. The stocky man who approaches is about his own height; their eyes are on a level. Half as heavy again as me, thinks the tourist, and a lot of it's muscle. The black, slightly-crumpled suit, the roll-collar sweater and the tattoos on the backs of large hands, all clearly indicate 'seaman'. The tourist looks at him unconcernedly. Got to show total calmness, he's reminding himself. The volume of voices in the background has tailed away. Now there's silence. He knows they are watching; the room's filled with expectancy. But he doesn't take his eyes off the other man.

His friendly look and relaxed posture have an effect on the seaman. A faint trace of puzzlement is not missed by the tourist who smiles benignly and says 'Hello'.

'You America?' The voice is rasping.

The tourist pauses. 'Well, England perhaps'.

'You holiday here?'

'Yes'. Then, with a strong hint of admiration, 'You speak very good English!'

The seaman's face shows that he's trying to find a response to the compliment; probably never had one before. 'I spik dem all,' he says finally, sticking his chest out.

Frank admiration continues to shine from the tourist's face and he smiles again. That extended summer job long ago in Marseille – not the first time the experience has come in useful. He'd felt confident of handling this situation and is now starting to enjoy the interaction. 'You live here?' he asks amiably.

The seaman is trying unsuccessfully to hide his nervousness as things continue to slip out of his control. His large hands clench at his sides.

The tourist drains his glass slowly, his eyes regarding the other man over the rim. He knows that they've never shown the merest flicker of doubt. The seaman's got to make a move now or he's blown it. They all know it. He begins to feel sorry for him, toys with the idea of offering him a drink so they'd think he got it by menaces. But no; that might open up something too difficult to handle. He smiles pleasantly once again.

The seaman turns at last, slowly, and starts back towards his companions. The local hard-man? A braggart challenged to tackle the money-flashing stranger? Surely both of these. He'll find it hard to explain his failure.

The tourist places his empty glass on the games machine and, winking at the painted blonde waiting patiently by the doorpost, strolls into the dirty, dark street. Round the corner, where they can't see him, he sprints some two hundred metres and, after listening and panting for a few seconds, continues at a fast walking pace. There's bound to be a more welcoming place

3

closer to the town centre. He giggles to himself as he searches for one.

Ah! Perhaps this'll be better. He hears the loud, expatriate-cockney voice summoning the few early-evening passers-by to enter 'The Club', promising drinks and girls inside. Oh well, just one glass; see what it's like. He tries to pretend to himself that the word 'girls' has nothing to do with his decision.

In contrast to the waterfront establishment, this is a very small room. A bar runs from one side to the other – on a shelf behind it, a mere half dozen bottles of spirits. A wine-cask stands at the end of the counter. He orders a glass of vino. Rejecting the barman's insistent demand that he pay for it with a credit card, he pushes a handful of coins across the counter. The drink is nearly finished when he's aware of the girl at his shoulder.

'Will you buy a drink for me?' She talks to him in perfect English.

The tourist inspects her. 'Yes', he says, catches the barman's eye, nods at the cask and holds up two fingers.

She's about twenty. Her face is stunningly beautiful in its frame of glossy black hair. The skin-tight trousers and half-unbuttoned blouse offer the promise of a body to match. She stands close, her shoulder and hip against him. He can't help turning his head and looking down the inside of her blouse; she's fully aware of it. Their eyes meet and they both laugh. She feels for his hand and, undoing another button, places it on her bare chest. He's holding a very firm, very warm breast. Her body radiates fitness. He rolls the hard nipple between thumb and forefinger. She gives a pained little squeak and he pulls her towards him, puts his forehead against hers and sucks air loudly through his teeth in sympathy. She resists his pull at first – he can feel how strong she is – but then relaxes. They move apart and smile at each other.

'Come upstairs,' she says quietly, 'and I will do things for you'. She mutters something in Spanish to the man behind the bar who shakes his head firmly.

4

'You mean sex?' asks the tourist who's beginning to regret wandering into something that could severely damage his career.

'Not sex, but – things.'

A young man comes through the curtains at the bottom of the stairs. He glances at them briefly, sheepishly, and hurries out. A very thin, almost grotesquely made-up blond woman has entered the room behind him. She eyes the tourist and smiles, showing gaps that look like they've been painted on. Her bare feet, with blue toenails, peep from beneath a long, green-silk dressing gown.

The tourist swallows the last of his drink and turns away. 'Sorry', he says. 'I've got to go now'. At the door, he turns briefly towards the brunette and smiles. She smiles back and shrugs her shoulders. He is sure that the empathy is genuine.

He leaves The Club followed by the woman in the dressing gown. She pursues him for some distance along the street, repeating something over and over in a cooing voice and flashing her awful grin. He can still hear her as he hurries round the corner.

*

The dozy customer dragged himself back from his reverie. The barman, still trying to assess how drunk he was, saw him sit erect and look around again.

At last! Something was happening. Two youngish German women were sitting at a table by the window, chattering and laughing over glasses of Sangria. A plump, elderly lady had seated herself opposite the tourist, on the far side of the horseshoe bar. Two Pekinese dogs sat on her lap, their heads on the counter, watching him. He bought all of the humans a drink. The stout lady thanked him in English with a strong Welsh accent. She lived in Spain permanently now and never thought of going back to Britain. The barman was her son. Oh no, not Spanish; just doesn't let on to the customers. The barman joined in the conversation, addressing him as 'Hey you, Jock' in a pretend Scottish accent.

The video was louder now. The bass notes, which had first attracted him from two streets away, could be felt penetrating the whole building. He was aware of someone dancing. A dirty-looking man in a thick black overcoat tied round the waist with string, trousers tucked into socks, was gyrating round the floor in time to the music. With his worn-out trainers performing a flurry of intricate steps, he disappeared through a door at the back of the room. The tourist accepted a drink from the lady opposite, the dogs still staring suspiciously. And then the dancer was back with a large overfilled garbage bin on his shoulder. He did some more fancy footwork on his way out into the alley.

The effects of the alcohol were becoming extreme. In the act of ordering yet another vino, the tourist saw the distance between himself and the barman increasing as he floated backwards off his stool. Picked up by the collar and seat of the trousers, he offered no resistance as he was dumped in the street.

*

He woke up to find himself being dragged from a municipal cactus bed by two armed policemen. His still-scrambled perception assumed that they were demanding to know what the hell he was up to and he made haste to tell them that he was Inglés. The long-suffering look exchanged by the men suggested that that was a plausible explanation. He fumbled for his driver's licence and the card with the name and address of the hostal, but suspected that the policemen were still less than satisfied and considering their next move.

'No habla Espanol', he said, pointing to the card. 'Hostal?' He raised his eyebrows and made a sweeping gesture with his hand. To his relief, the officer with the pistol pointed him down a narrow street and sent him on his way with a shove. With his mind clearing some more, he progressed by leaning forward at a steep angle. Hs legs, powered by the energy of the alcohol, moved rapidly to keep up. Soon he was totally relaxed again, enjoying his journey in automatic mode through the deserted streets. It crossed his mind that this was strange, that he would have expected Spanish streets to be thronged with revellers at this time of night. What time was it? Hell! His watch was gone. Well, fuck the time! No sign yet of that bloody hostal. He had no idea of where he was and he didn't really care much. However, another effect of the binge was becoming more and more pressing.

'Por favor, Senor,' he'd say when he met someone. 'Dónde es el lavabo caballeros?' He thought that's what the phrase-book said. But there wasn't a Senor to be seen and nature couldn't wait for one. There had to be somewhere ... . A narrow alleyway was the only possibility. Quickly now! He struggled with an awkward zip, leaning against a door for support.

With a loud crack, the door flew inwards and he staggered across the floor of a dimly-lit room. He held his breath. There was no sound in the house. Now, there must be a lavatory. There was, and he found it just in time – well, nearly just in time. By God, that was better. He realised that he was hungry and thirsty – very thirsty. The kitchen of course...

He woke up to a blaze of lights and a racket of voices. On his back on a sofa, he looked up at three strangers. The very large man was waving an empty bottle and glass, his face red with anger. His bottle! His glass! The small, furious woman, uttering a torrent of Spanish in which the word 'ladrón' was repeated over and over, struck his feet off her sofa. The blubbering child was looking in disbelief at a handful of biscuit wrappers.

'Christ,' the burglar told himself loudly, 'you're in the shit now, Danny boy'. His mind searching for answers was finding only irrelevances. Then, from out of the tumbling stream of disconnected data, came a vision of how Goldilocks had coped when she, too, found herself in the shit. The large man, galvanised by the burglar's hysterical laugh, sprang towards the telephone. The way to the door was clear. Three bounds and the ladrón was gone, echoes of his irregular steps chasing him down the empty streets.

*

(Norfolk, England):

Concentration gone, Archibald McSpake closed his notepad and lobbed another screwed up page towards the bin. He missed, as usual. Earlier, he'd convinced himself he was sufficiently motivated to scribble a first draft but all he'd produced was a title, the single word 'Scarr'. Oh well – the bloody poem would keep. The idea was promising enough but, once again, his mood was the problem. What he needed now was a shower, a glass of wine, – better make that a bottle, – and bed. Sleep was increasingly elusive these days and he found himself resorting to more frequent, and larger, boozy nightcaps. Aged sixty one, but starting to feel older, he knew that the underlying problem was the unaccustomed sameness of his existence. Retirement was much less attractive from this side of the fence. The mid-winter break in Florida might help but wasn't scheduled for another two months. He needed to do something now to tackle the depression and chronic lack of motivation that threatened to cripple him. Could he drag himself away from here? He bloody well had to before it became not worth the effort.

Some ten minutes later, on his way downstairs from bathroom to kitchen, McSpake halted, startled by loud knocking at the front door. Who the hell … ? The hall clock showed two minutes to midnight.

'Careful now, Archie,' he muttered and took several slow, deep breaths.

The knocking began again, louder and more persistently, but accompanied this time by a distinctly female voice – though you couldn't *always* be sure these days. He'd left his hearing aid in the kitchen, so the actual words were unclear. If you happen to be a retired spy living alone on a lonely stretch of coast, you will understand the caution with which McSpake approached the door, (an apparently ordinary door that enclosed two sheets of toughened steel), to check out his mysterious late-night visitors. He saw, with irritation, that he'd forgotten to reconnect the link

8

between his digital-stills camera and the security system. Hurriedly plugging the camera into its external battery pack, he switched it on. The viewing screen came to life slowly, giving a wide-angle view of the front yard. An empty sports-car was parked just inside the gate and he captured an image of the scene. A woman stood in the foreground, her face shaded from the light by the hood of a duffel coat. As he zoomed in, the camera readjusted its focus and exposure settings and he took a shot of her face. She did look vaguely familiar but he still felt the need for caution. He slid open the recess at the back of the hall-stand where he kept his late-father's old Walther P.38, removed the weapon from its makeshift case and dropped it into his dressing gown pocket.

Throughout his whole career, McSpake had tried not to leave anything to chance. Now, the weight of the pistol against his thigh was as reassuring as ever. More shouting from the visitor tailed away as he slid the three heavy bolts and opened the door.

It was only when the woman threw back her hood and said 'Hello Archie,' that he recognised Fractal, the daughter of his one-time colleague, Ernest Mandelbrot. Archie hadn't seen her since Ernest's funeral. She'd been at college then. That was more than twenty years ago. In the meantime, the shy young Fractal had changed into this confident woman who was drifting past him, trailing the subtlest sensation of perfume. As if it were an afterthought, she turned and planted a firm kiss on his cheek and he suddenly became aware that his visitor's self-confidence was a sham.

'Aren't you going to take my coat? Here you are. Are you on your own? Good, because I need to ask your help with a problem. I would have contacted you in advance but I believe I'm being watched. They're bound to be listening in on my phone calls as well'. Yes; Fractal was clearly under considerable stress.

'I'm not with you. What are you talking about? Who's watching you? Let's go through here, into the kitchen. Have a glass of wine'.

Archie opened the white Rioja and reached for a bottle of

the red as an afterthought. This could be an interesting night if he managed the situation well. Mmm. Perhaps. But don't rush things too much

'Are you sure you wouldn't like something stronger?' he asked. 'A glass of brandy, or a malt whisky?' Fractal nodded.

Archie went for a bottle of Glenscarr and poured his guest a measure, his optimism soaring. 'Relax if you can,' he said, 'and tell me who you think is watching you. And what's this problem you want to talk to me about without *them* finding out?'

'It began last month when I was approached by the Newton Mental Health Unit. I sometimes do outpatient counselling for them on a part-time contract. Recently, they'd had a most interesting referral; a boy who claimed he'd travelled off with aliens to a planet called – ah – Karos. He insisted that he hadn't been abducted but had gone willingly with the – um – beings. He gave a detailed and coherent account of the week that he was missing from home. No matter how often, or in what manner, he was questioned, nobody was able to trip him up. Was he *really* confabulating? I don't think so. The consultant psychiatrist said that, earlier, the boy had produced a small metal cube claiming that it was a *Communicator* given to him by one of the aliens so that he could keep in touch with them. It had been passed on by Doctor Ross to the Ministry of Defence and someone there had decided to retain it on the grounds that it fell from a secret test-aircraft flying over Newton.

'I'm to be involved in the boy's therapy, but that'll take a couple of weeks to fit into the Unit's schedules. In the meantime, they've agreed with his mother's suggestion that a change of scene will do him good. I'm not happy about it, but Doctor Ross thinks that his home environment is a major factor in the boy's problems and that a week or so at his grandparents' smallholding in Scotland may benefit him. The boy himself is keen to go.'

Fractal paused to finish her whisky. Archie reached for the bottle again but she placed her hand over the glass and pointed at the white Rioja. He poured each of them a good measure of the wine – his own imperceptibly the lesser of the two – and then, smiling encouragement, leaned forward to emphasize his curiosity.

'Well, Archie, the boy's story had been so consistent that I persuaded myself there must be some truth in it. So I got in touch with a local U.F.O. study group to ask what they could tell me about people who claimed they'd been abducted by aliens. Their secretary put me in touch with a writer on the subject. After a lot of questioning about my motives, the author, Guy, introduced me in strict secrecy to a government scientific adviser. She gave me enough information to make me realise the boy ought to be monitored carefully. I had to agree that my informant should remain anonymous and that any facts I uncovered would be passed back to her.

'Now, here come the strangest and most worrying parts of the situation: the scientist seemed already to know quite a lot about the boy and his immediate family and also that his grandparents live on the edge of a village called Scarr. Clearly there was something more that wasn't being shared with me. When I looked into the matter, I found that this village, by some strange coincidence, is reputed to be what's called a *hotspot* for – ah – Anomalous Aerial Phenomena. I'm so anxious about the boy's welfare that I've even considered giving up work to go and keep an eye on him. But other people at the Unit are depending on me. And, d'you know, I've experienced such odd happenings since I started making my enquiries, that I'm sure someone's watching me. Then I thought of you Archie, (you are retired, aren't you?), and remembered that my Dad once told me you came from that part of the country. Would you – could you – possibly – stand in for me? Keep an eye on the lad while he's in Scotland? Please, Archie!'

Fractal lowered her head and regarded him, wide-eyed from under long lashes. Archie, delighted by the signal and by this opportunity to get away and do something interesting, pretended to ponder. He refilled her glass from what remained of the white Rioja, dribbling the last few drops into his own. He did not tell her, and intended not to tell her until he'd thought more about the probability involved, that even stranger 'coincidences' had arisen. For example, he, Archibald Alfred McSpake, had been born in Scarr and had had his early education in its village school. And then there was that bloody poem about the place that he'd been trying to launch before she arrived.

'Let's consider the ramifications of what you're asking, Fractal. I've got some maps of the area in my study. Help yourself to another glass of wine while I pop up and get them. That red, by the way, is excellent.'

Archie stood up, turned the whisky bottle round to hide its label, and left the room.

'Maps and condoms,' he muttered on his way upstairs. He was unaware that, behind him, Fractal was tipping her last drink down the kitchen sink followed by most of the Rioja bottle's contents.

*

(Town of Newton, North of London):

Farther along the street a light came on briefly in the Wilsons' lounge, silhouetting the two occupants of an unlit car parked at the kerb. Marco had last seen it on the other side of the road when he came up to bed. There was always a strange vehicle in the street these days, although it was standing outside a different house every time he looked. He closed the curtains to a small chink, knowing that the watchers would be unable to see him in the darkness of the room – unless they were using one of those military night-vision things.

He went back to bed, sure that he wouldn't be able to sleep. His mother planned to set off early so they'd avoid heavy morning traffic on their way to the M1 Motorway. He'd be glad to get away from here. Scotland was a long way off and he hoped the mysterious watchers wouldn't follow. There was no doubt that they were trying to get the second metal cube. Doctor Ross had admitted giving the other one to the military people. He didn't trust Doctor Ross at all. Restless, he got out of bed again to check that the remaining cube was still in his backpack. It was. When he and his mother came home from the shops on Friday, he'd noticed that someone had been in his room. The signs, though very slight, were obvious to him. He had no doubt what the intruders were looking for. Good job he'd put it in his pocket before leaving the house. His mother, as usual, had dismissed fears of intruders and of watchers in the street, just as she'd dismissed everything he had tried to tell her about his trip to Karos. Only Miss Mandelbrot at the hospital had been willing to listen to what he had to say. He suspected that she believed him. Why couldn't others be so open-minded?

*

(Scarr Village in Northern Scotland):

The Reverend Solomon Stackpoole, (known to some as 'Slugpole'), was putting the finishing touches to next day's sermon. He hadn't composed it personally; he'd acquired it during his days in the American Mid West. All of the sermons he delivered in Scarr Kirk had the same origin. He simply changed and fine-tuned them to meet the requirements of any situation in which he found himself. He could write blistering tirades when he chose, but didn't see any reason to waste his talents on the folk of the village. The preferred target for his personal work was the small congregation of the exclusive and highly-secret chapel in Portlach.

At last the minister was ready for tomorrow and, pouring himself a large whisky, he tilted back the reclining armchair in which it was his habit to sleep nowadays – when he was unfortunate enough to be on his own. He relaxed weary muscles, sighed, and shut his eyes. He hoped that he'd dream again about the two eager 'nuns' who used to spice up his sex-life before he'd been obliged to quit New York.

*

At about the time that the 'Man From The Ministry' was running along a still-deserted Spanish street, Marc Powell, Archie

13

McSpake and Fractal P. Mandelbrot were getting into beds, (the last two into the same bed), and the Reverend Mr. Stackpoole was reaching out to drop his empty glass onto the study carpet. For the minister at least, it was just a typical Saturday night.

**

CHAPTER TWO

The Following Day: Sunday

(Southern Spain):

Daniel O'Donnel, head bursting from last night's binge, arrived several minutes late at the designated meeting place – a long-disused tailor's shop in Algeciras. He found that his contact, 'Hassan', had already swept the place for concealed observation devices. Hassan's new information was to be strictly verbal so notes, written or electronic, were forbidden. Any leak on this operation could negate many months of painstaking investigation and put Hassan and others in danger. As soon as Hassan had finished passing on the itemised data, he paused and offered to repeat it one more time. Daniel declined the offer. He was proud of his 'Memory Man' label. This title was often repeated by colleagues in the office when he was within earshot; he knew very well, of course, what they called him in his absence.

Task completed, the Moroccan agent made a hurried exit through the back door. Daniel waited for fifteen minutes, picked up his flight bag and left by the front. Reverting once more to tourist-mode, he spent a few seconds scanning a travel brochure and regarding surrounding features. Then, apparently satisfied, he locked the door and posted the key back through the letterbox. He walked along several streets, until he found a car-hire business open and managed to persuade a tired driver to take him to the railway station. On the way, he double checked his transport schedule for the time of the next train to Malaga. He had hours to kill before the evening flight and was beginning to feel thirsty. He would have a couple of glasses of vino tinto in the city by way of lunch, followed by a taxi ride to the airport where a nap on a bench until departure time would suit him fine.

*

(M1 Motorway, England):

At Leeds, Jenny Powell and her son left the Motorway for a break and a hot meal. Their previous fuel stop, at a very busy service station, had become alarming for the boy and annoying for his mother when a black limousine pulled in directly behind them. Their now-habitual 'Yes it is!' – 'No it's not!' argument had restarted and become increasingly bitter until both lapsed into resentful silence. Jenny was now having serious doubts about the wisdom of this Scotland interlude. As she drove off from Leeds, her son reverted to his sitting-sideways posture to watch the traffic behind. Each time a dark coloured vehicle moved to overtake them, he crouched down in an attempt to be inconspicuous. Jenny, with her teeth clenched, didn't trust herself to comment. Finally, as they passed under the River Tyne east of Newcastle, Marco fell asleep – a consequence, no doubt, of their early start. When they crossed the Scottish border beyond Berwick on Tweed, he was oblivious to the fact.

*

(Birch Cottage, Scarr):

As the Smiths relaxed after Sunday lunch, a squeak from the rarely-used front gate drew Bob to the window.

'Quick, Bessie. Switch off the tele. Slugpole's coming up the path. Get down!'

Footsteps crunched on the gravel and heavy knocking shook the front door. On their knees, Bob and Bessie faced each other behind the sofa, both worried that the unwelcome visitor might spot some evidence of their presence in the house. Nell, though totally deaf, was alerted to the threat from an interloper by the humans' behaviour. Vibration indicated that the front door was the site of attack, so she went scrabbling along the hallway to mount a defence. Once more the door shook under the minister's assault and Nell leaped at it. Bouncing awkwardly on arthritic hind legs, she clawed at the letterbox, barking as hard as aged lungs allowed.

'Shush doggie!' boomed the intruder. 'Shush now.'

There was a long pause, the Smiths hoping that the man was leaving. But the Reverend Stackpoole didn't give up readily on any task, most especially the task of wheedling money from people's wallets and purses for 'Church Funds'.

'What if he looks in at the window, Bob? If he sees that whisky bottle on the sideboard he won't leave.'

Bob considered dashing across to hide the bottle, but he found dashing a much harder activity nowadays. Though the Malt Whisky label was not an accurate description of the bottle's contents, Slugpole wouldn't know that. Bob, having discovered early in life that many people couldn't discriminate between the cheapest supermarket stuff and the real thing, had opted to replace the latter with the former for most occasions. On a previous visit, the minister had swirled the bogus malt round his glass, sniffed, sipped and smacked his lips. There was no beating the real Glenscarr, he'd assured Bob. Once you'd tasted it, nothing else would satisfy a connoisseur.

The crunch of footsteps on gravel removed the smile from Bob's face. He and Bessie tried to wriggle into as small a space as possible and they waited anxiously for the minister's next sally. And it came, louder and more prolonged and certain, they believed, to shatter the window pane.

'Mr. and Mrs. Smith!' bellowed the man. 'Are you there? Yes, I know you are. Bob, Bessie, I've come all the way up from the manse specially to see you. It's important. Can you let me in?' Getting no reply, he knocked with increasing force and then returned to the front door. He opened the letterbox flap and shouted, 'Yoo-hoo!'

At this first sight of the enemy, Nell leaped forward with a snarl. Her jaws snapped shut an inch from the man's nose. The flap dropped. For a short time the only sound was of Nell's growling. The Smiths were beginning to feel optimistic until Bessie remarked, 'I haven't heard his feet going down the path. What do you think he … ? Oh! The back door! He probably thinks … .'

Bob suddenly overcame his reluctance to move quickly. Half crouching, and with gritted teeth, he propelled himself across the room. His hand had nearly reached the knob when the opening door struck his head and shoulder. Stunned for a moment, he looked uncomprehendingly at the grinning face of the Reverend Stackpoole.

'Good gracious, Mr. Smith, have you been drinking? And what's Mrs. Smith doing behind the settee? Having a bit of the old Richard and Frances, were we?'

Bob pulled himself together sufficiently to signal 'Sit!!' to Nell who, growing tired of an unresponsive letter-flap, had returned to the room. She exposed her teeth in a soundless snarl. Bessie, red faced, explained that she'd dropped a pound coin, 'the only money in the house', behind the sofa.

'I'm surprised that you didn't hear me knocking. Perhaps the doggie barking? But I knew you were in. I've a kind of sixth sense for that sort of thing – unless the Good Lord is sending me messages. Haw, haw, haw! Is that the sublime Glenscarr on the sideboard?'

*

(McSpake's House, Norfolk):

After a late lunch of toast and scrambled eggs, Fractal headed her car southwards and a rather tired Archie walked down to the shore with his old beach-casting rod and some frozen peeler-crabs in a bait-tin. He needed time to think about the task that his new best friend had persuaded him to undertake. Things had gone nearly as well as he'd hoped last night. Anyway, he'd always found a deserted shore the ideal place for problem analysis.

Bird watching, (he thought they called it 'twitching' but he'd need to check that), was a possible cover. Childhood memories aside, birds weren't something he knew much about and overt ignorance might give him away. Could he perhaps pass himself off as a recently retired something-or-other trying out a new hobby? That seemed a plausible excuse for arriving at an exposed northern coast long after the tourist season had ended. Sea birds were, or had been, plentiful in the Scarr area and there would probably be migrants fleeing colder northern locations by this time of year. The more he thought about the birdwatcher plan, the more acceptable it became. It would enable him to wander at will, to use binoculars and to take notes.

Tomorrow he'd make all the arrangements. A trip to town to find a definitive manual on bird recognition would be a wise start. At the same time he could call at the repair shop to collect his car – if they'd fixed it yet. The mechanic, Ossie Harbottle, could give him a report on that if he was at the pub this evening.

The journey to Aberdeen and places north would need to be under way by Tuesday morning at the very latest. He had no problems regarding luggage; the second floor box-room offered plenty of choice from a lifetime's travel. But what the hell would a bird watcher wear? Archie was old enough to remember when outdoor hobbies were occasions for ordinary people to wear clapped-out everyday clothes, but now everyone seemed to conform to various dress-up rules. Image was important, ability less so. There was that group he'd seen in the Lake District last May. Quite clearly they were urbanites to whom the countryside was an alien place known only from lifestyle magazines. To amuse himself, and to practise some of his old skills, he'd kept them under surveillance for a whole morning. They'd spent their time walking around the streets of Windermere, dressed as if to climb Everest. But the only climbing they had done was up the steps of a café where they'd sweated over a mountain of cream-scones, washing them down with dainty cups of tea. Archie laughed loudly and looked round to make sure there was nobody within earshot. He supposed that he too would have to dress in a manner that supported his assumed persona. Must make sure he got the right gear – whatever that was. Doing Fractal a favour could be costly. She'd better make it up to him later, one way or another.

In the meantime, those were young herring gulls flying north and that was a cormorant, (or was it a shag?), on the end of the southern sand-spit. Words came readily to mind from a longish, unfashionably rhymed poem that he'd written last summer. There was a bit in it about diving-birds holding out their wings to dry. He had worried about possible adverse reactions by readers to the words 'shags on stony banks', but 'cormorants' didn't fit the rhythm of the piece. In any case, he didn't have any readers – hadn't yet attempted to air his verse in public.

When he'd retired from work and tried to revive his childhood interest in poetry, he'd found that values had changed. Poetry had swung away completely from classical rhyme and metre. He'd quickly realised that the High Priests of the obfuscation referred to as 'Contemporary Verse', wouldn't approve of the stuff *he* wrote – even if they could force themselves to swallow it without vomiting. (Archie recalled a group of children on a school outing gagging at the taste of fruit and vegetables served up to them in place of the 'fast' food to which they'd become habituated).

The unwritten rules of the verse-oracles were clearly infringed by rhyme. There seemed also to be a growing predilection for 'subtlety' of rhythm. To Archie and, he was quite sure, to the bulk of the population, this subtlety was often so rigorously contrived as to make its presence imperceptible. Vested interests were so insistent in their demands for the (inherently superior) contemporary verse that dissenters were gagged by publishers. He was sure that, if poetry were left to market forces alone, pretentiousness would shrivel markedly. For the present, prizes were being awarded so as to reinforce prejudiced perceptions of academic worth, – awarded to some really awful drivel. He had once transcribed a prize-winning poem – by leaving out its nonsensical line and verse placements – into a piece of contorted prose. Only one of the friends to whom he'd shown it thought it 'might' be poetry trying to explore unprocessed impressions.

And what had happened to creativity? How could creativity

have become shackled by the dictates of self-appointed 'experts'? Why did people allow themselves to be ushered sheep-like into irrational value systems? Could no one perceive the obvious – that this contemporary verse stuff had taken on all the characteristics of a minor religion? That the means employed by its academic High Priests, and their acolytes, bore a fair resemblance to the conformist demands of religious zealots? Archie, abandoning himself completely to this trend of thought, was certain that the verse dictators' reactions to criticism would be the same as those of committed priests whose 'only true religion' is being attacked, – i.e. rationalization. Attempts to engage them in logical and unshackled discussion of their certainties, would be manoeuvred into channels of intellectualization where they would feel less threatened. If you insisted on pursuing them there, demanded facts and challenged unfounded supposition, rage would inevitably ensue.

He had once been confronted by a church minister in a state of near-uncontrollable fury when trying to clarify the man's irrationality for him. He was certain that he had read hate and murderous intent in the man's eyes and body posture. Not what most people would expect from a clergyman. Archie breathed heavily then laughed at the thought of some enraged 'poet' raining blows on him – with great subtlety of rhythm.

The more irrational the value system, the greater the determination of its proponents that others accept it without question. McSpake's First Law of Exploitation of the Gullible. Archie hurled handfuls of stones towards the horizon. He was well aware of the element of stereotyping in his position but he was also aware of its good sense. It was a position arrived at through the application of logic, he assured himself, as opposed to tame acceptance of dogma.

Many people were oblivious to, or rejected, the fact that the number of aspiring poets far exceeded the number of those with the talent to perform the task adequately. In today's instant-fame culture, however, talent was less relevant than willingness to display one's inadequacies in the increasingly mediocre media.

He believed, (with fingers crossed irrationally), that poetry publishers were undermining their own enterprises. In order to find sufficient content for their booklets and magazines they were being forced to publish stuff so dire that no down-to-earth reader would give it house room. Just how many verbally-challenged arseholes would be going around calling themselves 'Poets' before the Contemporary Verse cloak crumbled and exposed them to the world's ridicule? Amused by his obscene metaphor, Archie imagined himself delivering it in a thundering voice to – well – to people. That is if he remembered it. It needed to be written down before it vanished into the chaotic box-room of once-important musings.

He was starting to consider the role of politically-correct poetry tutors unable, or too afraid, to tell students that they were producing bilge, (if, indeed, they even recognised it as such), when a slight twitch of his line indicated possible interest from a fish. He picked up the rod, his pulse-rate increasing. Holding the line gently between index and middle fingers, he tried to sense what was happening at the business end of the trace. But there was no further movement. Perhaps a small whiting had taken a fragment of the bait in passing. It was more likely, though, that the strong current scouring through the gully eighty metres out had washed a piece of weed against the line. He put down the rod.

Now where was he? He had let his irritation with today's so-called poetry distract him from the urgent need to plan the Scarr expedition. He'd need to check if there was still a hotel in the village. Once, there had been the moderately upmarket Bay House Hotel, favoured by summer visitors. Even better, from a local resident's perspective, had been the old Lobster Creel. Archie had often relaxed in front of its log-fires on winter nights in the nineteen fifties, listening to very old men in leathery skins and cheese-cutter caps telling and retelling exaggerated stories of voyages round the Horn at the turn of the century. He could remember some of their tales even now, although the faces of the tellers had faded into the mists of antiquity.

The tip of the rod dipped and line streamed out silently. Archie grabbed the tackle, flicked the reel into gear and wound hard into what felt like a good cod. He had really come out here to think, hardly expecting to catch anything but, if he landed it, this one might make an acceptable item to trade for a lift to town. It took him more than five minutes to beach the well-fed fish in the strong tide – a beautifully mottled seven-pound specimen. He threw the remaining peeler crabs into the water and, wiping his hands on a wet rag, plodded back up the deserted beach.

It was getting colder now and the sea behind him was taking on a leaden greyness in the late afternoon light. He lengthened his stride along the lane. A cup of strong coffee beckoned.

*

(Birch Cottage; Night):

The lights of a car coming round the curve in the road picked out the skull on the bookshelf. Its shadow stretched as it accelerated along the wall. When it reached the corner of the room, it disappeared. Marco wasn't bothered by it. He knew the skull was made of plastic. It had a slot at the top for putting in money and a trapdoor underneath for taking it out when you decided you'd rather spend it after all. Gran had told him that Uncle Bill got it one birthday many years ago when they lived in Essex.

But Marco couldn't sleep. He was far too tense, his mind busy struggling to make sense of his parents' problems. When his mother had stopped the car at Stonehaven so they could stretch their legs and have a cup of tea, she'd confirmed that the divorce was to go ahead. He recalled how Dad, when he came back from Australia with his broken leg in a plaster-cast, had moved into the spare bedroom. When the cast came off, he'd stayed there. The two of them rarely talked to each other when Marco was around. When they thought he wasn't, they argued almost all the time. He always wanted to shout at them to stop being so bloody stupid. But he hadn't been able to; he just didn't know how to handle the situation.

Oh well, it had all been decided now. This weekend, Dad was moving into a flat on the other side of town – to be nearer to his work, he'd said. Mum would remain at the house and Marco would continue to stay with her. He kept asking himself if his disappearance during the summer had played a part in their separation, but he couldn't be sure. One thing both his parents had agreed on was that there wasn't a planet called Karos and, therefore, he couldn't have been there. Marco had tried repeatedly to convince them that Karos was what the Karosians called their planet, so the fact that people on Earth hadn't heard of it didn't prove that it didn't exist. But the two of them just couldn't see the sense of his argument.

Again the lights of a passing car lit up the skull and again its shadow raced towards the corner. It disappeared at the same spot as before. Marco closed his eyes.

All that carry-on when he came back! The examination by the police surgeon and his admission to Newton Hospital had been annoying and embarrassing. He'd been questioned and prodded and poked and stuck with needles and X-Rayed. They had tested his blood, his urine, his reflexes and everything else they could think of. They'd even got him to shit in a container so they could take it away for some kind of inspection. When they hadn't been able to find anything wrong with him physically, they had, at last, started to listen. But that had led to his transfer to the children's ward at the Mental Health Unit. The only good things to come from all that nonsense were that he'd probably be off school until after Christmas and that, for a week or more, he'd be staying with Gran and Granda Smith here at Birch Cottage.

Again – a light; again – the moving shadow. This was a nuisance! Marco got up to pull the curtains but found them too narrow to close the gap. Well, no problem. He took down the skull from the shelf, put it in the cupboard of his bedside cabinet and returned to bed. Now perhaps he'd sleep. He tried to relax all of his body, starting with the feet, then the ankles, lower legs, knees … But he was still wide-awake. What if one of those vehicles passing the cottage was the big black car with the strange watchers? No; they wouldn't know he was here. They wouldn't, would they?

Once again headlights shone through the gap in the curtains. Again the shadow of the skull traversed the wall. Again it disappeared near the corner. Shadow? Skull? The skull was in the cupboard! Marco sat upright and saw that the door was wide open.

'Maaam!' He started out of bed putting his hand on the cabinet top. It felt very warm. An acrid odour was filling the room.

'Graandaa! Graan!' He ran for the door and stopped. Shadows were moving in the corridor. As he drew breath to yell again, the shadows changed into his grandparents.

'Now, now; what's wrong?'

'Granda. The skull! I put it in the locker and its shadow was still moving. And the door opened itself. And the cabinet's hot. And I can smell something.'

His mother had arrived, wide-eyed with alarm. 'Marc! It's your imagination again. You know what Doctor Ross said. You have to stop this.'

'No, look!' Marco pointed to the shadow which, though much fainter in the glow of the night-lamp, pursued the same course as before. 'I told you.'

Bob switched on the main ceiling light; Bessie went to the window and lifted a vase from the ledge. It held a single paper flower.

'That's where your shadow came from. You see? Don't worry. Try to sleep mow.'

'But the cabinet was hot and I can still feel the smell.'

Bob put his hand on the surface and took it away quickly, surprise on his face. He pulled the drawer open, looked, sniffed and poked in a finger. 'There. I've fixed it. You should know not to leave a powerful old radio in a closed space without switching it off.'

'But I'm sure I did,' said Marco, looking into the drawer. 'I remember -. Oh no! I think maybe -'.

'You must have turned the sound down and then forgotten

the radio was still on. See the holes in the back? The air couldn't circulate through them in the drawer, so it's been getting hotter and hotter. We're lucky you haven't started a fire.'

'I'm sorry, Granda. I didn't think.'

'You either don't think or your imagination runs away with you, Marc. You're always at one extreme or the other.' His mother was ranting again. 'Right then, back to bed now and let's have no more of this nonsense. We'll leave the door as it is. When I opened it earlier to see if you were all right, I thought you were sleeping.'

But soon they were all laughing as Bob made a show of carrying off the partly-melted radio in a bucket held at arm's length. He took the skull with him.

'Good night, Dear.' His mother's voice had softened.

'Goodnight Mum. Goodnight Gran, Granda.'

Although still embarrassed, Marco was relaxing. How could he have been so careless and so silly? And yet, that big car was worrying. He kept his eyes on the wall, waiting for the next vehicle to come along the road – just to be sure. Yes, there it was and no shadow.

*

(Bay House Hotel, Scarr):

The Reverend Stackpoole was the last customer to leave the hotel's public bar, just as he had been every Sunday night since coming to the village. That was nearly four years ago. He paused on the top step to inhale the smells of the sea and then strolled across to the crates of empty bottles piled in the corner of the yard. He urinated over them, shivering with pleasure at the sensation of icy air on his genitals. Zipping up, his eyes were drawn towards Whitescar Cottage away over by the sand dunes. A dim light showed briefly in one of the gable-end windows. The witches were up to something tonight. There'd been a lot of activity over there lately and they seemed untroubled by whether it was day or night. He was tempted to walk across to see what was going on. The last time he'd done that, he had observed the younger of the two silhouetted against the bathroom light. Not bad. Not bad. She must be well into her fifties but, witch or not, he wouldn't mind sharing a bath with her. Tonight, however, he didn't feel that the pleasure of watching would justify the effort involved. Something else was on his mind and he hurried along Shore Road to its junction with Scarr Brae.

When he turned the corner and mounted the steep slope towards the kirk, he was confronted by a nearly-full moon in the cloudless southern sky. The brilliant light turned the village into a cubist sculpture in black, silver and intermediate shades of monochrome. But the minister had other things on his mind than the haunting view. Picking his way carefully between icy patches, he scanned alleyways and gardens for clothes hung out to dry – with no luck. Even today, some people believed that hanging washing out on a Sunday was 'unholy'. Perhaps the middle-class area farther up the hill might offer some pickings. Yes. There, between the Mitchell's house and garden shed, were items pegged to a line.

Stackpoole looked around for signs of activity. The street was deserted. There were unlit windows on both sides but the thought that some sleepless observer might be looking out from one of them only made the situation more exciting. He vaulted over the low wall, walked rapidly along the shadowy side of the boundary fence and seized a pair of knickers from the line. They were frozen hard and would be difficult to hide, so he'd make do with one pair. He leaned against the shed's shadowy side for a moment as a car swept past on its way up the brae. Then he jumped back over the wall onto the street and tried to fit the awkward prize under his coat. Still no lights in any of the houses, so he'd got away with it again.

He grinned as he remembered coming face to face with old Mrs. Rogers when he'd snaffled some very large knickers and brassieres from her back yard. They'd looked at each other in silence until he handed the garments to her, raised his hat, wished her good evening and walked away. On the following

Friday, the postman had brought him a special delivery. The parcel contained the most enormous pair of red frilly knickers he could ever have imagined. He had worn them under his trousers for the Sunday evening sermon on 'Sins of the Flesh'. Mrs. Rogers was in the kirk and had been a regular member of his congregation from that day on. Indeed, it had become increasingly difficult to avoid her, as she seemed to materialise at the most inconvenient times. Just like her to pass away last year during one of his sermons.

At last the minister's trophy had thawed out sufficiently to fold, more or less neatly, under his coat and he hurried up Scarr Brae towards the kirk and the manse he called home – home only for the time being, he hoped. Half a mile away, on the crest of the brae, there was a light in an upstairs window of Birch Cottage. A figure appeared briefly and half-closed the curtains. Strange. Did the Smiths have visitors? He'd ask around tomorrow.

*

Half a mile beyond Birch Cottage, a dark-coloured Cadillac was negotiating a narrow gateway in a high wall. It proceeded slowly down a bumpy path between two conifer plantations. A keen human observer, if there had been one, might have made out two occupants dimly illuminated by the instrument dials. But the solitary fox that hunted along the wood's edge for fat partridges, barely gave the vehicle a glance.

*

(McSpake's House, Norfolk):

Archie was struggling with his usual insomnia but stubbornly resisting the pull of the wine rack in the kitchen. Two opened soft drink cans stood on the desk beside a copy of his poem, 'A Summer Spring'. He'd been trying to decide if the 'A' was necessary but his mind had refused to address the problem. Clearly, poetry revision was out of the question tonight. He

28

would just read the bloody thing through a couple of times and see if anything jumped out at him. He shook one of the cans, confirmed that it was empty and, surprisingly, hit the bin with it at the first attempt. He forced himself to pick up the typescript, resisting a strong urge to send that binwards as well. If he ditched it, he'd inevitably end up retyping it from the old scribbled notes when he changed his mind.

Now then, what about that bit he'd been thinking of down at the beach? It was the image of shags drying their wings after a spell of fishing. Whether the birds he'd incorporated in the piece were shags or cormorants wasn't really a problem at all. Whichever best suited the rhythm would do. He turned the pages. Yes here it was.

On either side rock-anchored kelp marks time in glittering ranks and shags hang out their wings to dry on far off stony banks.

Yes. 'Shags' was best and 'stony banks' rather than 'rocky banks' would avoid a clash with 'rock-anchored' in the previous line.

What else? Oh to hell with it! He could feel the motivation draining completely out of him. Leave it for another occasion. He couldn't be bothered going to bed either.

**

CHAPTER THREE

Monday Morning

(Surrey, England):

After heaving his suitcase into the car, Daniel O'Donnel went back to collect his rucksack and laptop from the doorstep. He glanced surreptitiously at the lounge window to see if Selina was watching him but she was keeping out of sight. Their blazing row hadn't been unexpected; pressure had been building for months. Now, finally, the explosion had come, triggered by him falling out of a taxi in the early hours. Selina's anger, once released, had been unstoppable and she'd screamed, with a certainty quite alien to her, that things were 'Finished!' Daniel felt relieved that she wasn't trying to stop him leaving; clearly no second thoughts. He guessed she would listen for him driving off before phoning her mother with the glad tidings.

The Witch would feel vindicated in her efforts to get this awful man out of her daughter's life. She'd hated him from the very first day he'd moved in with Selina, and had always made it plain that she felt her daughter ought to marry someone 'nice', someone of status, instead of setting up home with – well – how did she see him? A divorced African-American with a British passport, an Irish name and a Devon accent, who refused to join the cricket club and who hated horses! His defects probably gave her nightmares. (Daniel omitted excessive drinking from his list). In spite of the loud confrontation of the last half hour, he found himself completely relaxed, a heavy load gone. He kept his head down as he started the car so that she wouldn't see him smiling. If only Selina could find the sort of wanker that she and her mother, (especially her mother), believed deserved her, he would be delighted.

Daniel's aunt and uncle in Kent would be glad to see him and eager to put him up for a few weeks. Molly Green, who was his mother's step-sister, and Molly's husband Frank, had been urging him to bring Selina for a holiday at their place in Sevenoaks. As he'd foreseen, Selina's mother vetoed any such plan. Daniel had sometimes contrived to stay overnight at Sevenoaks by claiming at home that he'd be starting an assignment a day early. He had managed to remain sober (though sleepless) on those occasions, and the Greens had always been disappointed when he had to rush off to work. They always said the house would be his after they'd 'gone'. He hoped nothing he did would change that intention when he started commuting from there.

Commuting? He wondered if he'd have a job to commute to after tomorrow's debriefing session in Gurley's office. No doubt the old bastard would be fully informed by then of Daniel's ignominious removal from the plane when it arrived back at Gatwick. He'd been aware for a long time that the continuation of his career depended on him giving up the booze. He promised himself he would do so, starting this – or – well – maybe next week. As for the boss, Daniel had been told by Jackman in Communications how Gurley spent *his* weekends. Jackman's information was always more accurate than the usual office gossip, but Daniel believed that this piece should be treated with caution and reserved as a final weapon of desperation.

*

(Birch Cottage, Scarr):

Bessie Smith woke her grandson early so he could wave his mother off. His protests were brushed aside and he muttered resentfully all the way downstairs. It was essential that Jenny got back to Newton today, (the scheduled appointment with her divorce lawyer on Tuesday morning would involve the signing of documents), and Bob was to drive her to Aberdeen Airport for the flight to London. It had been agreed that she'd leave her own car at Birch Cottage until she flew back north. That, she hoped, would be next weekend. She hadn't mentioned it to Marc, but Jenny intended that the two of them should spend a few more days with her parents before going for a short tour in the west Highlands. Of course Doctor Ross and Miss Mandelbrot would need to agree to such a change of plan. The weather too would be an important factor.

Marco yawned as his grandfather's old Skoda turned right on Scarr Brae, away from the village and towards the main coastal highway. He was very tired after a second successive restless night and wanted much more sleep. No, he didn't fancy breakfast – maybe later. Bessie put on her comfortable boots and went to feed the chickens. She'd get Marc to collect the eggs when he felt able to cope with the task. Then he could help her gather fresh produce to fill the Bay House Hotel's vegetable hamper. It was due for collection in the afternoon.

A brassy sun had cleared the looming headland beyond Portlach and Bessie paused for a moment to watch its light flashing off the stream of traffic that entered the town from the west. That section of road was too far off for her to pick out the vintage Cadillac with its two occupants, but the customised charcoal and chocolate coachwork was undoubtedly being admired, and envied, by drivers in its vicinity. An hour earlier it had been stared at, (not always with admiration), by trades-people and other early risers in Scarr, as it moved slowly through the village in the pre-dawn light. Doubtless, most people had experienced feelings of puzzlement at the intrusive vehicle's progress along every street and lane wide enough to accommodate its bulk. The Cadillac's progress might well have suggested to observers that its occupants were familiarising themselves with local topography.

Bessie, however, was unaware of all that. She completed her work with the chickens and, shedding boots, started to prepare Marco's breakfast. A large bowl of hot porridge served with cold milk in a separate bowl, (she couldn't understand why everybody didn't have it this way), would give him plenty of the soluble fibre stuff that the nutritionists and food faddists were going on about these days. He needed building up after – well – after whatever it was that happened to him when he disappeared in the summer. Climbing the stairs quietly to see if he was awake, she found him half-dressed, scanning what he could see of the village from his bedroom window.

'Breakfast in five minutes,' she told him. 'Do you want one egg or two after your porridge? Two? I'll toast some slices of home-made bread as well.'

'Thanks, Gran. When can I go down to look round the village?'

'I'm going to the shops later and I want you to come with me, but you'll have to help here first. You can collect all the eggs in the chicken houses. I'll show you what to do after breakfast.'

*

(McSpake's House, Norfolk):

Archie was dithering again; this time about means of transport. Getting to the Moray Firth coast from here would have involved too long a journey for his forty-years-old Citroen even if it hadn't suffered a near-terminal stroke last week. Ossie had now estimated a month's wait for the very scarce spare parts to come from France. Flying, also, was out. Archie avoided air travel except in emergencies and, in spite of Fractal's anxiety, the Scarr expedition didn't seem like an emergency. So bus or rail offered the only reasonable travel options. But which? His breakfast was interrupted by the telephone.

It was Fractal! She wondered if he would be prepared to take a London-bound bus but get off at Newton. She'd fill him in on today's meeting with Doctor Ross. Archie could stay at her place overnight and she would drive him into the Capital in the morning to catch the Aberdeen train from Kings Cross. If she wasn't able to arrange official expenses for him, she'd pay for the undertaking herself. And how would he feel about eating out at Newton's newest restaurant? It would be her treat. She was certain they'd find some really nice way to round-off the evening. Could he? Yes he certainly could. Maybe her implied promises would bear fruit this time?

And so it was settled. Forget the bird-watching uniform; the old clothes would do. He'd need to expend some energy removing the blood stains from his waxed-cotton jacket to make it appear as new as possible. For him to look too much at home in well-worn gear would dispel the bumbling tyro image.

What now? Finish breakfast; get the cod fillets in the freezer; put out travelling clothes; pack good clothes for eating out; pack bird-watching gear; cancel newspaper and milk deliveries; turn down heating to anti-frost setting; put house lights on automatic timers; pack digital camera; ask Mrs. Dothray to cancel the cleaning for two weeks.

He put down the pen and scanned the list. That was about it, though he had a suspicion that he'd forgotten something. He rarely saw Jane these days so she wouldn't be likely to notice his absence. There was an afternoon bus to London. Oh yes, that was the other thing; he'd ask Dotty Dothray, when he phoned, if her brother Davy could drive him and his luggage to the bus station for three o'clock. They should leave here by two so he'd have time to withdraw some cash from the bank for general expenses. And, he'd nearly forgotten, a bird identification book.

Archie was beginning to feel quite lively now, even about the preparations. He hoped he might manage to find an hour or so to start that new poem. A change in its proposed title to 'The Village' seemed appropriate, although that probably wouldn't last through to a final version – if there ever was one. He wondered what the old place was like now. He'd find out tomorrow if it still had those:

- *houses crouching on the edge, stone gable-ends towards the sea* -.

Better incorporate that before he lost it.

*

34

(Scarr Village):

As they walked down Scarr Brae, Bessie gave a commentary on what she considered to be the most interesting features around them. That her grandson's view of 'interesting' was far removed from her own, appeared not to have occurred to her. Marco, therefore, listened selectively but tried to appear absorbed in everything she said.

Up here, on this southern edge of the village, Bessie pointed out, was the church known as Scarr Kirk. There, beside it, stood the manse where the minister lived. The minister was called Mr. Stackpoole but many local people called him Slugpole. The fact that some villagers either didn't know his name or deliberately perverted it, seemed not to worry him in any way. Dougie West once said the minister had told customers in the pub that he preferred Slugpole because of its 'uniqueness' and because there was a 'certain poetic quality' about it. The minister was very strange. Of course she didn't tell her grandson all of the things she'd heard about him.

'The homes up here,' said Bessie, 'belong to well-off people who've retired, or who have businesses or jobs in larger towns like Portlach. That big house over there, the one with pillars at the sides of the door and fancy trees in the garden, belongs to somebody important who works for an oil company in Aberdeen. If you look farther down the hill you can just make out the shops. That's where we're going. You'll see when we get there that some of them are boarded-up. A lot of people blame the supermarket in Portlach for their owners going out of business, but I agree with my friend Meggie Munro when she says it is the result of far wider changes to the world we live in. We can see them all round us. Mind you, it's change in the fishing industry that's had most impact here.

'Only a handful of small boats fish out of Scarr now. Meggie says that long ago there were more than thirty. Lorry loads of fish used to leave the village every day for markets in the south. She has no doubt that the success of fishing all over the North Sea, which led to people buying bigger and better equipped boats that had to operate from bigger and better equipped ports, started the decline of Scarr and other coastal villages. Fishermen were left with a choice: either change employment or try to keep up with new developments. Modern vessels were so much better at finding the areas where the falling numbers of fish were concentrated, that many people couldn't accept that the overall stock levels were going down. Meggie says it happened that way on the Grand Banks of Newfoundland. By the time the Canadian authorities realised how serious the problem was, it was too late; fish stocks had collapsed. They've never recovered and perhaps they never will. She says it was like cutting down the trees in a forest faster than they could re-grow. That's obvious to anyone who looks with an open mind and accepts facts – *all* the facts – without picking and choosing. Meggie believes that "downsizing" and returning to what she calls "old low-technology methods" should be a matter of urgency everywhere. She also thinks that local fishermen should be confined to, (and manage), their own sea areas.

'On top of all that, she says, average sea temperatures are rising across the world's oceans. Her great nephew, who's a biologist, told her that, in prehistoric times, fish moved in response to sea levels and changing temperatures and he believes this is happening once again. This time, however, Meggie's certain that the demands of a greatly increased population will be disastrous for all fish stocks everywhere. Why don't you come with me when I visit her? You're sure to like her.

'Marc? I said you can –'.

'Yes Gran. Yesss.'

'Anyway, Scarr itself declined as the harbour's importance declined. The harbour was Scarr's driving force and the only reason the village grew and prospered in the first place. Meggie's been keeping notes on it for most of her life. There's mainly leisure craft down there now.' Bessie paused with her hand on a gate-post to get her breath back.

'Gran, I can see the sea at the bottom of the hill – I mean the brae. Is that where the harbour is? Can we go and see it?'

36

'No, no. Not now Marc. We haven't got time. We'll just leave it for another day. Here's the butcher's shop. Mr. Mitchell runs his business in Portlach full time but opens this old shop three mornings a week. We phoned in our order on Saturday so the meat should be ready for us to collect. Al Mitchell's probably the best butcher in the whole area, and the most helpful. The supermarket can't compete with that or with the quality of his meat. Next shop down's the grocery store. The Portlach chemists leave prescription medicines there for collecting. We'll get your grandfather's tablets along with the groceries.'

'Gran, it's nice here in the sun. Is it okay with you if I just wait outside while you get the shopping? I promise I won't wander.'

'Well – all right. But stay here. We don't want you disappearing again. Do we?'

'No Gran.'

The air was motionless and the sun warm for the time of year. Marco leaned against the wall of a boarded-up shop and closed his eyes. As he breathed slowly and deeply, he felt as relaxed as when he'd stretched out on the pink rocks after rescuing Gavra Mog from the great Glop Hole on Karos. He could even hear the grating sound of stones moving in the racing river. Moving stones? He opened his eyes to find a girl showing off her skill on roller-blades. She saw him watching and, with one final, elaborate spin, came to a stop beside him.

'Hello, you're new here. Not at school?' She sat down on the pavement and began to take off the blades. The grubby plaster-cast that encased her left hand and wrist clearly made the process difficult.

'I'm Marc Powell but most people call me Marco. I'm staying at my grandparents' house up the hill. It's called Birch Cottage.'

'Know it', she replied. 'They do chickens. My dad stocks them sometimes. That's his shop.' She indicated the butcher's. 'So you won't be going to school here then? I'm a pupil at Portlach Academy. But I'm taking another week off.' She waved her plaster-cast in front of him.

'My school is Newton High', Marco told her. 'It's in a town north of London. They think I'm ill, though there's really nothing wrong with me. The hospital people sent me to my grandparents' place so they could keep an eye on my behaviour.'

'That's a good trick. How did you con the hospital staff? What did they think was wrong with you?'

'Well, I went off on my own for a week. When I got back and told them where I'd been, they didn't believe me. I had to see a psychiatrist, a real nut-case, who thought I was mad. I'm having a break here for a bit before they try to cure me.'

'You don't look mad to me. Why did you go away on your own? Where did you go? Did you walk or get a lift? You just – disappeared?'

'Yeh. Right off the face of the earth. They keep telling me I've not to talk about it. But you're nice. I might tell you some time.'

The girl blushed. 'Would you like to go fishing? There's a good place on Blackscar Rocks. Arc comes back with big fish from there sometimes. I've got a line and hooks.' She pulled a leather wallet from the pocket of her jeans. 'We could maybe get some bait at the harbour.'

'No, I can't go today. I'm with my grandmother. She's doing the shopping and I've promised to wait for her. My grandparents are going to be watching me like hawks, but if I mind my behaviour for a bit, they might stop. Who knows?'

'Bye then. I'm off. See you sometime.' She threw her rollerblades over the wall between the derelict shop and the grocery store and, in spite of her plaster-cast, scrambled after them like some tall thin monkey.

She was gone and Marco didn't know her name. All he knew was that her father was the butcher. The sign said 'Mitchell Quality Butcher'. What had his grandmother said? Was it Al Mitchell? He'd ask her when she came out. Maybe she'd know the girl's name too.

But his grandmother was taking her time. Marco peered through the window of the grocery store. There she was, one of four women chatting away at the end of the central aisle, just like they did in the supermarkets back home. They always picked awkward places for their gossiping – never saw the problems they were causing for other customers. He sighed in that long-suffering way his father did. And that changed his mood. The forthcoming divorce – it looked as if nothing could stop it now. He hoped he would manage to cope with all of it.

Suddenly, reflected in the store window, there was a car, a very large, dark-coloured limousine. Marco felt a rush of panic. He forced his shaky legs to propel him in through the shop door. From behind a shelf of breakfast cereals, he watched the vehicle drive slowly up Scarr Brae. There was only one person inside – a short, stout man wearing a hat. But the heavily-tinted glass made it difficult to see him in any more detail. Marco peered at the driver, who accelerated. By the time Bessie had persuaded her grandson to leave the shop the car had disappeared over the hill.

When they got home, a concerned looking Bob was waiting. He told them about the large American car that had come 'swooping round the bend' towards him as he turned off the coast road. When he reached the cottage, the back door stood open and Nell was sleeping, undisturbed, in the hallway. There didn't appear to be anything missing from the house but he'd like Bessie to have a look as well – just to make sure. He accepted her assurance that she had checked the front door and locked the back one before going down to the village. Marco confirmed that his grandmother had been very careful about security and that she had even locked the chicken runs.

But what about his bedroom? He waited until an opportunity arose to do a check. He found that somebody had searched the room and hadn't tried very hard to hide the fact. Huh! Did they really think him so stupid as to make it available to them? It was hidden safely in chicken house number two, in the third nesting box from the left, in the bottom row. Well, he hoped it was.

'Gran, can I do another egg collection?'

He must check up on the cube. And it would be a good idea

to spend the same amount of time in each of the chicken houses in case anyone was watching.

*

(Tottenham Court Road, London):

Daniel arrived at the pub early and decided to make do with a pint of lager. He was anxious to get this meeting over with and return to Sevenoaks. There was still that feeling of guilt about his treatment of the Greens. After dropping off his luggage there and making a number of phone calls, he had dashed off, promising Molly and Frank that he would be back by supper time. It was getting busy here in the pub with a rapidly growing lunch-time crowd and he'd have to be vigilant so as not to miss deWet. Daniel bought a sandwich, a vain attempt to make his drink last longer, and managed to squeeze onto a bench near the door.

The South African would know the solution – if indeed there was a solution – to the niggling little problems that still taxed Daniel's mind. He needed the information before tomorrow's debriefing. Pieter deWet, though no longer an agent of the diamond producers, still had contacts in England, Holland and Southern Africa who, he claimed, kept him well clued up on current business. What services did he provide for his informants in return? What was the information going to cost? Daniel tried to put those questions aside for now.

Suddenly deWet was standing beside him. Daniel hadn't seen him come in. No drink; no talking in the pub; they'd talk outside! As the South African led the way onto Tottenham Court Road, Daniel noticed that he seemed very nervous.

'Dannie, my friend, I have got most of the info I think you are requiring. Keep walking. Keep walking. I will tell you as we are going along.'

Daniel wondered if the nervousness was an act. The constant looking around wasn't the sort of behaviour he'd expect from someone of deWet's experience. Even passers-by were noticing it. However, the information he gave was plausible and, though still not quite complete, shed extra light on what Daniel already knew. He hoped there was now sufficient data to ensure the smugglers could be stamped on.

'Thank you, Pieter. You may just have got me out of a very tight spot. Is there something I can do for you in return?'

'We should leave it now, Dannie. It is good to be owed a favour. I will ask if the time comes.' He looked over his shoulder and hurried off down the road.

Daniel remembered his half-full glass on the pub table. It had probably been emptied by now so he'd better get another.

**

CHAPTER FOUR

Monday Afternoon

(Scarr Manse):

'Solomon Stackpoole DD'. With an Elizabethan style flourish, the minister appended his alias and bogus academic qualification to the hand-written sermon. He thought, however, that he might type it up this week for a change. It would really make their ears burn at the Portlach Chapel and it seemed wrong for such a masterpiece to be lodged in the archives in hand-scribbled form. It could be presented more artistically, in a suitable italic script, on that marbled mock-vellum stuff which had been gathering dust and cobwebs for years in the cupboard. Stationery in the stationary cupboard! Or even stationary in the stationery cupboard. Haw-haw-haw. Must tell them that one in the pub.

Stackpoole looked at the study clock. Quarter to three. Time to sort through recent acquisitions and lock them away so nosy Bella Tate, (he called her Tatey), wouldn't find them. Once he'd been careless and left out a pair of cami-knickers embroidered with the slogan 'Handle with Care' and they were the first thing the old bitch had spotted when she came in to do the cleaning. He'd had to explain that he was collecting items for a clothing-poverty campaign and couldn't turn down any charitable offering. Predictably, she couldn't wait to put the news on the village grapevine and he was all but swamped by a deluge of cast-off garments. Unwanted items were delivered to the manse and even to the kirk itself. Among the dross had been quite a few pairs of assorted knickers. He had also been gratified to find two of those thong things that had become all the rage. These more acceptable treasures were locked in the special suitcase under his bed.

And bed is where he'd relax for an hour before supper. Then, if he dropped in at the Mitchells' house at six o'clock, he shouldn't need to prepare his own meal. They always had liver and onions for supper on Monday evenings, though you'd have thought a butcher could feed his family on finer cuts of meat – like sirloin or fillet of beef or lamb chops. The minister felt saliva welling up. However, liver would do. He was fond of a nice piece of liver. If he put those knickers he'd nicked from their clothes line into his pocket before he went down there, it would add greatly to his enjoyment of the meal.

Maybe the Mitchells had heard some talk about the activity last night on the upper floor at the Smiths' place. If someone was visiting, he'd like to know. It would provide an excellent reason for dropping in at the cottage to introduce himself. What was it that Tatey had once told him about the Smiths' relatives? A son and a daughter, he recalled. The son was said to be abroad somewhere and the daughter stayed in the London area. Most likely one of those was visiting. It was strange that he'd seen no signs yesterday of the Smiths getting ready for a guest.

*

(Child Psychiatry Department, Newton Hospital):

As usual, the meeting was informal with Doctor Ross impatient to squeeze in nine holes before dark. Fractal looked in surprise at the man's old-fashioned plus-fours and brown brogues, the sort of gear that would have been nearing obsolescence even in his grandfather's day. Strange people, golfers. But a golfing psychiatrist? Weird! Quite clearly Ross was sinking deeper into his personal bunker. Luckily, he always left his clubs in the car.

MacDonald was starting to give his clinical psychology

report. He tended towards 'excessive verbosity', which is how he might have described the characteristic in a patient. He seemed oblivious to the fault in himself and to the impatience that it induced in listeners.

'Look here, MacDonald,' said Doctor Ross abruptly, 'could you cut out all the padding and psycho-jargon? Is the kid off his trolley or isn't he? The neurology report doesn't identify any signs of cerebral trauma. They gave him a thorough going-over and the E.E.G. is clear so far as Jenkins can see. That business about the little bugger falling from a tree in the old woman's garden is probably true; the police found clear signs of that. But with no evidence of injury, it seems that you are our main line of investigation. Is he nuts or isn't he?'

'Well, Doctor, far be it from me to criticise Mr. Jenkins, but I think his faith in the encephalography results could possibly be misplaced. Apparently he fails to realise that, sophisticated though the apparatus in his department may be, it's a long way from giving a detailed picture of cerebral functioning. I've read several reports from the United States about equipment far more advanced than ours and even they think that there's a long way – '.

'So what you're avoiding trying to say is that your psychological testing offers nothing that's of any use to us. Am I right? Come on man! Yes or no? All right, it's up to you, Fractal. When can you get young Powell talking? As late as that? Oh well. Follow-up meeting six weeks from today. Suit everyone? Fine. Fine. Mona, what date's that? Fine. Make a note and inform both parents of the change. Let's hope they'll make an effort to be here next time. Anything else that can't wait? Fine. I've got to rush.' Doctor Ross strode purposefully into the corridor.

Fractal declared that she too had to rush. She couldn't afford the time to listen to MacDonald's drawn out self-justifications; she needed to get back home before Archie arrived. He'd want to get settled in and have a shower before they got dressed for their evening out. Archie was still something of an enigma and she couldn't even be sure if he had a decent suit for the occasion.

She'd no doubt whatever about what she should wear. Even in Newton, the short black dress was the only option. Roll on the seven o'clock booking at the Restaurant Ursa Major. Very strange name that for an eating place!

*

(Birch Cottage):

The 'Market Garden' wasn't extensive. Marco could see that it covered an area equal to about three football pitches. Bob explained that, when he and Bessie had first seen the cottage, it had been surrounded by a tiny plot of land on which the then owner grew flowers. Before closing a deal on the property, they had come to an arrangement with the farmer on the adjacent farm to buy some extra ground from him – subject to obtaining planning permission for their proposed business. Permission was granted readily and the deal went through quickly. As for its size, this was as large an area as the two of them could manage. Income had been limited at first but was now increasing slowly and Bob thought another five or six years of development would enable them to resell the enterprise as a going concern at a decent profit. They had done the same previously with shops they'd owned in Kent and Essex. Their ambition was to retire one day to somewhere sunny – like Tenerife or Madeira.

The land had a thick hedge on the east side with two long polythene tunnels running down its length. On the opposite boundary, shelter came from a high wooden fence and an assortment of sheds. Along the bottom of the garden, there was a line of apple and pear trees. One stunted tree still carried undersized cooking apples. The extensive copse of woodland on the farm next door reduced sunlight as well as wind down there. Finally, the cottage, together with two garages and a large workshop, gave the land some protection from high winds that frequently swept up the hill from the cold sea below. Within these boundaries, the garden was divided by gravel paths into four main sections. Bob explained to Marco the methods that

45

he'd been using in his system of annual crop rotation. The system would have been comprehensible to Marco but for the fact that the chicken runs were not moved annually. They, it seemed, were moved counter-clockwise once every four years. Bob asserted that this special rotation scheme was the reason for the growing demand from local shops and hotels for 'Birch Cottage Organic Produce'.

'Come and look at these marked-off areas', he continued before launching into an extended description of how he had worked out his planting schedule. 'That plot over on the right, for example, is where we grew the potatoes this year. You can see a couple of rows still waiting to be dug up. I'll want your help with that later in the week. Those long mounds of earth cover the bulk of the crop which your grandmother and I gathered last week. That's how we protect them from frost during the winter. A small business like this just can't afford temperature-controlled storage so we do things the old-fashioned way. I dig an oblong trench about a foot and a half deep and line the bottom with a thick layer of straw. Next, I pile the potatoes onto it up to about this level' – Bob demonstrated by holding his hand at waist height – 'and then cover them carefully with plenty more straw. On top of that goes the earth that I dug out at the start, and as much more as is needed to keep out the heaviest frost. Frosted potatoes have a horrible, sweet taste and they're absolutely useless for eating. Nobody would buy them. When we take some out for sale, it has to be done on a frost-free day and the 'pit' repaired carefully. Nights can be very cold at this time of year and there's already been a trace of frost, so it's vital that we get the last of the crop out of the ground without delay That plot will become the fallow area next year'.

Marco had heard enough. Clearly, his grandfather and grandmother both suffered from the same annoying trait of boring listeners until *they* were forced to shut their ears to the torrents of unwanted information. He followed Bob around, nodding from time to time, and occasionally making what he hoped would sound like noises of approval. Information about organic fertilizers, summer tomatoes and winter greens passed over his head.

'Can you follow what I'm saying Marc? Marc! Oh, never mind. I'll sketch it on a sheet of paper for you. Would you find notes useful? Your grandma's a dab hand with the typewriter.'

And then he was off once more, talking of Bessie's home-made jams, jellies and pickles which were very popular and profitable.

'The well down in the bottom right corner gives all the water we need for irrigation. It has never gone dry since we moved here. A friend of your grandmother, Meggie Munro, insists that it dates right back to Stone Age times. Marc! Marc! I don't believe you've heard a word I've said. I can see horticulture won't be your chosen field. What are you planning to do when you leave school? Have you given it any thought?'

*

(Newton, near London):

The coach driver, anxious to recover lost time, was helping Archie to get his luggage onto the pavement when Fractal arrived.

'Hi, Arch! If you can hang on here, I'll bring the car round. It's in the supermarket car-park. No, no; just have a seat. I'll only be a few minutes.'

Archie heaved his rucksack on top of the small suitcase and sat on this makeshift seat to get his breath back. He felt for the notebook and screwed-up sheets of paper in his pocket. He'd never had such a serious word-block problem before and a bus hadn't been the ideal location in which to overcome it. Dare he ask Fractal's advice about the disjointed collection of phrases he'd scribbled down before his usual mental agility had gone on strike. Perhaps she wasn't interested in poetry or couldn't stand the stuff. Even worse, she might value that damned contemporary verse nonsense. Better play things safe, mention his problem only if he found signs that she'd take a sympathetic view of his writing. And there she was, stopped on the No Parking lines. He grabbed his luggage and staggered towards the red sports-car, hoping there would be enough room.

47

Twenty minutes later, they'd cleared the rush-hour traffic and were pulling onto the paved area in front of Fractal's block of flats. The building was clearly a fairly recent development and Archie could see two more identical blocks farther down the street. Across the road an older, much larger, building from the nineteen sixties was in the process of demolition. According to Fractal, its replacement would provide office space for an insurance company preparing to move some of its operations away from the city. She was pleased because the inevitable increase in demand for accommodation was already starting to push up local property prices. She'd arranged to have a revaluation done on her flat, bought less than three years ago. Affording a move to the seaside could no longer be ruled out. Even her home town of Brighton might be within reach.

Inside, an atrium gave access to two staircases, the one on the left leading to odd- numbered flats and that on the right to those with even numbers. Between them, a lift bore the warning OUT OF ORDER. Damn it! More luggage-lugging on the stairs. The lobby area was clean, in good repair and bright, the fading daylight from its high glass roof supplemented by the glow of warm-tone fluorescent fittings. They climbed up four flights to Fractal's flat, Archie lingering behind, examining the pretentious murals so she wouldn't notice his laboured breathing. There was a faint aroma of curry in the air. It reminded Archie of how the smell of boiled cabbage and wax- polish permeated tenement buildings in Glasgow during his sabbatical year in the early nineteen sixties. He had moonlighted for a firm of shady 'Investigators' and had always seemed to be the only private-eye available when tricky inquiries were required in the once-notorious Gorbals area. Although that part of the city was undergoing major redevelopments at the time, it had still been a risky environment for the solo agent. Nowadays, many people wouldn't possess the simple skills required to boil cabbage; probably most would never want to. The unstoppable march of takeaways and fast-food deliveries was pushing domestic cooking onto the sidelines of increasingly busy lives. And as for wax polish – well, if the stuff was still in use, he hadn't come across any. Dotty Dothray used some kind of aerosol spray – perhaps the modern equivalent.

Archie was worried when Fractal opened the door of her flat with a single key. He must have a serious talk with her about the security principles he'd always found totally effective – apart from that trouble with the television aerial fitter who'd got in through the skylight. The grainy security pictures were languishing somewhere in police files and they hadn't caught the culprit yet. He wouldn't mention that unless this building had some kind of roof access.

'Right then, Archie, we have our dinner reservation for seven o'clock, so let's get you settled in quickly. There's about fifty minutes before the taxi's due. You can get ready in the study. We'll decide on sleeping arrangements when we get back. I'll have the bathroom first while you unpack your stuff.' Fractal disappeared along the corridor.

In the study were two armchairs, a large desk with a swivel typist-chair and four bookcases. Below the window, an elderly music-centre sat on a low table. The loudspeakers were fixed to the wall on either side of heavy, lined curtains. Three of the bookcases were overfilled, one apparently with work-related information, and two others with popular paperback novels, literary classics and, Archie could see, poetry. He was disappointed that the contemporary crap items greatly outnumbered real poetry books. The last bookcase contained anything but books and clearly served as a general storage area in the absence of cupboard space. If Fractal made him sleep in here, there wouldn't be much room for a makeshift bed. Had she been made that anxious by her night at his place? He didn't think so. After all, she'd invited him here almost at once. He began to haul his best clothes from the battered rucksack. He could hear her in the bathroom and his bladder was hoping she wouldn't take too long.

*

49

Frank Green, with the very best of intentions, had poured Daniel a glass of dry sherry in the restful, old-fashioned sitting-room and was trying to stretch out a discussion about the weather. Molly, meanwhile, getting dinner ready in her new steel and marble kitchen, wondered if she'd added enough Burgundy to the gravy. Another splash wouldn't go amiss on such a special occasion. There, that was better. It was disappointing, of course, to hear of her nephew and his – ah – wife parting in this horrible modern way but lovely that he'd come to stay for a bit. She and Frank had been married for forty two years and had never thought of parting – well, almost never. Daniel seemed to be coping well with the situation. He was putting on a brave face, poor lad, even trying to smile about it. How time had changed things! People seemed to have less and less concern for others nowadays. Restraint was the key to happiness. Restraint! She added another splash of Burgundy.

Daniel's mind was as far from food as it was from his parting with Selina. He knocked back his second sherry, thinking with trepidation about tomorrow's face-to-face with Gurley. He had just spent more than an hour producing a schematic diagram of the problem's diverse elements with areas of intervention highlighted. Clearly, four agents would be required, acting simultaneously, to wrap up the case. The clarity of his plan was such that even Gurley would have to be impressed. But you never knew with Gurley. The mood in which he arrived at work seemed to warp his views of everything and he was apt to slap down the views of others without mercy. Jackman was sure the old fool was being pressured into taking early retirement. That would make the staff happy – unless it was a prelude to closure of the department.

*

(Birch Cottage):

Marco felt pleasantly tired at supper. His grandfather had kept him fully occupied and they'd dug up a whole row of potatoes and added them to the end of the 'pit'. For the final half hour, a boy called Raymond Meade had joined them. He had come to trade some edible brown crabs, (he called them partans), for a supply of potatoes. Digging them up personally was obviously the most enjoyable part of the transaction. Soon he sped off down the hill with a shopping-bag full of Golden Wonders balanced on the handlebars of a ramshackle bicycle that appeared to have been put together from an assortment of old pieces. Before leaving, he told Marco that everybody, except his mother, called him Arc and that a severe gale was expected later tomorrow.

As they mopped the last drops of soup from their bowls with chunks of wholemeal bread, the van from the hotel pulled up at the gate to collect the waiting hamper of vegetables. Bob hurried out to help the driver lift it on board. The second course was minced beef with carrots and onions, served with floury potatoes and garden peas. Marco sniffed the aroma of shortbread baking in one of Bessie's large ovens and wondered if he'd be expected to eat meals like this every day. Lately, they'd been having mostly pizzas and kebabs at home, not even bothering to sit at the table. His mother was so busy.

Later, a television weather forecast told of a depression approaching from the Atlantic. Winds of 'up to force ten' already driving ashore on the west coast of Ireland were certain to hit Great Britain tomorrow. Some structural damage was likely along the south coast of England and in the West Country. Oh, and there was a possibility of strong winds in Scotland as well.

*

(Restaurant Ursa Major, Newton):

As the Reverend Stackpoole wiped gravy from his chin in the Mitchells' dining room and Marc Powell settled down in front of his grandparents' television-set in far- away Scarr, Fractal Mandelbrot and Archie McSpake were being ushered to their seats in 'Newton's Best Restaurant'. The waiter handed them glossy menu cards and withdrew briefly while they made their choices. They decided on the Clear Chicken Soup for starters. Archie, 'not very hungry', was prepared to tackle the Italian Meatballs with Tagliatelle in Herby Vermouth sauce and Fractal opted for the Vegetarian Stir Fry. Both thought that Poached Pears in Ginger Syrup would round off the meal nicely. Oh, and wine? The list appealed to neither of them and Fractal's suggestion of ice-cold lager was endorsed by her companion. She nodded to the hovering waiter.

'You should have let me pay for the taxi, Archie; this is my treat after all. By the way, those scribbled notes you dropped from your wallet? Ideas for a poem, you said. You didn't tell me when I came to your place that you wrote poetry. Do you subscribe to any of the magazines? I get a couple of the better ones. Maybe you saw copies in my study. I do send them offerings sometimes but I've only had one published. Any luck yourself?'

Archie shook his head. 'They wouldn't want to publish the sort of stuff that I write. I consider poetry to have deteriorated to the point where it's just going round and round, unable to find any worthwhile direction. I think of it as having been trapped by the Black Hole of Contemporary Verse. I'd be delighted to see it break free before it plunges into oblivion.'

Fractal was disturbed by his bitterness. He had probably submitted material which had been turned down. She would have to proceed cautiously so as not to annoy him. She was reliant on his goodwill to complete the surveillance task in Scarr. The thought further reinforced her resolve to give him a good helping of motivation later tonight. Their starters had arrived and they switched to small-talk as they ate.

'There's a decent place to stay in Scarr,' Archie remarked as they neared the end of their main courses. 'It's called the Bay House Hotel. I remember it from my childhood and early life there. You didn't know, did you, that I'm a native Scarrian? I used to return there for holidays when I first moved to London, but my career soon made that impossible. Haven't been back to the place since making a flying visit – oh – it must be over thirty years ago. By that time most of the people I met were strangers. On a bus journey between Portlach and Scarr, some teenagers spotted me as an alien. They obviously wanted to bamboozle me when they started talking in a gross exaggeration of the old local dialect. At one time people knew a person's home village from differences in pronunciation and speech patterns. I was amused to think that I spoke like those teenagers before their parents went to school. However, I resisted the temptation to give a demonstration. Anyway, I've booked in at the Bay House for a week. It's not expensive out of season.' He put down his knife and fork and sat back in the chair.

Fractal, too, had stopped picking at her stir-fry and she caught the waiter's eye. 'Do you want another drink, Archie? No? Neither do I. We can have a nightcap later. I'll tell you when we get home about today's meeting at the hospital. And you can tell me about your plans for the Marc Powell surveillance. Ah, here come the pears. I almost wish we hadn't ordered them. I'm looking forward to an early night. Hope you are too, Archie.' She gave him that look again.

*

(Old Cottage, South East of Scarr):

The cottage, after standing empty for a dozen or more years, was showing signs of occupation tonight. Subdued light showed in a gap between the warped shutters of a downstairs window and the smell of burning wood drew the watcher's eyes to the cowled chimney. Barely perceptible in the darkness, smoke rose straight up in the still air to dissipate in the clouded sky. The gamekeeper peered at the scene suspiciously. He circled the building slowly and came on a large motor car half-hidden in a rickety barn at the rear. Alert to the possibility of the occupants having a dog, he approached the shuttered window using all of his stalking skills and peered through the gap.

A portable butane lamp on a table cast light on what was definitely a map. Seated at the far side of the table and facing the

53

window, a short, stout, bald-headed individual, in white shirt and red braces, talked rapidly as he drew a finger across the map. The gamekeeper could see the hands and arms of a second person. Squinting obliquely through the slit didn't bring any more of their owner into view. The only thing that might identify this person was a very large, oval, gold-coloured watch on his right wrist. There was talk in the village of strangers in a large American limousine but no one seemed to know anything about their identity or where they had come from. Now, however, the gamekeeper had discovered where they were staying. But why here? He'd keep a careful watch on them until he found out.

**

CHAPTER FIVE

Tuesday Morning

(Blackscar Rocks):

The tide was slack at the bottom of the ebb when Arc hauled two crab pots from the deep water at Blackscar. He transferred three keepable specimens into his sack to join the pair he'd winkled out earlier from crevices on the western side of the jagged promontory. His grandfather had often told him of the great hauls of partans that were common when *he* was a boy, but Arc didn't really believe that. Five was a pretty good catch. He lodged the sack temporarily in a pool farther up the beach and returned for the pots. He jettisoned the ballast stones and scraps of stale bait, carried the pots up to the road and loaded them onto his cart. He'd had pots smashed up in the past and didn't want it to happen again. Old men were saying that the storm that was expected tonight would be a 'snorter'. The pots would be safe in the shed while it lasted and he could do a bit of work on them when he had time. Geordie Moston at the hotel would be happy to buy these partans; he was unlikely to get any more shellfish for quite a while from any source.

Yesterday, Arc's mother had told him that some 'retired mannie' from England had a room booked at the hotel. He was supposed to be a bird watcher. That was fine if he liked looking at seagulls, though there weren't very many of those nowadays. Meggie Munro had been complaining to her that it was just another sign of Scarr's decline. Most gulls had 'disappeared along with the fishing fleet', she had declared angrily. As if she'd ever liked the thieving scunners in the first place! Better pickings for them in the garbage dump at the old Langmuir limestone-quarry. Of course they called if a 'landfill site' nowadays.

A visiting bird watcher? A skiver, more like! Anyway, Arc had no time for musing. Geordie and Annie would be up and about, so he'd get his catch over there as quickly as possible. If he wasn't delayed, he might manage to fit in some breakfast before having to drag himself off to school.

'I hope the mannie likes partans or Geordie might be left wi them on his hands', his mother declared when he got home and told her of his early morning transaction. 'Are you watchin the time for school? You canna be late twa mornins on the trot. He wants a what? Far does he think you'll get a salmon this late in the year? Can't he jist drive ower to the Portlach supermarket? Off you go then'. Effie Meade transferred the breakfast dishes to the sink and propelled her reluctant son towards the door.

*

(Fractal Mandelbrot's Flat, Newton):

There was guilt-fuelled tension between Archie and Fractal this morning which both would have preferred to put behind them. However, neither could summon up the motivation to apologise for the dispute. It was that damned poetry that had caused it. Last night, wonderfully relaxed after the most luxuriously extended copulation that Archie had ever experienced, he was asked by Fractal about his notes for 'The Village'. She'd chipped away at his reluctance to talk, until he had capitulated and explained that the fragments were intended to form the framework for a descriptive poem about childhood memories of Scarr. His imminent visit there had increased the urgency to get the poem down – in preliminary draft at least.

'I'm worried that, if I spend enough time there, the way that the place is now will start to distort my view of the way it used to be when it was the centre of the world. I go back a long way, you know. I went to school as a five-year-old in nineteen forty one. At the time, they were so worried about the possibility of bombs falling on the school that half of the classes attended lessons in the mornings and the other half in the afternoons.'

He had gone on to talk about exploring the beaches, the hills and the woods; about how children had freedom then to become part of the natural environment; about the supportive interrelationships which underpinned community identity. He spoke also about the ever looming realities of war: of families losing fathers and brothers in distant places; of bombers straggling back from raids over Norway and the Baltic with holes in fuselages and bits of wings and tails shot away; of great ships beyond the horizon, whose massive masts and funnels were all you could see from the shore. Then there were picnics in the woods on summer days with bread and home-made jam to eat and Ministry of Food orange juice to drink. But he was having difficulty of a kind he'd never met before in organising the images in writing. Even the poem's shape was a problem. He got up reluctantly to bring the notes from his jacket pocket.

Fractal peered at them in the subdued light of her bed lamp. 'Have you considered a different starting point', she said. 'I know it's about your village and about looking at it from a distance in time. That makes me think you could do the same spatially. Instead of looking about you in the village with its crouching houses, then up the hill to your picnic place and beyond, you could view things from the hill. What do you think? You could be standing up there in a dream, looking down and seeing things as they once were. And I'm not sure about your insistence on rhyming verse. I know that they used rhyme and metre more in those days; you still do as a consequence. But it might catch the interest of younger readers if you used a more contemporary style. All right! All right! I know that that'll eventually have had its day as well, but you should think seriously about what I've said.'

Archie had listened with interest which had turned to irritation and then to anger. He screwed up the notes to throw across the room, paused, and placed them on the bedside table. 'Why don't you write it?' he growled, lying down with his face towards the wall. They hadn't spoken again. Through a large part of the night they had lain awake, each aware that the other was doing the same, until both had slipped off sometime in the small hours.

'Are you ready, Archie? Are you sure a glass of apple juice is all you want? I must get you to Kings Cross before I go to work. A taxi? Please, Archie! Don't let's carry on this resentment stuff. I'm sorry I tried to influence your poetry beliefs. Kiss and make up? Mm? Mmmm. You've plenty of time for the train and I could go in to work late. Would you like-? Yes, me too!'

*

(Unidentified Office Block, Central London):

Daniel had been at his desk for hours, having felt a strong compulsion to leave the Greens' house before they got up. He didn't remember much about last night but was sure he had overdone things on Frank's Cognac. The need to alter his life's routine was a matter of urgency; the booze had become inescapable. Maybe the unfortunate events on the flight from Malaga would lead to imposition of change by others. What would his pension rights be worth if they demanded his retirement? Would there be anything reasonable by way of a lump sum? He'd never troubled to find out before. Despairingly, he envisaged himself drinking away all of his meagre resources and sinking into destitution. Christ! He could do with a drink now to cheer himself up.

Back to the planning. There must be no failure now. He finished typing his report. The diagrams were already drawn and there was just time to save it all to a disc. No time to make acetates for the ancient overhead-projector that Gurley insisted on retaining. If the bastard wanted acetates, he could bloody well arrange to have them done by somebody else. Jackman and two secretaries arrived. There was no doubt that they guessed

Daniel was engaged in a bail-out-the-lifeboat enterprise. Their sympathetic faces only served to anger him more.

When the intercom announced, 'Agent O'Donnel, Commander Gurley will see you now', Daniel stood up at once and strode purposefully towards the heavy mahogany door. 'The lion's den, Daniel', he muttered. 'The fucking lion's den'.

'I won't offer you a drink at this time of day, O'Donnel', Gurley said pointedly. 'You need to be alert for the meeting this afternoon. In the meantime, fill me in on the North African connection. We know you met the agent in Spain and I want all of the details. That's *all* of the details, O'Donnel. Leave nothing out'.

Daniel held up the disc and went across to the computer on the secretary's desk. As was usual at sensitive debriefing sessions, secretaries had been excluded. Daniel turned the equipment on and inserted the disc in the appropriate slot. He gave Gurley a verbal rundown on the essential information that he'd collected, as a supplement to the on-screen data. The old devil seemed interested rather than impressed. When the diagrams appeared, he sat up in his chair. The final piece of Daniel's work made him lean across his desk to take it all in. The 'Forward Strategy Proposal' clearly had him hooked. And why should it not? It was, Daniel believed, the best thing he'd ever produced for the department. But what meeting this afternoon?

'Right, O'Donnel, do you think you could add a bit more colour to the diagrams? Excellent!' Gurley was close to unaccustomed joviality now. 'I want you to make ten more copies of that disc, usual security precautions, and bring them to me. Make that eleven; the Prime Minister must have one. Don't put your name or identity code on them. I've a conference in Whitehall this afternoon. Top brass, or next-to-the-top brass, from all of the agencies involved. I want you to come along to operate the disc. And, of course, you can refresh my memory when facts require clarification. But I, myself, will brief the group on behalf of the Department. Good work, Daniel, very good work indeed!' He rubbed his chin vigorously. No doubt expecting promotion – or another gong!

Daniel returned to his desk to carry out the man's bidding. He wasn't too bothered about being consigned to the sidelines while Gurley tried to impress bastards even more self-important than himself. The forward-planning section hadn't been questioned. It had identified the need for agents to operate simultaneously in four -different locations, and he was one of only four agents attached to the Department. That should prolong his employment for at least another week. If Gurley's good humour lasted until the Whitehall meeting, Daniel might even claim the best location for himself.

*

(Scarr Manse):

The minister looked with pride at his Sermon to End all Sermons – although he did expect that, one day, he'd produce a better. In the meantime, however, this looked very impressive on the special paper. He unlocked the top drawer of the metal cabinet and filed it under B. He'd thought of G for genius, but brilliant would do. The irresistible need to shoot at ever-higher targets was, he believed, what propelled him through life. He folded the handwritten original and slipped into an inside pocket. It would do well enough at the chapel. In any case, having written and then revised it while typing up the exhibition version, he would remember each word with total clarity. At the sound of Tatey coming along the corridor with the coffee things, he looked around to make sure there was nothing lying about that he wouldn't want her to see. It looked all clear.

'Ah, coffee, Mrs. Tate. I always look forward to it. You make such an invigorating brew. Have you brought a spare cup? Good! You'll have one yourself then? And a biscuit of course; you must have a biscuit. Here, you sit in the armchair, take the weight off your feet, and I'll pour'.

Tatey flopped into the chair but sat leaning forward. The minister tried not to smile. Did she actually think that he—? Nah. Probably the 'fibrositis' she was always moaning about.

'Tell me Mrs. Tate, have you seen the Smiths of Birch Cottage lately? I popped in there on a pastoral visit Sunday lunchtime and found Mrs. Smith on the floor behind a settee. She looked quite flushed and I felt somewhat concerned for her health. However, she did manage eventually to sit on a chair. And Mr. Smith seemed not to know what to do about the situation. He looked bemused. It must be stressful at times for people of such advanced years to try to cope with visitors. So, after ensuring that they were not in any imminent danger, I had a small glass of water and left. I hope they coped with the visitor later in the evening. I can't remember if it was a son or daughter they were expecting. Did you hear if Mrs. Smith recovered enough to manage? Do you think the visitor would mind if I dropped in for – well – for a progress report?'

'Bessie Smith must hae recovert gey quick. I saa er gaan inti Mitchell the butchar's aboot thes time yistardy. Shi'd a grandsin wi er. He cam up wi's mithar fae Ingland on Sundy nicht, bit the mithar hid ti ging back hame on the Mundy. Annie McPherson says Bob Smith drove er ti the airport ti catch a plane. The loon's bidin for a week. He hisna been verra weel.'

'Mrs. Tate, why are you talking like that? George Moston says you come from Shropshire and, though I haven't actually been there, I'd be most surprised to learn that that's a Shropshire dialect. Have you picked up some of the local lingo from your husband? He was born here, wasn't he?'

'Na, na; I mean no, no. Meggie Munro's started a group for the protection of the ancient Scarr dialect. Once they spoke like this everywhere up here but, Meggie says, it was a little bit different in every village. Only the old Scarr people know what it sounded like locally and every year there's fewer and fewer of them. I'm sure Meggie would be pleased if you came to a meeting.'

'Alas, Mrs. Tate, I'm such a busy man. Much though I'd like to attend, I couldn't verra weel neglect my parochial duties. When did you say the boy's mother would be returning? This Mrs. – Mrs. – what was her name again?'

(A railway Carriage, East Coast Main Line):

Archie was fretting. The train had been stopped for forty minutes and nobody seemed willing to give a reason. He'd been flustered when he arrived at the station with seconds to spare and he was worse now. That early morning session in Fractal's bedroom had stretched away beyond what he'd expected, or was fit for these days. His fantasy of taking her off to the Florida Keys was beginning to look less and less enticing. Anyway, what the hell! Why would she want to ditch her career to go off with a man twenty years her senior? Especially a man who was beginning to show early signs of decrepitude.

The belief beginning to circulate among passengers was that an electrical fault had caused the breakdown. Someone with a mobile phone and access, apparently, to relevant sources said that a 'replacement loco' was on its way down from Doncaster. To escape the stress of the situation, Archie smoothed out his crumpled poetry notes and fished a reporter's notebook from his rucksack. The disagreement with Fractal over the content of his intended poem was slighter than it had seemed. He could appreciate the advantage of an elevated viewpoint, looking at Scarr as if from another world. But rhyme and classical rhythm couldn't be swept aside. From a high position, he'd be looking down, in memory, on the very school where he'd first absorbed the beauty of such verse. He could recite many of those magic words even now. But the school had been demolished years ago. Mmm. It might be worthwhile trying to preserve the spirit of it, if not in this poem, then in another.

He had once been shown an ancient photograph of the school foundations being laid. The workmen had been dressed in collarless shirts, waistcoats, crumpled black trousers and flat caps – the near universal clothing of late nineteenth and early twentieth century labourers. The one in front, his grandmother had said, was her long-dead husband, his grandfather.

Now, about this 'Village' piece; what should be included in the poem?

Identify viewpoint: i.e. top of hill.
Look down on houses: Type of houses and their appearance.
Sea: Ever present, looming, threatening.
Look south to woodland: Physical appearance, atmosphere.
What else is needed? War-time with ships and planes.
Enough? Perhaps.

Archie began an uncharacteristic struggle to produce lines that fitted together within a coherent rhyme-and-metre framework. Unlike the usual verse that came from somewhere in his unconscious mind, fully formed and without effort, this was turning into a tangle of impressions. He was trapped in something new and worrying and there was no possibility of going back to the clean slate stage. The argument with Fractal had probably killed that. Or was there some deeper psychological reason? At least the train had started to move and was picking up speed. Good. It had looked for a bit as if Scarr would beyond reach today.

*

(Backhame House, Outskirts of Portlach Town):

The Cardingtons' house stood out even among the most palatial residences in Portlach's West End. Jonathan Cardington had been educated at Portlach Academy, Durham University and the Sorbonne. It surprised his parents when their son, after two terms in Paris, decided to abandon French Literature and become a banker. Cardington senior, a well-off fish merchant, was always ready to indulge his highly intelligent, (if erratic), son and supported Jonathan's further studies in Finance, Commerce and Banking in the United States. On completion of those studies, Jonathan joined the New York office of an international banking corporation where he worked for nine years, gaining rapid promotion and a wife along the way. Clearly heading for dizzy heights of international finance, he was appointed Head of Development at the bank's expanding London operations in nineteen sixty seven.

Jonathan's wife, Marietta, who had played a few minor roles in Broadway productions, overcame her reluctance to move to England when Jon's growing financial muscle secured her a part in a British comedy film. With the promise of more, maybe even better, parts to follow, she had been packed for the journey before her husband. It was during the transatlantic voyage, chosen instead of a flight in lieu of a second honeymoon, that he saw the first signs of Marietta's infidelity. That she had constantly sought out the company of a bald, overweight Second Engineer had been shocking to him. For a few months he'd tried to be more attentive towards her but, eventually, he'd allowed himself to sink into a state of acceptance. Nothing must interfere with his work. Anyway, he could only guess what she got up to at the studios. An acting crowd! The nineteen sixties! They were all at it.

Jonathan looked disapprovingly from the elevated study window as Marietta got into her Porsche. Trying to persuade her to drive a more age-appropriate vehicle had been just the waste of time he'd expected. She was off today to have lunch with friends at the Portlach Arms Hotel's Riverside Gardens. That outdoor facility had always closed for the season at the end of September but the new owners were intent on seeing how much extra business a month's extension would bring. Bunglers! Financially competent business people wouldn't have considered the plan. They were supposed to be heavily mortgaged. How had they found a bank willing to support such a naïve scheme? He turned to the terrestrial telescope and watched as Marietta's car disappeared over the bridge.

Recently, Jon had made a lot of use of this particular scope. Last Thursday he'd observed her during her morning walk on the shore. Instead of going along the sandy beach at the edge of the tide, which was her invariable routine, she had taken the path across the old, abandoned golf course. She'd looked back at the house in the most blatant manner before disappearing behind the large, gorse-covered sand dune in the centre of the links. Puzzled and suspicious, he'd swung the telescope round and caught a fleeting glimpse of a figure in black vanishing behind its far end. Observing one end of the mound and then the other, he'd become increasingly angry when neither of them reappeared. It could be that two people had stopped to pass the time of day but that was a far-fetched possibility. He knew Marietta too well to believe that. Thirty five years ago he would have marched down, bristling with belligerence, to see what the hell was going on. Now, after many years of frustration, that just hadn't been an option. He'd continued to watch until, twenty minutes later, Marietta had emerged from behind the far end of the dune. Jonathan had waited until the other person appeared at the nearest end: that blasted minister from Scarr!

The new camera was here now, still in its case, waiting to be set up. He would start on that today. He'd be ready to shoot a film if her encounter with the Stackpoole man was ever repeated. 'Film star? I'll give her bloody film star! And show it in court along with the other evidence – unless she agrees to go on *my* terms.'

Jon, marital problems uppermost in his mind, didn't look towards Inch Greele. As president, secretary and treasurer of the Portlach Anomalous Phenomena Society, he had declared himself responsible for observing the islet. He had logged nothing since Sunday night when there had been the merest hint of a light out there. The women at the cottage must have been disturbed by it too. At least one of them had been poking around with a lantern but even the large reflector scope and the light of a near full moon hadn't revealed anything specific for him to report at the next A. P. Society meeting.

*

(Static Train; East Coast Main Line):
Archie, returning to his seat with a cheese sandwich and a cup of tea, could see that the woman sitting next to him had been reading his notes. Clearly, she hadn't formed a favourable opinion and leaned against the window as if to avoid any possibility of contact with him. He thought she probably felt threatened by the scribble of disjointed phrases about 'The

Village' that he'd left on his seat. He could quite easily understand someone viewing them as the product of a disturbed mind. Well, he was a bit pissed off with them himself. He pulled a packet of sweets from his pocket, held them out to the woman and asked innocently, 'Would you like a mint?' She didn't reply and pushed herself more tightly against the glass.

Having one stoppage on a train journey was bad enough; a second was outrageous. When he had bought the tea, they'd told him that a landslip had blocked the line ahead and that buses would be arriving to transport passengers to Edinburgh. Bloody hell! He shoved the scribbled notes into his pocket, reached down a copy of 'Summer Spring' from his rucksack and attempted to relax. But soon he began to experience the usual anxiety that came from reading his own work.

The woman, who must have been watching after all, said 'Ooh, poetry! Did you write that? What does it say?'

Archie nodded and spoke quietly into her ear:

'*There is another, subtler, force that cannot shift the sea*
but wraps me in seductive bonds of curiosity
that draw me down the shingle beach, across the rough strand-line
of tangled weeds, and twigs, and shells, and scraps of nets, and twine
where strutting, hands-in-pockets crows forage for easy meals
among the ticks, sea-lice and shrimps, dried crabs and shrivelled eels'.

'That's lovely', she said. 'I like the bit about seductive bonds'.

The bus arrivals were announced and Archie managed to give her the slip.

**

CHAPTER SIX

Tuesday Afternoon

(Birch Cottage):

Bob was digging up the last of the potatoes which Bessie and Marco collected in pails and tipped into the trailer. The trailer was attached to a very noisy miniature tractor that produced choking clouds of smoke every time Bob revved its engine. The protective ear-muffs that they all wore couldn't quite shut out the racket and Marco was relieved to see the second, and final, load being emptied at the end of the clamp.

Bob uncovered his ears. 'Right then, Marc, you and I have to open the pit for this lot while your Gran goes inside to put the kettle on. After a cuppa, we'll fasten everything tight against the storm. High winds off the sea can be very bad at this time of year. They often bring sleet or snow. When we've got the potatoes clamped, we'll put some old sails over the top and peg them down until the weather improves. We're going to use that pile of ropes to anchor the sheds and the nets will help to secure the polythene tunnels. The garages are tough enough to stand up to storms but the chicken houses need special care. Willie Morgan's son lost all his chickens in a storm last January. When he looked out in the morning, his car was still there but the garage he'd parked it in was gone. Blown away! He never found any of the bits and had to build a new one. He decided that a brick one like ours would be worth the expense in the long run.'

The storm warning had sent all but the very largest ships hurrying for shelter. Television news was announcing that Local Education Authorities were to close schools an hour early. As he demolished a wedge of cake along with his tea, Marco could hardly believe such measures justified. The newspapers, and even the television channels, often exaggerated small problems. They tended to be what his school friend, Ziggy, called 'historical'. Out in the yard he'd had to take off his sweatshirt, so it wasn't very cold and there wasn't even a breath of wind. He really would like to see this supposed storm they were banging on about. However, it was clear that his grandparents were concerned – and they didn't seem to be historical types. That and the thought of chicken sheds disappearing over the trees, taking the metal cube with them, encouraged him to take a more serious view of the weather forecast.

'Come on, Marc. It's time to get busy again. It'll be dark earlier than usual and the work must be finished by then. Look there, out to sea. That boat heading for the harbour looks like a line fisher. And do you see the bigger one that's just rounded the Ness? It must be heading for Portlach. They'll be glad to get ashore, although there won't be any fish buyers about. People wouldn't be expecting landings today.

'Have you noticed seagulls flying inland? They're better at forecasting weather than we are. And look at the flock of smaller birds coming down from the north. I reckon there could be thousands in that one. They could be fieldfares or redwings – or maybe both. They migrate here in the autumn and leave again in the spring. They're fond of fruit and you should look out for them in the wood and the hedges after the storm's past. Your grandmother's friend, Mrs. Munro, says that a small number of them stay here all the year round and raise families. I've never seen it myself. But we've no time for gawping. Gran will be shouting if she sees we're not busy.'

They worked in silence, Marco imitating Bob's actions until he knew exactly how to proceed with the pit covering. Bessie, having put a casserole into the oven, joined them to help with the chicken houses. Marco managed to recover his metal cube from its latest hiding place and worked nearly as hard as the adults. The calm of the last few hours was at an end. Wind was rising in gusts in the rapidly fading light as they pegged down pieces of old fishing nets across the tunnels. They added a few building blocks round the edges for extra security.

'Now for the sheds! Marc and I will fix them, Bessie, if you lock the garages. And would you bring a pair of storm lanterns. We'll need them before we finish this. If the electricity fails we may need them in the house as well.'

The gusts were getting stronger now, becoming more prolonged and, even in the shelter of the buildings, threatening to propel Marco down the garden. Eventually, Bob thought it wise to send him indoors to help his grandmother get the supper table ready. Half an hour later, Bob himself came in wearily and went to wash and change clothes. The wind was rattling the window frames, bombarding the panes with hailstones, and Nell, who'd been lying on her favourite mat under the hallway table, was persuaded by draughts to join them in the kitchen. Bessie brought the chicken casserole from the oven and Marco decided that he didn't ever want to see, (or eat), another hamburger.

*

(Russian Factory Ship, East of Shetland):

Captain Vladimir Radek had retired to his bunk with a three-quarters-empty bottle of vodka; quite sufficient in the prevailing circumstances. He needed to be fully ready whenever the First Mate called him to the bridge. In any case, tension was making him restless and probably ruled out the possibility of sleep. It was inevitable that severe weather would disrupt operations for a day or two, maybe even longer. The reduced speed that he'd ordered should continue to support his cover story of an ailing engine, but sailing too far and then having to turn back would draw unwanted attention from the American spy-satellite system. The nosy crew of the Scottish Fisheries Protection vessel had seemed satisfied with Radek's 'nursing the engine' explanation and with his assurance that no assistance was required. They'd shadowed him for forty minutes and then headed off south into the gloom.

What the Russian didn't know was that a Special Investigator assigned to the fisheries vessel had taken high resolution images from various angles and transmitted them to a recipient in Whitehall. These, when compared with pictures taken previously by a French destroyer on patrol off the west coast of Africa, had confirmed that, apart from minor superstructure alterations and paintwork changes, this Nikolai Rykov with the St. Petersburg registration was the very same vessel that had passed Cape Verde as the Leon Chuikov of Archangelsk. After travelling up the west coasts of Ireland and Scotland, the ship had rounded Shetland and set its course south east. It looked increasingly likely that the Russian was heading for the Baltic – just as the experts had predicted.

Only one fishing vessel had accompanied the factory ship on its voyage from the West African fishing grounds. All the others had been sold off to local African interests by the owner. This one remaining trawler had sailed ahead of the Nicolai Rykov and was continuing its course northwards in the direction of the Lofoten Islands – under the discreet surveillance of a Norwegian deep-sea tug.

*

Meanwhile, in far off St. Petersburg, rising business tycoon and fishing fleet owner, Yevegeny Zhirkov, sat alone in his heavily curtained study, monitoring the movements of the South East Asian stock markets on a row of desk-top computers. But Zhirkov had only part of his attention on the cathode ray tubes in front of him. He was also replaying in his mind the plans he'd made for the reorganisation of his entire contraband-diamond operation. The fishing-fleet cover had served well for a time but he was now ready to open up other means of transport.

The battered factory ship and fleet of trawlers had been bought cheaply from their previous owners at a time when the Russian fishing industry was switching operations away from the West African coastal shelf. Eventually they'd started to look even more out of place there and Zhirkov had decided on major changes. His new air-freight business would give a faster, more secure and more profitable way to transport fish and, covertly, uncut alluvial diamonds to where there was most demand. The same kind of 'persuasion' which had prompted the previous ship-owners to part with their assets could be applied to the matter of finding new buyers for the Nikolai Rykov / Leon Chuikov.

The ship *was* beyond economic repair and ought to be scrapped but it should be fairly easy to persuade a compliant buyer to think in terms of loss at sea and an inflated insurance claim. She had rounded Shetland earlier on her way back to St Petersburg with a skeleton crew on board, her other workers having returned home by air. The one remaining trawler might be fixed up for sale to a company fishing the Barents Sea – if a buyer could be found. She was already on the way there to avoid the forthcoming winter freeze in the Baltic. However, there would probably be minimal profit and ship-breakers might yet provide the boat's graveyard.

There was also the bigger problem of a swindling captain. How did the man expect to get away with skimming off some of the best stones? Zhirkov's personal assistants had met crew members at the airport and brought them back for questioning. They'd left him in no doubt that Radek had agents in Scotland who were part of the scam. That was the trouble with diamonds. The fools always convinced themselves that they didn't have enough. This final voyage of the decrepit factory ship was the last opportunity to call Radek to account. Zhirkov could only guess at the value of the rough stones that had been stolen. Ten percent might be a reasonable guess, but the truth would be forced from the thief very soon. The Second Mate would be able to give him details of the captain's operating methods when the ship docked. Ivan Konev (ex-navy and ex-KGB) was a stickler for factual detail and could probably be trusted. Zhirkov regretted not having planted him earlier.

*

(Whitehall, London):

While information and pictures of developments at sea were being pored over in offices in European capital cities, Agent O'Donnel, at a meeting in London, was being filled-in on the next moves in the operation. It amused him a little and annoyed him greatly that some desk-bound fool was giving him instructions on the very plan that he'd produced for his boss. He volunteered himself as the north of Scotland shore link in the slowly closing noose, a proposal supported reluctantly by Gurley but strongly endorsed by representatives from the Spanish, Portuguese and French embassies. The United States diplomat asked no questions and offered no views. Clearly he was there only to observe.

*

(Bay House Hotel, Scarr):

The hotel owners had given up on their expected visitor from England. It was evident that he wouldn't be arriving today so Annie Moston was about to send Sally the parlour maid home. And then a battered white Mini, covered in stylised images of red and green flames and bearing the legend, 'Yardley and Cheever, Custom Car Specialists, Aberdeen', pulled into the car park. A stiff, elderly man hauled himself from the driving seat and leaned wearily against the vehicle. Refusing Annie's help, the man wrestled a suitcase, a large backpack and two plastic shopping bags from the rear seat and struggled to carry them through the wind and rain to the front entrance. Eventually, he had to concede defeat and accept assistance with the plastic bags. He was clearly in no condition for conversation, so his helper introduced herself as co-owner, with her husband, of the famous Bay House Hotel and led him into the lobby. There, he flopped so wearily onto a chair that Annie began to wonder if he would manage to climb the stairs.

'Just you sit there, Mr. McSpake. I'll bring you a brandy if you like. Or would you prefer whisky? Oh hello, Minister', she said to the new arrival. 'Could you keep an eye on this gentleman for a minute or two while I bring him a whisky? You'd like one yourself, of course?'

The minister nodded his assent and sat down opposite Archie. 'Elements getting the better of you?' he inquired. 'Some of our more pious villagers might declare the rising storm symbolic of the Lord's growing wrath at man's manifold sins. Don't believe it myself, of course. There's no doubt that stormy weather existed long before people dismissed their multiple deities and invented Him to take all the blame. Your luggage indicates a resident guest and your name's McSpake. Are you here on vacation or business? A bit late in the year for holidays so I bet a penny you're on business. Bird watching? Good God! I owe you a penny. I'll put it in the kirk collection box for you. You can do your own praying – if you're so inclined.'

Archie was edging towards the inner swing-door to escape his large, volcanic tormentor when Geordie Moston, (Just call me Geordie), arrived. He handed a small glass of whisky to each of the two men. The minister sniffed his and then downed it in one gulp. Putting the empty glass into his coat pocket, he held the door open for Geordie and Archie to carry the bags through.

Placing his own untouched glass on a table in the lounge, the elderly guest declared his need for a shower and a rest. Geordie carried the luggage up one flight of stairs and pointed out the locations of fire escape and extinguishers. He hoped the old guy's memory was in a better condition than his physical appearance.

'You'll find a bathroom along there at the end of the passage,' he said, 'but all the rooms have their own showers. You're in Room Two. Here we are. I'll get Sally to bring up a cup of tea for you. Or would you prefer coffee? There's a menu on the bureau – if you'd like to give her your order for dinner. On special offer tonight we have dressed crab.'

'That's fine,' said the guest. 'I'll certainly hae the partan; if the quinie would fess up a coffee jist noo. And the gless o' whisky. I left that in the lounge.'

Geordie looked at him but said nothing. The man had certainly been in this area before. The lingo sounded authentic, at least to the alien ears of a Glaswegian. It might be a good idea to encourage him to talk over a drink or two. He wondered if any of the regulars knew anything about this man.

*

(Whitescar Cottage; on the edge of Scarr Village):

Four hundred yards west of the Bay House Hotel, Maggie MacPhail fought strong gusts to put up shutters on the north and east facing ground-floor windows. As usual, her upturned rowing boat was lashed down to the metal rings embedded in the hard-standing beside the front door. Earlier, she had secured the laboratory at the back of the house against all possible, (she hoped), eventualities. Maggie knew from years of experience just what severe weather was capable of doing to their exposed house down here by the sand dunes.

Her grandmother, Emmeline, was always tapping at the barometer in the lobby and attempting to read it through the magnifying glass that she wore on a cord round her neck. Today, Emmeline had declared that: 'The weather glass is diving like a lead-sinker so you better shorten sail and batten down the hatches.' Maggie had heard similar warnings from her grandmother on previous occasions and events had rarely proved the predictions wrong. More expenditure on damage repairs probably. Insurance was unaffordable for such an ancient property teetering on the sea's edge. However, a very good run of business would be needed before she could escape to somewhere with plenty of sunshine. Southern Portugal would be nice. So would north Africa. But her grandmother would never agree. Emmeline had declared that the only place she would consider moving to was somewhere in the Southern Ocean; preferably South Georgia. Maggie thought she was just saying that to be awkward, but couldn't be sure. Even after all these years she still found it hard to tell when the old woman was serious and when she was joking.

'Hatches battened, Grandmother,' she told Emmeline, bolting the heavy oak door. 'I'll make you some cocoa before you settle for the night. You'll enjoy a tot of rum in it as usual, won't you? If you just wait a little while, I'll pop into the office to catch the television weather forecast. The aerial surely won't stand up to this wind long enough to get the ten o'clock report. Would you like me to bring some toast and honey with your drink? Yes? Okay. You just rest for a bit and listen to the storm shaking the rafters. You always like that. Better pray that they don't cave in.'

Maggie's breathing returned gradually to normal and she began to relax while watching the programme. The presentation was gloomy as usual, but there seemed to be little worthy of hype tonight. Some objective statistics were presented subjectively, giving viewers a distorted picture; an ongoing famine in north eastern regions of Africa seemed no longer to be newsworthy – the sacking of the first football manager of the season was teased out to fill the vacuum; slates being blown off houses and trees blocking roads in the West Country were keeping outside broadcast teams busy in several locations. Maggie turned the set off. She'd get a shipping forecast on the radio later. Selecting one of the Dark Jamaica Rum miniatures from the bottom drawer of a filing cabinet, she headed for the kitchen – the galley, as Emmeline insisted on calling it.

The aborted mission tonight was a nuisance. Everything had been ready here as it was over at Bolson Hall. Victor had expressed his annoyance on the phone about the rapidly deteriorating weather that would rule out the use of his new motor-cruiser. A rendezvous at sea would be impossible during the next day or two; maybe not at all. 'Captain R.', he informed Maggie, 'Still refuses to consider that strategy. He's certain that the risks couldn't be justified; says he'll call off the whole operation if I don't do things his way. Anyway, Sis, pop across for a chat when the wind moderates. Don't want to say too much on the blower. See you.'

*

(The Greens' House, Sevenoaks):

Daniel was scanning the pages of two paperback books on British bird recognition. Trust Gurley to come up with such a daft idea. Why the hell couldn't his cover have been that of a tourist engaged in learning the specifics of malt whisky recognition? He'd have a head start on that. But he knew that Gurley would never consider letting him loose on such a scheme. The operation might determine the future of the department and, indeed, the future of all of them.

Back to the books. 'Eider Duck'. They seemed to frequent that coast. Points of recognition were: outline at rest; outline in flight; colour; diet and feeding behaviour; flocking habits; yes, okay. What about nesting? Nah. Though it wouldn't surprise him if the little bastards *did* nest at this time of year. And as for little, – the book said fifty to seventy centimetres in length. Mmm. But what was this about another type called the King Eider? Ah, fuck the swotting! Do it on the plane tomorrow – if the Airforce bods could get their arses off the ground.

'Expect a phone call', they'd said, 'sometime in the early hours'. How was that for precision planning? The smallest book was the one he'd take with him, – heavy on illustrations and light on written detail. He was to pass himself off as a beginner. The garb they'd provided looked like cast-off jungle uniform from the Second World War, so it might do. But the bloody binoculars were clearly ancient naval issue – probably dating from the battle of Jutland. Christ, he'd better not slip into the sea with those round his neck.

The Greens had gone to bed. They'd probably locked up the booze but that quarter bottle of blended whisky from the supermarket should help him through the early part of the night. He'd have the Export Pale Ale by way of a starter. He placed the opened bottles on the maple-veneered coffee table along with his mobile phone, and leaned back in the leather chair.

*

(Restaurant Ursa Major, Newton):

Fractal's date had looked steadily into her eyes after helping her into her new winter coat. It was chilly tonight and a strengthening wind was starting to whip empty beer cans and chip bags along the street. She was glad that she'd wrapped up for comfort as well as for style. She had worried about splashing out so much on the coat but Guy was clearly impressed. He had insisted on paying for the meal – as she'd expected. The vintage champagne was beyond her normal lifestyle and she'd tried not to show surprise at the size of the tip he had given the waiter.

'Thank you Guy', she said as he armed her into the taxi. 'Are you coming back to my place for a cup of coffee? I've got a spot of Armagnac if you want.' She lowered her head and looked up at him through her eyelashes. 'I'd like to hear more about your Alien Conspiracies book.'

'Delighted, Fractal', he said. 'Then maybe you can tell me more about this old buffer who writes doggerel and who's monitoring the abducted child at Scarr village. A contact of mine, chap called Jon Cardington, runs a group in the nearby town of Portlach. It's called the Portlach Anomalous Phenomena Society. Apparently Jon can observe half of Scarr from his study. He's very rich and spends an absolute fortune on optical equipment. He arranged finance for the publication of my first book. Now, he and I are to be involved in talks with an American movie production company about a definitive film on alien abductions. It's clear from your serious interest in this Marc

77

Powell case that you could fit into the psychological profiling team. If you're interested, I'm well placed to pull strings. I'll give old Jon a ring in the morning – if you'll allow me to use your telephone.' Fractal's eyes confirmed that her telephone would be entirely at his disposal.

*

(Bay House Hotel):

After a plate of 'organic' vegetable soup, the partan made a satisfying main course. Served in its shell, liberally seasoned with pepper in the way that he remembered from all those years ago, and accompanied by crisp oatcakes and a glass of cold water, Archie just didn't feel the need for anything else. On his way out of the small dining room, he looked into the public bar. Good. The minister wasn't there. Telling Geordie Moston that he was having an early night and would probably sleep late in the morning, he headed for the stairs. The background moaning of the wind rose briefly to a roar as the last of the drinkers left by the front door and a gust of cold air urged the hotel's solitary guest up to the landing. He was glad that he'd turned up the heating in his room before going down to supper and he knew that he was going to sleep soundly tonight, even if it was still only nine o'clock.

*

Suddenly awake, Archie sat up in bed, listening. For several bemused seconds he was back in the Scarr of fifty years earlier and the detonation of a maroon had just put the lifeboat on standby. Even dawning realisation of where he was didn't entirely curb his anxious wait for the second bang, the one that would signal an imminent launch. But today's larger lifeboat was stationed at Portlach and it seemed unlikely they'd use maroons to summon crew members in this age of electronic communications. Better not ask anybody; they'd probably laugh

78

at him. Clearly, the noise had been a product of the storm, and *that* had gained substantially in strength while he slept. He got out of bed and wiped a pane of the steamed-up window. Great rollers were powering out of the darkness, exploding up the beach opposite and roaring backwards in preparation for further assaults. Four hundred yards to the east, with the tide nearly full, periodic 'lumps of water' were sweeping over the breakwater and deluging boats in the harbour basin.

So far, this was an ordinary storm. Over there in nineteen fifty three, entire waves – not just spray – were engulfing Scarr lighthouse. A sixteen-years-old Archie had watched sequences of them with crests fully forty feet in height. More than a mile inland, people could feel wetness on their faces and taste salt on their lips. After giving up on attempts to shelter from the wind, he had allowed it to propel him, (running to keep his balance), from the bottom of Harbour Lane to the top. He'd risked the same exploit on Scarr Brae and soon found himself, leg-weary, hanging on to a telegraph pole on the brow of the hill. Up there, flying sea-foam was piling against Birch Cottage before whipping away to the woods beyond. There, skeletal trees were being torn from the ground by the shrieking elements. Tonight he could feel the tension growing in his neck and shoulders at the memory of that day.

Archie had experienced many storms in his lifetime but never one like that – well, not outside of the tropics. Wind force was away beyond the piddling Beaufort scale. It had been measured at a steady (not gusting) speed of one hundred and twenty five miles an hour in the Hebrides and, he was convinced, must have exceeded even that on this coast. There hadn't been sustained winds of that intensity in modern times. They had inflicted enormous loss of lives and of ships, including the Stranraer to Larne ferry which sank in the Irish Sea. Fishing boats had been wrecked even in harbours and severe damage caused to buildings. Inland, vast areas of forests were laid flat.

The ensuing storm surge down the narrowing channel of the North Sea had produced devastating floods on the unprepared east coast of England causing many more deaths. A change in wind direction piled the storm surge east towards the European mainland where it burst through protective dykes. Several hundred deaths occurred in and around the British Isles and nearly two thousand people were drowned in Holland.

Statistical probability would indicate only a miniscule threat from a storm of that magnitude tonight; but you could never trust statistics in relation to individual episodes of severe weather. Another loud bang had him heading for the corridor where he found Geordie on a stepladder inspecting a trapdoor in the ceiling. His offer of assistance turned down, Archie returned thankfully to his room.

He began to recapture the feelings he'd had as a child in the old house round the corner in Simpson Close. That was long gone, its location now part of the library car park. He was experiencing once again remnants of the anxiety that used to trouble him when he contrasted his indoor comfort with the harshness outside. Words were tumbling in his mind, coalescing, aligning. He knew he must get up and write them down before they evaporated in sleep – just as countless pieces of verse had done in the past. He switched on the lamp on the bureau and rapidly produced:

I strained in vain to see beyond the window
where outdoor-blackness vied with that inside
and stars had slipped away behind the blanket
of storm-cloud scrolling southwards from the sea.
I listened to the wind scale up the Beaufort,
hurling hail against the shuddering panes
and penetrating gaps between the roof slates
to slam the heavy loft-hatch in the hall.
I curled myself into a foetal posture
with woollen bedclothes pressed against my ears,
relaxing limbs in sequence, breathing deeply,
letting sleep defocus childish fears.

Not a completely-finished verse but it would do for now. He

could tinker with it tomorrow, if he felt in the mood, but it would be better left until improvements came of their own volition. He lay on the bed and started worrying about the lack of rhyme. It didn't want to rhyme. It must be the bloody Fractal effect.

*

(Birch Cottage):

Having decided that he mustn't miss any aspect of the storm, Marco was still awake. He was enjoying the sensations of the wind roaring over the hill, shaking the cottage from end to end. Fusillades of hailstones rattled against the windows at intervals and a persistent howling noise came from the kitchen chimney. He couldn't have slept even if he'd wanted to. Tonight he felt safe at last from the threatening strangers in the big car. Even they wouldn't be mad enough to be out in this. Would they? Out from where? Somebody must know their hiding place. Maybe Arc would have some idea, or the Mitchell girl with the blond hair. She was really nice. If he could get away for a bit, he'd take up her offer of a fishing session. It was Blackscar rocks she'd said, wasn't it? There was an old fishing rod in one of the sheds out at the back, but he was sure his grandfather wouldn't lend it to him. On Sunday evening he'd heard his mother giving strict instructions about what he was permitted to do. Fishing wasn't included.

He shut his eyes, relaxed and listened to the fury of the elements.

*

(Scarr Kirk):

The Reverend Stackpoole had forsaken his comfortable study chair for an oak pew in the kirk. He hadn't put the lights on, (he didn't want to attract attention), and he was careful not to let the beam from his torch stray onto any of the windows.

Painstaking planning was vital for the success of the ceremony. Diagrams and a timetable should ensure that everything would go smoothly. Tomorrow he'd check who would be attending and give each of them instructions on dress and reminders about ritual. He started at the sound of the vestry door crashing open. But it was only Tatey's husband, Wullie, come to make sure that the kirk was secure against the storm. Wullie was very conscientious – especially when you didn't want to see him.

'It's all right Mr. Tate. I've just checked everything. You can't be too careful in this weather. Thank you for your trouble. I'd ask you across to the manse for a drink but I'm clean out of supplies at the moment. Maybe another time?'

**

CHAPTER SEVEN

Wednesday Morning

(Russian Factory Ship, Northern North Sea):

On the bridge of the Nikolai Rykov, Captain Radek was riding out the storm with his usual patience. Four and a half hours until dawn and the shipping forecast offered him little reassurance. There was no chance of completing the operation tomorrow night. Friday could be a remote possibility, but he knew that it would be wiser to defer things for yet another day. The people ashore wouldn't risk taking the transfer before the sea had subsided, so he should reschedule the drop to Saturday night. Then, it was essential for him to head eastwards without further delay.

There was little doubt that his position and course were now being monitored as a matter of routine by those who believed they owned this part of the sea. The captain didn't want that routine to turn into something more specific. The 'stealth' aircraft was lashed down securely under cover, as it had been all the way from the West African coast, and it really needed a test-flight before the operation went ahead. He'd remind Yashin to give it a check over tomorrow and take it for a short outing on Friday. Then, on Saturday night, it would carry ashore the usual ten percent skimmed from Zhirkov's diamond cache to be put into the care of Bolson and MacPhail. If he followed the established routine, it would appear to confirm that this operation was the same as previous ones; i.e. that the stones that were landed should travel in small lots, via Bristol, to the shady European cutters. And so they would.

This time, however, the captain wasn't going to settle for ten percent. It would be his very last chance to have the whole cache from a two year operation. He'd been preparing his plans over many months and had revised and refined them until he was certain they were as close to faultless as could be. When he and Yashin returned from the Scarr delivery, they would refuel the aircraft and, after sending the remaining crew members to their quarters, bring all of the diamonds up from the strong room. By the time the crew realised they'd gone, they should be well on the way to Scandinavia. Later, Yashin would drop him in Norway with the stones and then deliver the aircraft to the Americans. In return for the acquired Russian technology, Yashin had been promised asylum and enough dollars to last a lifetime. Or, the captain thought, for as long as it took Zhirkov's agents to find him.

The plan that Radek had put in place to ensure his own safety, required that Yashin, the aircraft and himself should appear to be 'lost at sea'. The diamonds missing from the Nikolai Rykov's strong room would reveal the deception but, with sufficient head start, he was confident, (well almost confident), that he'd get away. Retirement to wealthy obscurity in South America seemed more desirable every time he thought about his future. The surgeon in Canada had promised: 'Even your own mother won't know you Vladimir'. But it wasn't his mother he'd be hiding from. Zhirkov's reach was very long and his enemies invariably vanished without trace – or explanation. His agents were all former KGB men and the rising billionaire could afford to employ a great many. As an extra safeguard, therefore, Radek had arranged for a second image, and identity, change to take place in Thailand. When Zhirkov's hit- men found Doctor Digby in Ontario, the information and photographs they persuaded him to give up would send them off in pursuit of someone who didn't exist. There were never certainties with changes of identity, but the captain couldn't think of any scheme that would give him a better chance than this one.

That is what Vladimir Radek had planned. The pilot, Yashin, had his own plan which foresaw a very different ending.

Radar showed that the ship was getting closer to those oil-rigs. The captain altered its heading two degrees to starboard.

*

(Whitescar Cottage):

A hundred and seventy nautical miles south of the Nicolai Rykov, Maggie MacPhail was trying to sleep on her office couch. Ever since she had given up the nightly struggle to get Emmeline to her favourite 'crow's nest' bedroom on the upper floor and had installed her in the one next to the kitchen, Maggie had had to watch that the old woman didn't try to get up on her own. She needed a lot of help with mobility but could be sufficiently headstrong to try to cook something on the gas stove in the kitchen. Even worse, she might decide to wander outside to 'cast a weather eye forrard'. A Care Home could never be an answer to the problem. Maggie was certain that Emmeline wouldn't survive such a restriction for long.

When Maggie was five weeks old, her parents had died during the London blitz. Her grandmother had taken on her care and that of her eighteen months old brother, Victor. She owed so much to the old woman that she couldn't possibly do anything to make her unhappy. Maggie switched on the reading lamp and reached for the photograph album on top of a bookcase.

There, was a picture of Maggie and Victor with Emmeline. It had been taken in Peterhead in nineteen forty six. That was the year Maggie went to school and Victor was taken off to live with his late father's sister, Lena MacPhail, in Whitby. Snapped with an ancient box camera on some kind of sub-standard film, the badly fixed print had soon become very faded. Maggie had had it copied many years later but the degradation had only been halted. Maybe Victor could do something to improve it with that new-fangled digital technology. It did seem unlikely but she'd ask him anyway.

And here was a wedding photograph of her father, Hector, and mother, Yolande, taken in Whitby in nineteen thirty nine. Hector MacPhail was in his Petty Officer's uniform while Yolande, who must have been just sixteen at the time, was wearing a white wedding dress. Her veil was thrown back to show her dark Latin looks, – looks that would be wiped away for ever two years later when she and Hector died in a German bombing raid on London's East End.

Emmeline, devastated by her only daughter's death, had got the two young children away from London at the first opportunity. They moved to the Peterhead area when Emmeline's late-father's brother, Barney Hill offered them the tenancy of a run-down cottage in the tiny village of Burnhaven. Five years later, after Barney's wife had died, Emmeline and Maggie went to stay with him in his house in Peterhead. At the same time, Victor was formally adopted by Auntie Lena.

Maggie always remembered those days as the happiest and most exciting time of her life. Uncle Barney owned a fish-transport business in Peterhead and a butcher's shop in Fraserburgh, and had, (like many others), been described in the local paper as 'a pillar of the community'. When Barney retired in nineteen fifty three, he sold his pre-war Austin Ascot and bought a new Alvis saloon with dove-grey and deep- burgundy coachwork. Twelve years old Maggie had thought it the most beautiful motor car in the world. She always looked forward eagerly to her weekend picnic outings in it with Barney and Emmeline. One afternoon they'd visited Scarr and fallen in love with the place, Emmeline declaring it to be nearly as good as South Georgia. But it was not until nineteen seventy five, after Barney had died at the age of ninety and left them a modest sum of money, that they'd been able to buy the cottage beside the Whitescar sand dunes, the site of their picnic on that high-summer Sunday twenty years before. Maggie was then a biochemist of thirty four and Emmeline was approaching her seventieth birthday.

Maggie listened to the turmoil in the darkness outside. There had been many worse storms during the years they'd stayed here and she was hopeful that things might improve before dawn. The clock showed that that would be in four hours or so. She got up to make a cup of tea.

On the way to the kitchen, she paused to peer at the sepia photograph in the ornate golden frame on the sitting room wall. The low-wattage bulb of the night-light didn't show it very clearly but Maggie had lived with it for so long that she was familiar with its every detail. It had been taken in Montevideo in nineteen twenty one at the marriage of Emmeline Hill and Victor Borges.

It was on the way north, after the end of that season's whaling operation that Emmeline's father, Charlie, had disappeared from his whale-catcher off the River Plate. His sixteen years old daughter, who had been accompanying him on her second voyage, took command of what was now *her* boat and ordered the crew to put into port at Montevideo. That's what she'd always maintained, though Maggie remained sceptical.

The American whaling co-operative, which Charlie had joined after the Great War, had started operating in nineteen-nineteen with three catchers and a two thousand ton merchantman converted into a factory ship by a Norwegian company that had gone bankrupt in the process. When the co-operative's catches were so poor for the second year running that it was unable to meet its hard-won contracts, it became clear that the enterprise had failed. Under the threat of ruin, members agreed to sell off assets for as much as they could get. In the event, they were to get very little.

Emmeline, however, had fallen in love with a trawler skipper called Victor Borges at their first meeting in Montevideo. Twelve weeks later they were married and the young couple set out on Victor's boat on a voyage from Uruguay to the United States of

America. It had long been Victor's ambition to run a fishing operation in New England. Once there, the husband and wife team rapidly gained a reputation for honesty and resourcefulness and their business began to prosper. In nineteen twenty three, a pregnant Emmeline settled ashore near Portland, Maine, to raise the expected baby. There, the Borges' daughter, Yolande, was born. Tragedy struck two years later when Victor Borges died at sea of 'heart failure'. Subsequently, Emmeline sold up and took Yolande to London.

Maggie peeped into the old lady's room and listened to her loud, regular breathing. Better not to disturb her with an offer of tea. She tiptoed into the kitchen and reached for a jar of instant coffee.

*

(Bay House Hotel):

The storm had forced its way into Archie's dream. He woke up, wet and shivering, still struggling to keep his head above water, his hands still cramped from hanging on to the duvet. Bloody hell! He sat up, switched on the bed-head light and waited for his pounding pulse to calm down. It felt as if he had been on the verge of a heart attack. In a minute or two he might have a cup of tea. On the table, beside the electric kettle, was a half-sized bottle of white wine that he'd looked at earlier but decided not to open. Chardonnay certainly wasn't his drink of choice. However, … . He got up at last, wrapped the duvet round his shoulders and switched on the kettle. While waiting, he unscrewed the cap and poured some wine into a tumbler.

The image of towering seas and a foundering ship demanded to be banished from his mind but Archie hung on to it determinedly. He shuffled across to the notepad on the bureau, feeling himself enmeshed in wind and waves, wind and waves, and the persistent rhythm that stitched them together – as if at sea in a tempest.

I opened my eyes   to the rage of the storm,
in the avid embrace   of that ravening beast.
With sail gone and mastless,   stout oars torn away,
we jettisoned cargo   and weapons and mail-coats.
Sheer cliffs to the eastward,   great ice-peaks beyond,
in steepening seas   that outstripped our bailing,
we sped past deep inlets,   unable to reach them,
until the last haven   had vanished astern.
Ahead of our tall prow   a gap in a lee-shore
was rapidly merging   with gathering night.
On the edge of our passing,   as timbers were riven,
dead men shrieked their hate   at the maw of the Maelstrom.

For a time, Archie wasn't really aware of what he had scribbled. He breathed more slowly, more deliberately, waiting for his stress to subside, and then tried to read the scrawl critically. Setting it down had been just like producing examination answers from the unconscious. He had never been able to remember back then which questions he'd answered, let alone the information contained in his responses. In later life, most of his creative writing stuff had emerged in a similar way. He started to examine the structure and content of this piece.

There wasn't much doubt about its Viking background. He'd once read somewhere of long-ago battles with Danes on these very beaches. Local folk tales seemed to give credence to those. However, the Maelstrom was the great marine whirlpool among Norway's Lofoten Islands. So this could be about seafarers returning from a voyage to the far north who'd been caught in a storm on the Norwegian Sea. Sail, oars, mail-coats, high prow, could all support a vision of armed Norse traders.

The rhythm of the piece might have become embedded in his mind from fragments of ancient sagas. It brought back the memory of a scholar who'd paid a visit to the English Department when Archie had been a pupil at Portlach Academy all those years ago. The man had tried to interest a press-ganged audience in the words of his new translation of the ancient saga of Beowulf.

Archie, like everyone else, had been bored by the performance. But, when the man declaimed lines in what he said was the Old English of the original, his chest had threatened to burst his tweed jacket and his reedy voice had boomed out with a power that induced crawling sensations in the nape of Archie's neck. Suddenly the rhythm had seemed to fit and there had had been the sound of heaving waves and of fierce battles in a twilight-world of monsters and demons. That had been a transporting experience. He'd even considered trying to learn the lingo. But schoolboy preferences are fleeting where work is concerned and he had found other occupations more attractive and far less demanding.

Archie had never heard Old Norse spoken but didn't doubt that the rhythms of sagas declaimed in Norwegian longhouses, during interminable winter-nights, would be equally grounded in those of the natural world.

A trading long-ship returning from the far north to its home anchorage in southern Norway, or Orkney, would almost certainly have carried seal skins, wolf pelts and fox furs – and maybe valuable walrus ivory and hides. But the bulk of the cargo, he believed, would have been dried cod. He remembered his father's generation still preparing such supplies for the winter fifty years ago in these very coastal villages. Of course, those were usually haddock and small codling, salted and sun-dried rather than freeze-dried as they would be in the icy north. In his nightmare, he had seen a vision of the long-ship's crew heaving overboard all of their prized cargo in a frantic bid for survival.

The piece that he'd written earlier, (where was it?), could be the foundation for a first verse. This, with its oceanic rhythms, could be a second. The poem's completion would require a third verse that reverted to the original metre. Perhaps it could be about waking up in the morning and finding the real storm still raging. The ending might be tricky – subject to anticlimax. Let it simmer away for the present. Something might emerge eventually. Again, no rhyme! The piece was away beyond that stage now but was, in any case, probably better without it. Archie accepted the idea very reluctantly.

Nearly four o'clock but the sleep interruption certainly hadn't been a waste of time. The kettle had gone cold, damn it! He drained the last of the wine and, as he did so, the lights went out. From the window, he could see that everything was in darkness out there, apart from the Scarr lighthouse which continued to operate on its emergency power supply.

*

(Bolson Hall, East of Scarr):

The Major lay awake in his large bedroom at the Hall. His wife had long-since moved permanently to the one next door. Victor rarely slept now, perpetually worried by the debts that threatened to destroy him. He hadn't been able to pay Tradwell this month and the gamekeeper was becoming surlier by the day. Apart from Maggie and Radek, only Tradwell knew of Victor's deception, of how he had taken the dead Major's place in nineteen seventy six, after their mercenary group was wiped out in a skirmish with Cuban mercenaries in Angola. Sergeant Victor MacPhail and Corporal Lachlan Tradwell had been the only survivors. They had escaped with the unexpected assistance of a covert Soviet 'Military Adviser' attached to the Cubans. Sergeant MacPhail had found it convenient to vanish at this point, ('believed killed somewhere in Africa') and to reappear as Major V. Bolson R.E.M.E. (Retd.).

The bogus Major bought a small cottage in rural Dorset and retired there with his newly acquired wife, Davina, and his 'batman', L. Tradwell. Now, owner of Bolson Hall, (formerly Blackscar House), and its estate, together with the mothballed Glenscarr Distillery, Victor was regretting the deception that had brought him here. But there was no possibility of going back. Radek just wouldn't let him off the hook. Victor could produce no definite proof that the real Major Bolson had died in an illegal military operation. What if he were accused of killing the man for his own profit? Profit? The Major's measly pension? Tradwell, too, was becoming so pissed-off that he might cause serious problems. It was the word of one individual against another. When Tradwell, in his role of gamekeeper and field-sports instructor, had taken that last party of Austrian grouse shooters to the airport in Victor's aged Bentley, he'd claimed that the usual generous tips had been withheld. Yes, Tradwell was a problem for which Victor had no answer. Not yet, but he was giving it a lot of serious thought. He intended that the stuff in the study safe should be shared with Maggie alone. Tradwell knew it was there but he couldn't possibly know how much.

Victor remembered that first holiday in Turkey. Meeting once again with his Soviet rescuer, Major Radek, by then a civilian, had seemed the product of chance, but Victor had long since realised that he'd been targeted. They'd had a few drinks together, talked about Angola and Africa generally. Radek had claimed to have business contacts on that mineral-rich continent and that he was in the process of arranging a business scheme to trade in uncut diamonds. Victor, looking for an opportunity of his own, was interested. That's how it had started. Now, he just wanted to get out, preferably with profit. However, Radek's refusal to let Victor sell his miniscule share of the diamonds was crippling business here at the estate. Victor had had enough of being dictated to. He'd been working on a plan of how it might be possible for him to change identity once again and disappear from his creditors.

That bloody wind was a problem tonight. The old distillery and its outbuildings could be at risk from storm damage and it was no longer insured. At least the remaining casks of whisky could come to no harm. They'd been stolen last year when 'robbers' had got past the warehouse security system. A police operation hadn't found any trace of the missing whisky. Tradwell had made sure it was well hidden on the moor and, after the search had been called off, brought it back to the secret cellar beyond the cellars at The Hall. To sell it, however, they would need to bottle it under a different name, perhaps blended so that connoisseurs wouldn't recognise 'The Unique Taste of the Real Glenscarr'. A pity to lose so much of its value.

Victor had become increasingly concerned during the last few months about what Tradwell got up to when he went out at nights. He certainly visited the bay House for a drink or two but discreet inquiries convinced Victor that these drinking sessions didn't account for all of the missing time. He'd naturally assumed that the man had a lady-friend somewhere nearby. But doubts were nagging away at his mind. What if he were meeting police or customs officials to set Victor up? The prospect of arrest for involvement in smuggling was alarming. And, with the husband in prison, there was nothing to stop Tradwell stepping into his shoes – and into his wife's bed. He'd seen how the two of them had been looking at each other when they thought he wouldn't notice. Christ! They didn't need to shop him. They were welcome to go off together whenever they wanted. Could that be the answer to some of Victor's problems? Perhaps a share, a very small share, of the diamonds might induce them to get out of his life. It was a price that needed careful consideration. But before he could consider, sleep waylaid him.

*

(Sevenoaks):

Daniel, having left the Greens' bathroom as quietly as possible, tiptoed to his bedroom to make final preparations for the journey. He'd been given an assurance on the telephone that an unmarked vehicle would pick him up in half an hour and take him to the air base. Of course he'd have to wait there until weather conditions 'Up North' had improved sufficiently to ensure a risk-free landing. That could be any time today – but the meteorologists were predicting late afternoon. Shit! Hours of sitting around waiting – and they probably wouldn't be too liberal with the drinks. It had been agreed, without consulting him, that arrival in Scarr by public transport would best support his cover story. In the event of his being delayed for too long, missing the last bus, they'd lay on a taxi for him.

In Whitehall, the general consensus was that Scarr would be the scene of the smuggling operation's last act. Naval assistance was being deployed on that premise. Daniel looked forward to being at the hub of things when the trap was sprung, believing that his future would probably depend on it. However, within the Department's general plan, to which he had contributed so much, early glimmerings of a scheme of his own were beginning to crystallize. He resisted the temptation to take that any further at present. It would have to be finalised on the spot after analyzing local circumstances.

Gathering his luggage together, he moved quietly down the hallway and unlocked the front door, leaving it slightly ajar on the security chain. He didn't want the Greens getting up to see who could be knocking so early in the morning. The brief note on the table would give them all the information that he wanted them to have. With a measure of success, (to Daniel the term 'luck' was meaningless), he wouldn't be seeing them again. He might send them a bottle of brandy at Christmas so they could celebrate their freedom from his alcoholic presence. A small, battered, blue van pulled up at the kerb and a scruffily dressed individual, ignoring noise legislation, beeped the horn. Damn! Daniel scrambled to get his luggage out before the Greens came to investigate.

*

(Birch Cottage):

By the time Marco awoke, faint greyish light was showing at the gap in the curtains. The wind still buffeted the house, still threatened to blow the windows in but, he thought, it wasn't *quite* as strong as it had been in the middle of the night. His grandfather knocked at the door and came in with tea and toast on a tray.

'Sorry, the toast's a bit black round the edges. There's a power cut so I had to make it the old fashioned way. Your Gran and I think you should stay in bed for a bit. She's stoking up the cooker and she'll give you a shout when it's breakfast time. I'm off to have a look round outside, see what damage there is. There's definitely a hole in the roof of that farthest shed. That'll need an emergency repair. But there might be other problems I haven't seen yet. I'll know when I've done my rounds. You'll be safer in here till the wind's gone down. I'll bring in some extra firewood later if it calms a bit and you could maybe help. But let's wait and see.

'Thanks, Granda. I'll do some reading when it gets lighter. I thought my bed lamp was broken but it's the power cut of course.'

Marco bit into the first slice of toast. He didn't mind that it had scorched edges; he could hardly see them in the gloom and they gave the toast a nice salty taste. The home-made butter from Harry's farm was brilliant. He paused for a moment to listen. Yes, the wind was definitely going down but probably not enough for them to let him go to the harbour. He'd been here for two whole days, not counting Sunday night, and hadn't even seen the harbour yet. It didn't look promising. Maybe if he nagged them a bit they might take him down later. But he knew the chances were slight. And he daren't sneak off on his own. They'd start to watch him all the time if he did that.

Actually, Birch Cottage wasn't too bad. There was a lot that was good about it. At times though, it felt like a prison. He missed the company of people his own age. So far he'd only met two for a little while. There was Raymond something, the one who liked to be called Arc, (or Ark, maybe), and that nice Mitchell girl. He'd forgotten to ask his grandmother if she knew what the girl's first name was. There must be lots of kids in the village, unless the Pied Piper had come on a visit. That reminded him – there was a tin whistle thing in the cupboard, though it was made of green plastic. He found it, took it back to his bed only to find it much harder to play than he'd imagined, producing a high pitched shriek on every note. A pity about the radio.

*

(Scarr Manse):

The minister stretched his ample frame and emitted a low-pitched growl from the back of his throat. His companion stirred beside him.

'Oh Solomon, you're so deliciously masculine. I've loved

being with you.' She turned and rested her head against his chest, rather too near to his armpit, so she took it away again. 'When do you want me to bring Tricia over to meet you? Would an hour before the ceremony be all right? She's thrilled with everything I've told her and she's looking forward to the initiation. She saw you having a drink one night at the Brakeside Arms and would have introduced herself if you hadn't hurried off. Her husband's in Geneva this week so she'd be happy to stay here for the night. She says that you only have to ask.'

'I might well do that Marietta. Twenty seven did you say? Great! If she's all that you tell me, you might advise her to bring her toothbrush, – and her frilliest underwear, of course. Speaking of frilly underwear, here are your lovely knickers. There's nothing quite like the feel of silk. I'd have enjoyed trying them on but they're too – um – petite.'

Solomon, steeling himself, kissed his companion. This hadn't been his most memorable night. Still, she *was* willing enough. It surprised him that Jonathan Cardington hadn't divorced her long ago. He listened as she called her husband on a mobile phone, apologising because the storm had prevented her getting home last night and assuring him that she'd spent the night at Dolly's place. She would see him when the wind abated. As soon as she'd rung off, she called Dolly with instructions on how to respond if her husband tried to check up on her. The minister noted that the routine wasn't an unfamiliar one. However, she should have put the deception in place in advance. But never mind. It was most unlikely she'd ever stay here again.

This Tricia sounded like hot stuff. He hoped that he'd be up to the challenge. Tomorrow night would reveal all. The minister rolled out of bed and padded, naked, to the bathroom. Marietta wrapped a pillow firmly round her ears.

*

(The Meade House, Scarr):

Taking his creels in before the storm broke had enabled Arc to relax and he had fallen asleep as soon as he got into bed. It hadn't always been like that. After his father's accident on the oil rig, he hadn't had an unbroken night's rest for more than two years. Night after night his mother would hear him getting out of bed and walking about his room. Sometimes he would play tapes on his music centre with no apparent concern for the neighbours. Effie, very concerned for her son's state of mind, had tried to persuade him to cooperate with the child psychologist. Arc had declined even to speak to the woman. There had been some discussions about in-patient assessment but these foundered when Effie backed up her son's rejection of the proposals. Now, however, he seemed to be getting along by keeping busy with all his schemes. Doctor Murray believed that he was going to be all right.

Effie prepared a cup of tea and carried it through to the sitting room. She wouldn't waken the boy as usual; he'd brought his creels up to the shed and there wouldn't be any school today. The clock above the fireplace said seven twenty. Normally she went across to open her shop on the junction of Middlefields and Scarr Brae for eight thirty, but today there were no hairdressing appointments before eleven. Just as well. It would be rather pointless for people to have their hair done in this sort of weather. She was almost glad that she'd turned down Mr. Stackpoole's invitation to the mysterious 'Special Ceremony' that he was having at the kirk tomorrow evening. It was unlikely that the wind could blow like this right through until then but, in any case, Effie had got into the habit of spending her evenings at home. She sighed, relaxed and wondered if the minister would call at the shop today. Lately, he'd been dropping in quite often. 'In passing', he'd always said, but Effie found that she was beginning to look at him in a slightly more interested way. He was a bit old, really, but – well – she'd see.

**

CHAPTER EIGHT

Wednesday Afternoon

(River Scarr Valley, South of Bolson Hall):

Tradwell was in full gamekeeper mode. The two springer spaniels needed a proper outing and he was walking them up the Scarr valley towards its junction with the Strath Boggach Burn. Although Glenscarr Distillery had manufactured the product that bore its name for nearly two hundred years, the peaty water that contributed so much to its alchemy had always been piped directly from the uncontaminated upper reaches of that burn. At one time, the distillery had exported a special 'Strath Boggach Highland Malt Whisky (Limited Edition)' in fancy bottles, at premium prices. That particular product had all gone to the Italian market until the outbreak of the Second World War brought an end to shipments.

That was in the days of the previous owners who had, subsequently, let the distillery decline. They'd operated sporadically for forty years or so after the war, selling their product to blenders, but had been on the verge of ruin by the nineteen eighties. When the naïve, would-be entrepreneur Major Bolson turned up, it must have been like winning the pools.

Recently, Victor had been talking about possible ways of getting the 'stolen' Glenscarr on to the market labelled Strath Boggach, (after all it was the same whisky), but he knew that the customs people would be onto the ploy pretty quickly. To carry the matter through, he would need to reopen the distillery to provide cover and the funds for that were, it seemed, non-existent. No, Tradwell thought, the booze would have to be sold to a shady dealer with its taste and colour subtly altered. Maybe old Jock Tavish or Andy Watt would bring their years of experience to such a plan in exchange for a few hundred tax-free pounds in the back-pocket. It was certainly a job for professional whisky tasters. Jock and Andy also had a reputation for repeatedly outsmarting the most suspicious of excisemen in earlier times when such officials lived on site. The current downturn, arising from overproduction, made it uneconomic for anyone to buy the business as a going concern. A Japanese distillery company had offered to do a deal but Victor had declined their meagre offer. That offer was still on the table, however, and Tradwell knew that they could be forced to accept it – if finances were really as bad as Victor had been griping about. The bastard had diamonds in his safe but was keeping quiet about the number and their value. An aggrieved Lachlan Tradwell wouldn't put up with this treatment for much longer. He'd need only one chance and the high-life that he craved would be waiting for him. It was only this prospect that had stopped him shopping the bloody 'Major' long ago.

Having reached the Junction Pool, Tradwell began to climb the steep slope down which the burn poured in a series of cascades. The higher he went, the less shelter there was from the wind and, all around him, stunted birches and alders thrashed at the sky. He was pleased to see ragged openings appearing intermittently in the cloud cover. At the top of the slope, he could make a rough estimate of wind strength: down from last night's force eleven to about seven this afternoon. A sudden shower of rain spattered the ridge as he left it behind. With the subdued dogs at his heels, he began to follow the left bank of the burn which now meandered towards him down a gentle incline from the high moor to the south east. In taking this route, he was leaving behind the Bolson Estate for that of Lord Leithland, but he was eager to see if the strangers were still present at the old cottage. If he couldn't get to the bottom of the mystery, there was the option of quizzing one or other of the Leithland keepers. Nothing could ever happen within their preserves that they didn't know about. This was Wednesday. Nesbit, one of the under-keepers, sometimes drank at the Bay House on Wednesday nights. A 'chance' meeting, the offer of a pint of Export, and Nesbit would give Lachlan all the estate gossip.

For the next two miles, the Strath Boggach Burn took the form of a network of smaller streams and rivulets. These drained the high-moor bogs and converged from various directions on three tiny lochans. They all had Gaelic names but Lachlan had no idea what they were. He couldn't be bothered with that nonsense. Too bloody difficult for a grown man to learn; and, if you did learn it, there would be hardly anyone around here to speak it to. He glanced towards the low dome of the collecting cistern which provided the distillery's water. This supply, it was wrongly claimed, was secured in perpetuity by ancient royal charter. Lachie led the dogs across the channels to where a depression two hundred yards beyond steered another runnel of water off to the south west to feed the Belter Burn. The strangers and their vehicle had been holed up at the old cottage down that particular valley.

The dogs were becoming somewhat cheesed off, he thought, and it was raining more heavily, so a quick look would do for now. Victor was having a business meeting later and Davina had indicated that, as usual, she wouldn't be attending. After all, it was only with his sister Maggie who was a bit of a fool. She was supposed to have a Doctorate in Biochemistry but nobody really believed that. Everyone knew she was dabbling with witch's brews. Davina couldn't stand Maggie. But she did like Lachlan Tradwell. She liked him a lot. With her, he'd found, there always seemed to be the unspoken promise of something more than casual talk. He had made up his mind to discuss the matter with her. After he'd had another look at the old cottage and its skulking inhabitants, if they were still there, he would hurry back to The Hall and invite Davina to his rooms to share a drink. He imagined himself standing in front of her, whisky bottle in one hand, glass in the other, asking if she'd like a small whisky or, (and here he'd pause and stress the words carefully), would she prefer a large one? He should probably raise one eyebrow and smile suggestively at that point. Carried away by his mental picture, he was nearly on top of the cottage before realising its proximity. He signalled 'sit down' to the dogs and crouched with them behind a large clump of gorse. A chuckle from the other side of the bush froze him like a pointer. Peering between the thorns was Drew Forsyth, Lord Leithland's Head Gamekeeper.

'You're a bit outside your boundaries the day, Lachie. You're the second snooper I've seen so far. Caught the young Meade lad, him they ca Arc, no half an hour ago. I skelpit his lug and telt him he'd get the jile if he spoke aboot onything he'd seen. I made him swear an oath on the Official Secrets Act. Actually it wis my hymn book, but he took it gey serious. I suppose you're on the same quest. Well, his Lordship wants me to mak certain the mannies in the cottage dinna get disturbed. He says their business has the highest level o secrecy. I saw you last time, snoopin in the dark, and guessed you'd be back. Now look, Lachie, there wis a government minister flew up in a helicopter last week to mak sure there'd be nae breaches o' security. So if ye say a word aboot it, the police will be visitin The Hall.'

'Right, Drew, I was just curious. Nearly everybody I've spoken to in the village thinks they must be spies. There's a lot of chatter about it. If they were genuine visitors, people are saying, they would be staying at the hotel. You can expect a lot of prying around the estate if news gets out that they're here. How are you going to explain things then?'

'Well, it's nae to be pushed ower fast. Folk need to find oot a wee bit at a time. That way it'll be mair believable.'

'Find out what, Drew?'

'The story is that they're surveyors workin for a construction company and lookin for a place to build a deep-water cargo terminal. Aye, ye may lauch Lachie, but that's what the folk in London want as a cover for the operation. You and I ken fine that the watter's ower shallow hereabouts for something like that but the government apparently hasnae a clue. Mind, I've been thinking, maybe that'll be the excuse for closin doon the operation when they've finished whatever it is they're up to. Ah well. Here's Jakey Parker for the next shift. Cheerio, Lachie. Mind fit I said.'

The dogs were on their feet and ready to go as soon as Lachie stood up. His glance took in the distinctive oval gold watch on Parker's wrist. He had already noted that the large limousine was no longer at the cottage and that there were several satellite-dishes on a lattice-work mast half hidden among birch trees on the opposite slope. Whatever the mystery-men's intentions, their planning seemed to be serious. Oh well, in spite of the warning he'd just been given, he would continue to pursue the truth of the situation, and the truth now included Parker's recent meeting with the strangers.

But Davina must be lonely. The thought spurred him on his way. The now-optimistic spaniels padded off ahead.

*

(Leithland Castle, South East of Scarr):

Lord Leithland and his guest had just ended their meeting with the two American agents and his Lordship rang for the maid to remove the tea things. He rose from his desk to see the men to the door personally.

'Thank you, Mr. -um- Ollie and Mr. -ah- Buster. It is, as you point out, s-second base. We must now spring forward to - ah - to hit the bulls-eye. Yes, the bulls-eye. Good after-afternoon and good luck.' He watched them until they drove off in the Cadillac and then returned to his study where the Under Secretary of State was running skilled fingertips across the keys of his laptop computer.

'What do you think, Dickie? Do those men know wh-what's

102

at risk? They seem to be very self-assured about the whole - ah - business but conditions in the United States are very different from ours. Won't the P.M. think again and assign some of our own people? In the - um - absence of Security Service personnel, could we not draft in men from the M.O.D.? No? Oh well. They'd better get it right. I'd h-h-hate to be the one who has to own up to the deception. The - ah - little people will start throwing g-googlies if it ever comes out.'

*

(Bolson Hall):

Major Bolson was busy in his study with the door locked and curtains drawn. This was a situation where it was impossible to be both secure and inconspicuous, and security had to take precedence. People could wonder all they wanted about what he was up to, but no one was going to walk through the door or look in at the windows to find out.

He had done his best to sort his own uncut stones. Sorting them for size was reasonably straightforward, but visualizing potential gems hiding within the rough was absolutely impossible. Quality issues were a matter for experts. He slipped six stones into each of the little suede pouches and locked these in turn inside their steel delivery boxes. Putting the boxes back into his blue leather briefcase, he replaced that on the upper shelf of the heavy safe.

Captain Radek's black case, now nearly empty, neatly filled the lower shelf. Victor had the key for that case as well and he opened it now to look at four locked boxes inside. Each, about the size of a pack of twenty cigarettes, was colour coded. The four individually matching keys were in his desk drawer. Those keys had been delivered – one each month – by a visiting sportsman from Austria. Although these remaining boxes now took up very little space in a case which had once been full, Victor knew that its contents made each box worth a large sum of money. There should be none of them left by now but the dispatch pattern, of one box every month of the two year cycle, had been interrupted by people nosing around Maggie's place. Radek was impatient about the delay but Victor had insisted that there was no alternative to retaining some of the Bristol-bound deliveries until the risk had decreased. The captain should be more aware than anyone that putting too many smuggled stones on the market over too short a period was a danger to him and his operation. He had accepted the delay but was becoming very anxious.

Now, Victor was waiting for another delivery of twenty six boxes, two of which would be marked out as his and Maggie's share. For a short time he would have in his possession the eight accumulated boxes of their own stones plus twenty eight of Radek's. That would be enough to solve anybody's financial problems for a lifetime. He had often tried to think of a foolproof way to get his hands on some of Radek's diamonds which, he had no doubt, would be of better quality than his own. The ideal solution to the problem would be for the captain to meet with a fatal accident, but Victor was in no position to bring that about. If only the bloody sea would do to him what it had done to his, (and Maggie's), great grandfather, Charlie Hill, in the South Atlantic in nineteen twenty one, – swallow him without trace.

There was a knock at the door and Maggie's voice shouted, 'Hello Victor. Let me in.' He locked the safe hurriedly, spun the dial and slid the wall panel back into place.

'Nice to see you, Sis. This damned storm has screwed things up badly. Radek's fuming out there. I'm sure he thinks we didn't get the last four shipments off for cutting because of incompetence, and that the risk from snoopers was just our excuse. This month was to be the absolute deadline so we have to do something quickly. One of the Austrian grouse shooters said Radek wants me to know I'll be 'dead meat' if they haven't reached the lapidary workshops by the thirty first. It seems the courier will be in Bristol to take delivery on the twenty ninth. When are you sending your next crate of plant extracts?'

'The day after tomorrow, Victor. The Drugs Squad people, if

that's who they were, poked around for the best part of three months as you well know. Every time I went out to collect plants, there was an 'ornithologist' or a 'botanist' with binoculars. What would a botanist want with binoculars? I made a point of revisiting the same sites on the way back and usually found people examining the plants that I'd been interested in. But now they seem to have accepted that I am what I say I am: a producer of plant extracts for the cosmetics industry. Did I tell you that Jimmy had a raid on the Bristol depot? Of course they didn't find anything. He says he could sometimes see signs that crates had been opened during their journey. However, the last lot went through untouched. Nobody seems to have levered off the corner batons on any of them so they won't know about the secret compartments. How many of Captain Radek's boxes are left? Once we get them on their way, that'll clear the decks for the new delivery. God, Victor, I hope this one will be the last.'

'There's another party arriving tomorrow, Maggie, to try for a late salmon. The fish'll be a bit dark in colour but the Austrians don't seem to mind – especially after we have them smoked. One of the visitors is supposed to be bringing special instructions about sending off a larger-than-usual number of stones to Bristol. I don't know what that's about. Christ, Sis, I'll be as happy as you when the whole shenanigan's over. All we'll have to do then is make arrangements for unloading our own share for as much as we can get. It won't be easy. They'd be hugely more valuable if we had them expertly cut first, but I can't raise the sort of money *that's* likely to cost. You, Maggie? No, I thought not. I'll give you a phone call when it's all set up and say something as a signal. How about "It's going to be frosty next month"? Then you can collect the stones from me, take them back to your place and get them into the crates. If Radek lands the next shipment in good time, we might have to do something with part of that as well. He's getting more impatient every voyage.

'Oh, I meant to tell you last week – but forgot – that if anything happens to me, my solicitor has a personal package for you. It contains a spare key for the safe and instructions, which will let you work out the code for the combination lock.'

'Victor, I can see you're still depressed. You shouldn't be thinking like this. Nothing's going to happen to you. Nor me neither, I hope. Now I have to go in case Grandmother decides to visit the beach. Are you sure you don't want her to know you're still alive? If she mentioned it to any of my visitors, they'd just think it was a dotty old woman's imagination. I doubt she'd believe it anyhow. She thinks of you as just one more tragedy in her past. No? I think you're right. Let's forget it altogether.'

*

(The Sea Pool Bridge, River Scarr):

It was nearly two o'clock when Arc reached the bridge and the tide was slack at high water. Any salmon impelled to run the river to reach the spawning grounds would already have entered, or be getting ready to enter, the sea-pool. There, Arc's experience of the Scarr had taught him, they would wait for the ebb to get under way. When that occurred, the water level in the pool would begin to drop and the river would start flowing with increasing force, providing the fish with an irresistible invitation. From the precarious ledge under the bridge, it was sometimes possible to catch one when you got the timing right. At a particular volume of flow, a bunch of lobworms could do the trick if it was allowed to wash downstream beside the near bank. To have a fair chance of success, the bait had to be placed exactly on the dividing line of the current and the still water.

Arc had already unrolled his hand-line and laid it in loose coils on the ledge beside him. He dipped the piece of jute sacking into the river and wrapped it round his bait-tin to keep the worms cool in their bed of sphagnum moss. As he tied a hook to the line, he heard the sound of footsteps approaching on the road above. He recognised the heavy, long-striding gait of the minister heading towards Portlach. Arc had never known the man to make this journey in the middle of the afternoon; he invariably went in the early evening two or three times a week.

Sometimes Arc had seen him returning to Scarr before six o'clock in the morning. Most people believed that Stackpoole had a lady friend in Portlach and that his night-long outings were visits to that unknown person. Only a few villagers knew the real purpose of the minister's journeys and none of them dared talk about it.

The footsteps stopped on the bridge and Arc began to fear that the intruder's presence would make him miss the ideal fish-catching window. However, after alternate fits of coughing and gasping for air, the man began to breathe more and more easily. Finally, he spat a large gob of respiratory mucus into the river and strode onwards again. His voice could be heard fading into the distance in a tuneful baritone rendering of:

'*I'll taaake you hooome agaaain, Kathleeeen...*'

Hurriedly, Arc baited the large hook with a bunch of lobworms, made a quick assessment of water-flow and clipped his selected weight to the bottom eye of the three-way swivel. He stretched his arms apart seventeen times as he measured an appropriate length of line to reach the top of the lie where fish should be waiting in line astern, – if there were any fish on this tide. He knew he wouldn't have to wait long if one decided to bite. In another five minutes or so, they'd all be running up the Scarr with a firm sense of purpose, and the opportunity to hook one would have gone until the next tide. He watched as his line straightened downstream and waited with unwavering concentration.

*

(Shore Road, between Scarr and Portlach):

Again the minister paused to recover his breath. He had lost a little bit of his body-weight over the last six months, almost certainly due to these extended walks and to the frequency of his sexual encounters, but there was still a long struggle ahead if he was to regain a reasonable level of fitness. He was quite determined, however, that cutting back on food wasn't an option. He loved food even more than he loved sex and both were essential to counterbalance the deeply entrenched sadness of his nature. Trying not to think below the surface of that particular matter, he resumed his walk. The cinder track here had deteriorated into a muddy pedestrian path crossed by deep ruts from 'off-road' vehicles. The fickle wind, gusting from a variety of directions, blew sand round the minister's ankles. He shivered and refastened his coat.

To the right was that irregular bumpy area which, Meggie Munro had been telling anyone daft enough to listen, was the location of an early Bronze Age 'kitchen midden'. She insisted that Victorian investigators had excavated the place and had found ancient fire-blackened bone fragments of deer and goats along with hundreds of years' accumulations of limpet and mussels shells. The supposed site was covered with marram grass and sparse, ground-hugging gorse bushes and looked as if the only people likely to give it more than a glance would be the most determined of courting couples. However, Marietta Cardington had told him in bed that gangs of teenagers danced, naked, round bonfires here. Well, the ashes and scraps of charred driftwood were certainly in evidence. But dancing nude at night among all that gorse? They'd have to be very well tanked-up on illegal substances to do something that stupid. He would ask Mason's girlfriend if they got many gorse-related injuries in Accident and Emergency at weekends. Haw-haw-haw!

Stackpoole strode across the abandoned golf links towards that central sand dune where he'd first encountered Marietta. He looked up at the house, wondering what kind of reception she'd got from her husband on returning home this morning. There were no signs of people at any of the windows, although the one at the top of the turret did have its curtains pulled shut. Was that a twitch of the fabric? No; probably just imagination.

He reached the western edge of Portlach's ancient sea-town where centuries-old stone cottages still defied the elements. Most were empty now, having been upgraded to summer-holiday homes. Turning into an opening between two locked and shuttered houses, Stackpoole sidled along the narrow gap known as Annie Croaker's Condy, until he reached the rusty fence that bordered the long-dismantled railway line. Scrambling over the wire, he paused again for breath before setting out in the direction of Mason's house. He left the overgrown cutting eventually, for the more secure footing of Herry Baxter's Lane, and soon reached the rear entrance to Mason's yard where he wiped his brow with a linen handkerchief and looked at his watch. Five minutes to four. The fastest time yet. Negotiating the spaces between a lorry and piles of building materials, he knocked at the door, certain that nobody had observed the latter part of his journey.

*

(Birch Cottage):

Increasingly fed-up with the weather and finding the afternoon television programmes totally uninteresting, Marco asked Bob several times if he could visit the harbour. The answer was always 'No!' For a while he watched his grandmother baking cakes until he couldn't stand that either. Declining her offer of a spoon to finish off the remains of the mixture, he went to sit in the front hallway. Nell sat at his feet, her head on his trainers. He heard Bob come in again at the back door, having completed what he'd been attending to in one of the polythene tunnels. The sound of muffled voices in the kitchen was interrupted by Bessie calling for him to join them.

'Marc, your Granda fed the chickens earlier but left the eggs for you to collect. We think the wind's gone down enough to do it now. But we need to talk about your thirteenth birthday. Had you forgotten that it's tomorrow? I thought so. That's why I'm doing some extra cakes. We could try to organise a party if you want; maybe invite some people of your own age up from the village. What do you think? They'll be able to tell you all about Scarr. You've met Raymond Meade already. I'm sure he could think of others you'd find interesting. Mitchell? Oh, you mean Alison Mitchell, the butcher's girl? Yes, I'll try to get in touch with her parents. Maybe some of her friends would like to come too. Off you go and collect the eggs. I'll phone as soon as I've put this last cake in the oven.'

When Marco came back indoors with two full egg-baskets, Bessie was waiting for return calls from Alison's father and Arc's mother. He was anxious at the thought of meeting strangers, but Arc had been all right and Alison Mitchell had been lovely. Maybe they could have a disco – if there was enough room.

'Gran, I'll just go upstairs for a bit and look around. Is that okay? Will you shout when the people ring back?'

'Don't be too long. And have a look in the room at the end of the corridor. We thought you might want to have your party there tomorrow evening. Here's the key. See what you think. I'll tidy it up a bit in the morning when you go down to the beach for seaweed. You did tell him Bob, didn't you?'

'Sorry. No, I hadn't got round to that yet. I meant to wait another couple of hours to see how fast the waves are going down. Marc, after Grandma has talked to the kids' parents, we could have our tea down at the Bay House. That way, we'll have a good idea of sea conditions. What do you think?'

'Great! I haven't seen the shore yet. Will I need to dress up for tea?'

'Of course you won't! The Bay House isn't that kind of hotel. But make sure you have a wash and change those jeans. The trainers are fine. I'll call Mrs. Moston now to make sure it's all right – though it shouldn't be a problem at this time of year. We'll leave here in an hour. Try to be ready.'

*

(Bay House Hotel):

Geordie Moston was talking to the hotel's lone resident in the lounge bar when the Smiths walked in. They were accompanied by a boy of about twelve or thirteen. Archie watched them, confident that the boy must be Marc Powell. Earlier, he'd braved gusting winds to walk up Scarr Brae and had seen the man working in the greatly-enlarged garden of Birch

Cottage. His deduction was confirmed almost at once when the youngster started to ask his 'Granda' questions and the man addressed his responses to 'Marc'. The newcomers went to sit at a window table overlooking the beach. Archie adjusted his hearing-aid slightly and waited for the group to order. The adults decided they'd settle for tea and scones and the boy asked if he could have shepherd's pie. It was a bit early for cooked meals, Geordie pointed out, but he'd ask the Missus if there was any left over from lunch time.

Archie realised that he too was hungry and would enjoy some shepherd's pie as well – if there was enough to go round. He took his drink across to the next table, said 'Hello' to his neighbours and buried his face in the current issue of the local newspaper. During the next half hour, he collected some useful information from reading and a great deal more from listening.

The electricity supply had been restored in the early afternoon and now the streetlamps began to cast widely-spaced pools of illumination along Shore Road. From where he sat, Archie had a clear view of a light at Whitescar Cottage. But it was a moving light. In the gathering gloom he could just make out a figure among the dunes and guessed it was likely to be one of the 'witches' that Annie Moston had been discussing with a group of young women at lunch time. He smiled. As always, supposition was more interesting, and more believable, than boring facts. And he did intend to find out what the facts were. He had a strong suspicion they'd be linked to Scarr's 'U.F.O. Hotspot' reputation.

The people from Birch Cottage were getting ready to leave, the boy talking excitedly about his planning for a birthday party. Archie returned to the bar.

*

(Northern North Sea):
The captain had handed control of the ship to the First Mate with a warning to keep an eye on that unknown vessel showing

on radar southeast of the Nikolai Rykov's position. The stranger had appeared to be holding a parallel course with them. While that was not unexpected at the height of the storm, improving conditions should have sent him off about his own business – unless he was suffering an engine malfunction. That would be an unlikely coincidence. Radek had watched with growing suspicion, waiting for a change of course and speed that hadn't come. A slight adjustment to the Nikolai Rykov's heading had been answered by an identical one from the 'shadow'. He thought it not unlikely that the Fisheries Protection vessel had returned to keep a watch. If so, he had a surprise waiting for them.

But now, at last, radar showed the stranger altering course. The captain relaxed and went below to catch up on his lost sleep. First, though, he'd have a quick glance at the treasure chest. The whole trip's diamond collection was in there and just waiting to be snatched away from Zhirkov's grasping hands.

**

CHAPTER NINE

Thursday Morning

(Shore Road, East of Blackscar):

Archie, keen to reinforce his ornithologist cover story, had set out well before dawn with binoculars and bird-recognition book. It was after half-past six now and the sky was lightening over the horizon. The sun would be up in less than an hour. At the end of next week, clocks would be turned back again to Greenwich Mean Time and the resulting lighter mornings paid for with darker evenings. The sea had calmed a lot overnight and Archie felt relaxed in a way that he never did when away from its restless presence. He peered in the half-light at illustrations of cormorants and shags in the manual, unable to read the small print. Why hadn't he remembered to bring a torch? Never mind. It would soon be bright enough. The cloud cover in the east was beginning to fragment, giving promise of a fine day.

He became aware of someone approaching from the direction of the harbour. The person was pushing a handcart stacked with crab pots; it wouldn't be lobster pots at this time of year. He made out a boy of about twelve or thirteen who stopped on the roadside verge above Blackscar and began to tie stone weights into the bottoms of the pots. He followed those with pieces of bait – they looked like frozen flounders – and then carried the pots, one at a time, down the dark finger of rock which had been well exposed by the ebbing tide. With old memories awakened, Archie looked in the slowly brightening light at where he, himself, used to set creels nearly fifty years before. There had been a particularly prolific spot for crabs where the end of the promontory dropped away abruptly. The hard bottom lay six fathoms below spring tide high-water mark. He watched as the boy heaved two of the creels into the depths there. With the floats at the ends of the retrieval-lines bobbing in the surface, (drably coloured to attract as little attention as possible from casual passers-by, Archie noted with approval), the boy carried his third creel to the western side of the rocks and placed it among the boulders at low-tide mark. Although much had changed here over the years, there was clearly a great deal that was just the same. He watched the lad collect several large plastic flagons that had been stranded on the beach during the night, and stack them on the cart.

It was almost fully light. The sun, though screened by the headland, was heaving itself over the horizon beyond. Now Archie could see the boy clearly and thought that he had a vaguely familiar appearance – but couldn't be sure who he resembled. Digging deeply into his memory didn't bring anyone to mind. Perhaps Archie had known a grandparent of this boy during his early life in Scarr.

The boy set off towards the harbour and Archie walked in the same direction until he reached a wooden bench above East Beach. Clearly, it had been sited here to give a view across the bay towards Whitescar. He sat, looked and remembered. At its outer end, the promontory sloped down into the sea. It continued under water for some eighty yards and resurfaced as the barren islet of Inch Greele. The seam of gleaming quartz, after which Whitescar might have been named, continued right across the islet. What were the birds that used to nest out there? Archie was becoming more and more certain that they must have been eider-ducks. He opened the bird-recognition book, hoping once more to find something to jog his memory.

A sudden beam of light glared on the glossy paper. He pocketed his reading glasses and looked eastwards to where the sun was now peering across Portlach Ness. Peering? Away to the west, the brightening sun was overwhelming its own reflected light on the moon's face above the sand dunes. Paling? Sun peering; moon paling.

The sun peers over Portlach Ness, the moon pales in the west
and dawn-struck houses on the shore blink off their short night's rest.

Archie scribbled the couplet, (which seemed rather insipid), into the 'Notes' section of his manual. He really must remember to carry a notebook at all times.

There was traffic on Shore Road now and a number of people appeared to be busy at the harbour. He turned his binoculars in that direction and then focused on the hotel. He could clearly see Geordie talking to the driver of a milk-delivery van. Much farther west, he picked out somebody walking across the undulating surface of the dunes towards Shore Road. It was clearly a woman. From conversations overheard in the hotel, he had no doubt that that was the famous Maggie MacPhail. No sign of her broomstick but she did appear to be carrying a bundle of something that looked like vegetation. Archie, smiling, recalled tinkers knocking on doors, selling the besoms they'd made. His grandmother had always insisted that there was nothing better for 'gettin the stue oot o the corners'. Their heather-stem pot scrubbers, too, put modern plastic equivalents to shame – and they didn't poison the environment.

But, with his wristwatch showing ten minutes to eight, he'd have to get moving. The sea air and good food were rapidly restoring his appetite.

*

(The Whitescar Sand Dunes):

Maggie MacPhail had spent half an hour collecting plants to be turned into stock materials for use at a later date. Today's consignment of extracts was waiting in her largest refrigerator for the addition of Victor's diamonds. The foreign sportsmen were due to arrive at Bolson Hall around eleven this morning. As usual, one of them would be carrying instructions about despatch of the contents of one of Radek's boxes. That meant the designated stones would be ready for Maggie to collect before twelve. She would follow her old routine of dropping in for an informal snack-lunch with Victor in his study. Her picnic basket would conceal the diamonds on her way back home. Once the stones and plant extracts were crated up, she would drive them to the Portlach Transport Company. They'd be in Bristol first thing tomorrow morning. But Maggie had a feeling of unease about this particular operation. There could be no doubt that Victor was keeping back information about likely variations in established practice. Uncertainties could be done without in such a risky undertaking. At least, there was no sign now of the prying drugs investigators. It seemed they'd taken themselves off somewhere else to target more culpable suspects. Just to make sure, however, she would have a brisk walk along the shore to note any non-residents.

At the harbour, her curiosity was aroused by a man coming towards her from the Blackscar direction. As they converged, Maggie could see that he was a stranger of about sixty. He wore outdoor gear that had been subjected to moderate wear. There was a brownish mark on front of the jacket that could have been dried blood. Work wear or leisure wear? Perhaps a shooting or fishing jacket? The man stopped and made a show of training his binoculars out to sea.

'Hello'. Maggie smiled. 'See anything interesting out there? There should be one or two boats going out shortly. The forecast's good.'

'Actually, I've been looking for eider-ducks. But I haven't seen any so far. Mr. Moston tells me that they often swim out there. I retired recently and I'm trying to get an outdoor hobby going. I thought bird watching might be worth a go. Are you a local resident? Please tell me that you know all about eider-ducks.'

George Moston's right. Eiders do swim in the bay in groups.

They dive to feed on the mussel-beds between Whitescar rocks and that little island farther out. It's called Inch Greele, though nobody seems to know why. That's my house over there, Whitescar Cottage. You can often get a very good view of eiders from the edge of the property. I'm on my way back now. Why don't you walk with me? I'll show you the best observation point.'

'That's nice of you but they'll be expecting me back at the hotel for breakfast. *You* can join *me* if you like. Maybe you could fill me in on some of other sea-birds. As a beginner, I am really quite ignorant about them. By the way, I'm a retired accountant. My name's McSpake – Archie McSpake.'

'I can't take up your invitation today Mr. McSpake – Archie. I look after my grandmother. She's over ninety and she'll be getting agitated if I stay away too long. My name is Maggie MacPhail. Please call me Maggie. I'm a self-employed biochemist. If you'd like to come over for tea or for a drink some time, phone me. Here's my number.' She handed him a gold-bordered business card.

*

(Bay House Hotel):

Daniel, unable to open his eyes against the strong light that glared between the curtains, fumbled for the office-issue watch on his bedside locker. The whisky bottle toppled over at his touch and a plastic tumbler rolled across the floor. A knock on the door was followed by a woman's voice asking if he was all right, and did he want breakfast in his room or downstairs. He struggled to orientate his consciousness to where he was and what he was there for, and decided he was unfit to do anything at present. The watch was showing twenty past nine.

'I'll give breakfast a miss today.' His head felt as if it was being crushed when he shouted. 'I'd like to lie in for another hour if that's convenient,' he added more quietly. 'I had a long busy day yesterday.'

The voice informed him that he'd be given a call at ten thirty.

Busy day? He didn't try to fool himself. It had been one of the most boring and frustrating days of his life. Sheer Bloody Torture! There had always been someone with him at the base in Suffolk and he'd had a solitary pint of beer at lunchtime. They'd got him off on his flight north in the late afternoon. Thank God, he'd thought. Whisky country was waiting to iron out his stresses. But things got worse. The officer who'd been appointed 'minder' at the Scottish base had carried the secrecy brief to a greater extreme than his southern counterpart. Daniel had been picked up from the fighter-plane at the far end of a runway by a Land Rover with blacked-out windows, and taken straight to an old hut well away from any other buildings. The bastard even put a sentry on the door. A meal of tea and sandwiches was delivered by a miserable looking man in civilian clothes whose status was a mystery. He did not answer Daniel's questions or respond to his attempts at casual talk. Name rank and serial number? No response from the tight lipped ... -. Daniel couldn't find a word with sufficient venom to describe him.

The remainder of the evening, with nothing to do, or to drink, had brought him to a state of sweating near-despair. The taxi, which somebody somewhere had authorized to take him along the coast to Scarr, arrived after ten thirty. Although it was said to be the property of a private hire company, Daniel didn't take that for granted. Its barely cooperative driver had stopped on the journey, with an overdone display of reluctance, to let him use a hotel lavatory. Five minutes and two double whiskies later, he had been on the road once more with a full bottle of Speyside Malt in his luggage and a look of contentment on his face.

This morning, the overturned bottle on the locker was about a quarter full. No wonder he had a headache. A hair of the dog, he thought, sitting up in bed. Again there was that feeling of nausea that he'd been experiencing over the last few weeks. It came on when he was preparing to have a drink. As soon as he swallowed the first mouthful, the feeling disappeared. Trying to recall why the sensation was reminiscent of something in the past, took him back to the time, (he must have been about seven or eight years old), when he'd been sick with what his mother referred to as 'the jandeez'. Hepatitis was the commonly understood word now, even among laymen. Hepatitis! Liver damage! Alcohol! Cirrhosis! Fuck! How could he give up the only thing that made his life bearable? He looked at the bottle again; again there came the feeling of nausea. The tumbler had rolled away somewhere so he pulled the cork and swigged the pale golden liquid from the bottle. It went down smoothly and the nausea passed off at once. Boy! That was needed. Daniel wiped his mouth and lay back on the pillows. Already he was starting to feel optimistic about the day ahead.

When the chambermaid announced 'ten thirty', Daniel got up at once. He even felt like eating something not too filling. A packet of crisps, perhaps. And maybe another packet for lunch, washed down by a few bottles of beer.

*

(Scarr Beach):

When Bob and Marco arrived on the foreshore west of the harbour and looked down on their chosen part of the beach, the sea was flowing up the scars. With the spring tide two days past its maximum, however, there was no special urgency today about harvesting the reddish-brown seaweed. Torn from its rocky moorings in large quantities by the storm, mounds of it had been stranded by the waves at, or above, the high-water mark. Obviously the tide wouldn't reach up this far today. Bob tried to explain the different heights of tides and their relation to phases of the moon. From his grandson's expression of boredom, he doubted if anything that he said was registering in the boy's mind.

In fact, Marco was thinking about his birthday party in the evening and looking forward to Alison Mitchell being there with two of her friends. He couldn't remember *their* names. Arc would bring along someone called Jimmy. Jimmy had a large collection of compact discs and a portable player at home and

Arc was sure he could be persuaded to bring them to the party. Marco, who'd been unable to wait, had opened his presents before breakfast. When she left on Monday, his mother had secretly left two packages for him with Bessie. The first contained a digital 'Astronaut's Watch' from her, while the second, from his father, held that pair of trainers he'd spent ages staring at in the sports shop in Newton town centre. Again he experienced the sad, helpless feeling about his parents' separation. Bessie, conscious of his pain, pushed one more parcel towards him. She and Bob had splashed out on a pair of designer jeans and a tee shirt for him to wear at the party – but only if he liked them. After breakfast, Bob had had to wait for him to open the birthday cards that the postman had just delivered.

Their delayed start meant that the very best position on the beach had been taken by someone else. 'Never mind', Bob had said. 'There's plenty of room left – and plenty of seaweed'. With the truck backed onto the beach-top verge, Bob manoeuvred a battered old wheelbarrow down a broad, two-inch-thick wooden plank. Several more planks were laid end to end to form a temporary pathway on which the barrow could be wheeled across the pebbles. Marco was assigned the task of throwing seaweed towards his grandfather with a large, unwieldy potato-fork. Bob then loaded it onto the barrow with a similar implement. When the barrow was full, Bob retraced his path up the boardwalk and inclined plank to empty the seaweed into the back of the truck. After a few minutes' breathing space, he did it all over again. As the third barrowful was being emptied, Arc appeared and offered to lend a hand. His offer was gratefully accepted and the truck was fully loaded in less than twenty minutes. The slimy cargo was ready to be driven up to the cottage and tipped out in the garden. Bob had intended Marco to go with him until Arc suggested the two boys should stay on the beach to collect weed from a wider area and pile it up ready for the next truck-load. At first, Bob was opposed to the proposal.

'Granda, I promise not to wander off. Let me stay. I want to find out more about the seashore and Arc can tell me all sorts of stuff. Please! I'll work hard.'

'I don't know exactly what your grandmother's going to think when I arrive without you, but I've a good idea of what she'll say. Anyway, she should be with me when I come back down. She's having her hair done at Arc's mother's shop. Afterwards, we'll be having tea and sandwiches at the hotel. Arc, you can join us if you like. Yes? I'll get Bessie to tell your mother. By the way, why aren't you at school today? The assembly hall? What; the whole roof? Well, well. I didn't think the storm was as bad as that.'

When Bob drove off, the two boys started to pile up seaweed on either side of the boardwalk. They talked about the party, Arc referring to Alison as his 'girlfriend'. Marco felt really awful; he couldn't begin to understand the mixture of negative feelings that suddenly became attached to everything. He talked to Arc only to answer questions and did so with as few words as possible. Arc looked puzzled and moved farther away. Marco saw him go across to where a large piece of stranded wood was about to be re-floated by the rising tide. Arc, looking pleased, dragged it up beyond the high-water mark and covered it roughly with stones and weeds. It was a door complete with decorative glass doorknobs

'Marco, d'you see that auld mannie wi the binoculars? Look. There! I saw him oot early at Blackscar. He's a stranger fae England, bidin at the hotel. He keeps looking at us. Wonder what he's aboot. Better keep an eye on him.'

In fact, Archie was observing the incoming tide as it advanced in gradually increasing rivulets between the fragmented stacks of sedimentary rock. Tide-watching was an occupation that he'd revelled in even before he was old enough to go to school. He would never forget the day his mother caught him wading in the bottom of the harbour at low tide. The embarrassment of receiving a thrashing below a gallery of grinning fishermen had stayed with him for a very long time. He'd made certain she never caught him again. Perhaps, he mused, the skill in misdirection that led him to become a professional spy, (and amateur conjuror), had taken root back then. Again he focused on where the edge of the advancing water was constructing patterns – forming fractals. Yes, fractals.

I realign divided thoughts to where I want to be;
that interface of fractured land and fractalating sea.

*

(Shore Road):

From the edge of the fish quay another, younger, man was also peering through binoculars. He was trying to observe his rival in the bird-watching business. Fuck! An expert would soon see through his disguise and that bastard certainly looked like an expert. Must avoid him completely. Wonder where he stays. He noticed the Moston woman from the hotel walking along the road with two young children. Daniel who had no interest whatever in children and their incomprehensible behaviour, made a rough guess that they might be about six or seven or eight and maybe twins – possibly. The woman kept looking in his direction. What the hell was wrong with her?

Annie Moston was taking the twins, Millie and Polly, to the library. She dreaded the days ahead. Last week had been the mid-term school break and that had been quite tiring enough. She'd looked forward to having some respite from her demanding little girls from now until the Christmas holidays, but storm damage at the school had upset things. Geordie believed the damage wasn't as serious as local gossips were saying, but that it could still take a week or more to get the roof repaired. Builders were in demand everywhere. Child minders were in short supply and expensive too, these days, – especially reliable ones. The extra income from those two guests would go only a short way towards paying the bills. She was lucky, she supposed, to have anybody staying at this time of year. Lucky? Well, maybe she should keep an open mind on that. Both guests were supposed to be bird watchers but neither seemed to know anything about birds. That one across the road was the most peculiar. He had arrived late, slept till

122

nearly eleven this morning and then came downstairs smelling of whisky. No, it probably wasn't lucky at all.

That gear of his looked like something from an old film. He was trying to watch things through a pair of enormous binoculars that nobody could possibly hold still without a tripod. In fact, they were the sort of item you might find gathering dust in an antiques shop or on display in a museum. As the man manoeuvred the binoculars in the direction of Shore Road's junction with Scarr Brae, Annie turned to look. A large American car had just turned off in the direction of West Beach. But the twins were getting excited about books and Annie steered them up the library steps.

*

(West Beach):

The two boys were shifting a lot of seaweed and didn't notice the car until it had reached the end of shore road. At that point the path westward turned into a rutted grass track through gorse thickets and on across the dunes. Confronted by Maggie MacPhail's van coming along the track, the Cadillac stopped and the driver blew his horn impatiently. Maggie halted and looked at the two men inside, but didn't give way. By the third beep, Marco was stumbling across the pebbles, shouting 'Run Arc. Run!' Before he reached the sand dunes, Arc had caught up with him. They stopped and looked back. A very tall, thin man in a dark suit had got out of the car and was racing towards them with long, loping strides. He was covering the ground extremely fast. As the boys got ready to run once more, they saw the tall man reach the bird watcher's position. The old man appeared to lose his balance and stumble in front of the runner. The runner tripped over him and landed face down in a gorse bush. He lay there for several seconds, declining the offer of a hand up. Indeed the offer seemed to enrage him. He got to his feet at last and, after an exchange of words and waving of arms, strode back to where his companion waited in the Cadillac. He had to step aside smartly as the woman in the van came up behind him and blew her horn repeatedly. The car driver backed up slowly and executed an untidy six-point-turn in the narrow road near the hotel. Marco and Arc watched the vehicle drive away and turn up Scarr Brae. They returned reluctantly to their piles of seaweed.

'What was that aboot?' asked Arc. 'That's the mannies I saw at the cottage on the Leithland estate. They've a hideout there – like gangsters. Some folk say they're spies. Leithland's gamekeepers have got orders naebody's allowed to speak aboot them or they'll be arrested.'

'Here comes my grandfather. I can't tell you now what they're after. But I promise I'll tell you tonight at the party. We've got enough seaweed here for two more loads so it won't be long till sandwich time. A good job because I'm starving.'

*

(Effie Meade's Hairdressing Salon):

When Bessie entered, the Salon was empty but sounds of animated voices and laughter came from the back shop. Effie soon emerged, looking flushed, followed closely by the grinning minister. She steered Bessie towards one of the two washbasins and prepared to wash her hair. Minister and hairdresser, meanwhile, kept up a constant chatter about 'the Special Ceremony' – whatever that was. Stackpoole was trying to persuade Effie to attend it and Effie, while refusing to comply, was clearly enjoying his attempts to change her mind. Oh, Effie, Effie! How can you be so completely blind to the threat of this man? Bessie struggled to control the urge to shout it.

The door opened and three young girls entered, the girls who would be coming to Marc's birthday party. Bessie and Effie said 'Hello girls'; Stackpoole just nodded. They went to sit on the row of chairs arranged along one side of the room and Bessie watched in the mirror as they all gave the minister the widest possible berth in passing. Effie could learn from these girls' instincts, but it was evident that she wouldn't want to do so.

'Well, I must be getting on,' said the minister. 'I'm very busy. Think about what I said Mrs. Meade. If you want to attend next month's Ceremony, I'm sure we can come to some mutually beneficial arrangement. Glad that you've recovered Mrs. Smith.' He left the shop, letting the door bang behind him.

'What does Solomon mean, Bessie? Have you been ill?'

'Don't ask Effie. It's a long story. He makes me feel ill-at-ease when he drops in unannounced. Bob's not happy about it either.' In the mirror, she saw all three girls nod in agreement. Effie shook her head in astonishment at such a sentiment.

As he turned up the brae, the minister went over in his mind the list of old and new club members who'd agreed to be at the kirk at eight o'clock sharp. Apart from himself, there would be Jackie Mason with his girlfriend, Lorna. Then there'd be Lizzie and Donald Malcolm from the Scarr grocery store. That was five. And Marietta Cardington had promised to be there with her friends, Dolly and Tricia, – the very promising, very eager Tricia. Great as far as it went, but one person short of the nine he'd specified when drawing up the plan for the ritual. He didn't have a lot of time to fid someone. Tatey or Wullie? Out of the question! In any case, this was the night they went to their line-dancing class in Portlach; the very reason why he'd been able to move the ceremony from the chapel to Scarr Kirk. Suddenly he burst out laughing. Tatey and Wullie line dancing! 'Haw-haw-haw-haw'. Jessie Alexander finished sweeping her front step abruptly and slammed the door behind her. 'Haw-haw-haw'. Maisie Weston, on her way down to the shops, halted nervously then gritted her dentures and retreated rapidly up the street.

The minister didn't see Maggie MacPhail drive past the bottom of the brae on her way back from Bolson Hall. However, she was almost the last person he'd risk in the club – notwithstanding that tantalising bathroom-window silhouette. She'd be much too dangerous an involvement.

**

CHAPTER TEN

Thursday Afternoon

(Shore Road):

Daniel, intending to enter the hotel, and Archie, in the act of leaving it, halted face to face on the front steps. The eyes of each shifted to the book that the other was carrying. Finally, Archie said 'Snap! We both appear to be on a hunt for the coast's avian residents. Or are we? If so, a pooling of information would be appreciated. I'm a rank novice, unknown in bird-gazing circles. How about you? From your gear, I'd guess you're a switcher of note.'

Daniel, inwardly alert, regarded the older man impassively. Was this a very crude attempt to probe his cover, or was the old bastard taking the piss? The term 'bird watching' had been used throughout the books he'd looked at. 'Bird gazing' brought to mind a very bizarre picture, and 'switcher' was just silly. He allowed a look of mild interest to block the puzzlement he felt and asked, 'Do you stay locally?' Getting no reply, he volunteered, 'I'm a visitor. I saw you earlier getting entangled with an aggressive bast–, sorry, – I mean aggressive *person*. He clearly had some reason for chasing those kids. At first I thought he might be a paedophile but now suspect I was wrong about that. You did a good job of stopping him. Made it look like a complete accident. Bit of a Jujitsu man, I think, and not just an amateur.'

'All right,' replied Archie. 'I'm not what I seem. And it's very obvious that you're not what you're trying to seem either. I overheard Mrs. Moston and the chambermaid talking about you

126

when I was having breakfast. You are Mr. O'Donnel, aren't you? I'm in the room next to yours but one. They were saying you might be a spy. I've no doubt that they've got me marked down as some kind of snooper as well. Those men in the car, they're Americans. At least the one I talked to was. He threatened to kick my ass. When I laughed, he looked like he was going to have a fit.

'I don't believe they're FBI. They could perhaps be working for some kind of private investigations group. But what the hell they're doing hereabouts is a mystery to me – and to the locals. I've heard some very strange suggestions about them. It must be puzzling to have an influx of aliens to a small village. Everyone here knows everyone else and most of their business too.

'Look here, we're obstructing the doorway. Let's go over to that bench and talk. I'm prepared to put my cards on the table if you'll do the same. No sense in us being diverted from our individual, ah, enterprises. I'm making the assumption, of course, that we *are* on different missions.'

'Yes, all right,' said Daniel. 'But let's take it step by step. And my very first step is to the bar. I need a drink.'

Archie, who had noted Daniel's tremor, nodded his head gravely.

*

(Whitescar Cottage):

Maggie loaded the crates into her van. She wasn't in too much of a hurry to reach the depot as the transport company would accept assignments until four o'clock. And they were expecting her. However, Victor had received another of those rare, coded messages from Radek, to say that they should expect the next delivery of stones to be landed in two day's time and that the entire shipment must be sent on to Bristol on Monday. The outstanding part of the previous delivery, from the study safe, was to go as well. Maggie was anxious about the sudden need for urgency. What was Victor not telling her?

There were some unused crates in the lockup behind the lab

but she was a bit short on concentrated extracts. She sighed. It would require many hours of work to meet the conditions that Radek was now setting.

As she drove past the hotel, Archie McSpake and that other man were on the front doorstep, deep in conversation. She must try to find out from McSpake who his companion was. The man probably did resemble a bird watcher in a remote sort of way, but Maggie had doubts about both of them. Undercover policemen? No. One was too short and the other a bit too old. Private investigators? Customs men? Radek's spies? It was pointless to speculate. More information was needed. She'd phone the hotel when she got back from Portlach, and invite McSpake over for tea this evening. She needed to discover more about him and his motives. Maggie was *especially* uneasy about the *other* man. Even if he *was* just an inquisitive visitor, the fact that he was wandering around with binoculars made him a potential source of disaster. She felt concerned at not having time to investigate him more thoroughly. There was just too much work to be done over the weekend.

Driving up Scarr Brae, Maggie saw the minister crossing from the manse to the kirk's vestry door carrying a large black sack. Not another clothing relief project! After the last one, Jock Wilson claimed he'd found piles of old clothes thrown down the dried-up well behind the byre. The minister had identified them as definitely the garments that some thief had taken from the African charity collection. The stolen money, it seemed, had vanished completely.

As she drew level with Birch Cottage, rain started to splatter on the van's windscreen. The very large drops were surely forerunners of a thunderstorm. Farther along the road, just as she was passing a stone gateway that gave access to one of the Leithland Estate's timber plantations, a lightning flash lit up a large dark limousine parked at the edge of the wood. It must be the one she'd had trouble with this morning. Then came a loud crash and Maggie switched her eyes back to the road ahead. Rain became a deluge and thunder rolled.

*

(Bay House Hotel):

Archie and Daniel had started back from the beach-top bench as soon as the first raindrops hit them. By the time they'd reached the door, both were soaked through. The two men agreed to continue discussions later. Archie hurried upstairs to shower and change his clothes while Daniel, shaking water from his hair, turned into the bar. Each knew a great deal more about the other but doubts persisted and many questions remained unanswered.

At least, Archie mused as he unlocked the door to his room, the two of them were on different missions so they should manage to avoid conflict. Sharing of resources, (O'Donnel's laptop computer and satellite phone and his own over-decorated hire car and camera, for instance), would give each one a greater breadth of surveillance than he'd have working on his own. It was a pity that the bloody phone was on the blink.

When the rain eased, he would drive up to Birch Cottage to check that everything was all right with Marc Powell. Those men in the Cadillac were clearly focusing on the boy. Was it really the supposed communicator that they wanted? If the Ministry of Defence had one of the two that young Powell said he'd obtained, perhaps they did want the other one. But that man at the beach was clearly American. Why did Americans want the mystery object as well? How did they know about it? Were they working with the Ministry's approval or independently? There didn't seem to be any other stalkers around – unless O'Donnel was their accomplice. Perhaps his 'smuggling investigation' was just a cover story. Archie had no doubt that his own vigilance level must remain high. Thoughtfully, he stepped into the shower.

Meanwhile, in the bar, Daniel was starting on a packet of potato crisps and another double whisky.

*

(Effie Meade's Hairdressing Salon):

With the coming of the rain, Effie had closed up shop at three o'clock. There were no more appointments in the book and no prospects now of 'on spec' customers. She sat in the back-shop drinking a cup of instant coffee and thinking of Mr. Stackpoole. He had really wanted her to attend his ceremony at the kirk and had made her feel that things wouldn't be quite the same without her. Guilt, (and something more), began to prompt a change of mind. He was such a lovely, attentive man and he made no attempt to conceal the fact that he liked her. That kiss which he gave her before Bessie Smith interrupted things, showed that his feelings were deeper than she had supposed. Perhaps he'd been on the point of asking her to marry him. Effie gasped for breath and her heart thumped on her sternum at the thought of it. She could feel her face and neck flushing and was thankful that she had locked the door. She leaned back in her chair with eyes shut and let imagination carry her away:

'The Reverend Stackpoole and Mrs. Stackpoole', the announcer would say as she and Solomon walked, with great dignity, into the meeting of the General Assembly of the Church of Scotland in Edinburgh. Perhaps one day the announcement would be 'The Moderator of the General Assembly and Mrs. Stackpoole'. Effie saw herself in a wonderful silk gown and glittering jewels entering the room down a broad marble staircase, escorted by Solomon in top-hat and tails, to deafening applause from ranks of obsequious clergymen.

Effie's dreamy smile vanished suddenly, her reverie interrupted by loud knocking at the shop door. She would wait until whoever it was had gone away and then she'd get off home. There was that nice dress she had bought in Aberdeen last summer for her niece's wedding. It would surprise and thrill Solomon if she turned up unannounced. She would remain behind when the others, whoever they were, had left. And, when he asked her, she'd say 'Oh Yes!' She wouldn't call him 'Darling' right away, but let him take the lead in that.

'Maam! Let me in.'

It was her soaked-to-the-skin son demanding to know where he would find a clean shirt for the party. Yes, of course. She'd forgotten. It was that boy Marco's birthday and the party was to start at four o'clock. Al Mitchell would be picking up the bairns in his car. What time was it now? Twenty past three already.

Archie McSpake, driving past, caught a glimpse of the Meades leaving the shop on the corner. They turned into Middlefields Road under Effie's flimsy umbrella. He continued carefully up Scarr Brae, peering through a streaming windscreen across which wipers thrashed with minimal effect. The party, which he'd heard the Smiths and their grandson talking about, was to start at four o'clock. He'd park in that lay-by opposite the wood, then watch the cottage until he was sure things were under way and that the men in the Cadillac weren't nosing around. He still didn't know where they appeared from or disappeared to, but Geordie had told him at lunchtime that somebody called Lachie had been dropping hints about knowing where they had their 'hideout'. Hideout was it? They were up to something seriously wrong if they needed one of those. He had no doubt that they were a clear threat to the Powell boy. If this Lachie was in the bar tonight, he would try to get some information out of him. He wished too that Fractal had felt able to pass on more of her government scientist's confidences – even if she had promised not to do so. Oh well, just stay alert Archie. For now, it would be a relief to get off the road until the bloody rain had stopped.

*

(Parking Lay-by near Birch Cottage):
Archie, beginning to shiver in the chilly dampness, turned on the engine and the heater and rummaged for a cloth to wipe condensation from the glass. He'd positioned the car carefully so that he could see the main gate of Birch Cottage in one of his rear-view mirrors. It was evident, however, that intruders would be able to approach the house on foot from other sides. He

131

didn't really want to get out of the car but felt a pressing need to scout around. Zipping up his leaky waterproof, he dragged himself out onto the slippery grass verge. A vehicle approached from the direction of the village so he wriggled back into the driving seat.

A large Volvo full of people pulled up on the paved area outside the cottage. When the driver blew his horn, Bob Smith and Marc Powell opened the gate and the Volvo disappeared inside. Archie turned up the volume control on his hearing aid, lowered his offside front-window and wiped rain from the wing-mirror. Now he had to wait. Somewhere an engine started. A vehicle, the presence of which he'd been unaware, emerged from under overhanging branches at the far end of the wood. It purred past him, slowed down briefly opposite the cottage and then sped away down the brae. That Cadillac again! A few seconds later, Archie heard Bob Smith telling Al Mitchell not to worry about collecting the kids after the party as he would give them a lift home himself at seven o'clock. Al drove off back in the direction of the village.

Archie was reassured that young Powell would be safe for the next three hours at least. However, before going back to the hotel, it would be wise to do a bit of scouting around the cottage. He believed it unlikely that anyone else would be about now that the Americans had left, but there was no harm in making certain. He shivered again as he got out of the mini, recalling the trouble he'd once had with guards on the East German border. This would be a stroll in comparison.

He was still very puzzled about the Americans. It did seem that they were targeting Powell but things might be more complicated than that. Was the item that the boy had acquired really some kind of communication device? For communicating with whom? And did it require two conspicuous men in an even more conspicuous car to target a child? Archie was starting to consider the possibility that they could be working on a diversion, and that their real mission was something completely different. Had it anything to do with the diamond-smuggling racket that

O'Donnel was investigating? Or that O'Donnel *said* he was investigating.

*

(Birthday Party at Birch Cottage):

Marco was trying hard to overcome his shyness in the presence of so many people he'd never met before. Well, there were *three* strangers. The boy in the mock military trousers and bomber jacket, who was lugging a heavy backpack, was Jimmy. His father, he said, was on a mission overseas with the S.A.S. Alison said 'Hello Marco' and introduced her friends Mary and Margaret.

All three girls wore party dresses and makeup and, when they took off rain hoods imprinted with the logo: 'Meade Hair Salon', revealed immaculate hairstyles. Marco thought that Mary's jet-black hair went well with her olive skin and brown eyes. They were a marked contrast to Alison's fairness. Mary seemed totally at ease with her surroundings and turned away to talk to Bessie about cake decorating. Margaret, who was hanging back shyly, also had dark hair. Gravely, she shook hands with Marco, wished him a Happy Birthday and blushed. He realised that he was blushing as well. He wanted to talk to her, to tell her that he thought she was lovely, but found himself mumbling something ridiculous about the weather instead. He realised that he was still holding her hand and let it go suddenly. He was completely speechless when she kissed him on the cheek and handed him a small package in fancy wrapping paper.

Bob ushered them all into the front room where two tables had been placed end to end and covered with a linen cloth. Along one wall, a sideboard was loaded with soft drinks and dishes of food: a cold buffet that could have fed twenty hungry kids with lots to spare. Marco helped Bessie to uncover the food and to distribute the empty plates. The guests jostled about selecting things to eat from the sideboard and then went to find places at the table. The seat beside Margaret was free and Marco

133

moved towards it but hesitated. With his face red, he backed away and sat opposite her instead. Margaret, realising that she'd really meant to have a tuna sandwich as well, went to get one from the sideboard. Marco, anticipating what was about to happen, was seized by a surge of confused emotions. But when she came back and sat on the chair beside him, he was overjoyed. Muted applause from the other kids showed that they'd been aware of the interaction.

From outside, McSpake noted proceedings. He was positioned against a dark background and far enough from the undraped window to be invisible to the people inside. The wind-blasted bushes along the top of the ridge would ensure that passers-by on the road didn't see him silhouetted against the cottage lights and report him to the police as a prowler. There was almost no chance of anyone creeping up on him with firearms. A flash behind him lit the low cloud. By the time the sound of the explosion reached him, he was already cursing the fireworks-fiends who began their Bonfire Night nonsense earlier each year. Better get back to the car and change out of these muddy boots. No point in giving them something more to speculate about at the hotel.

The car was cold and wet again and it took ages to get away down the brae. No more signs of the men in the Cadillac. Where the hell did they keep disappearing to?

*

(Bay House Hotel):

Billy Rolph, the relief barman, was chatting with early-evening customers about the influx of strangers to the village. The general consensus was that these were not ordinary strangers, but odd, potentially-dangerous, snooping strangers. They'd stand out even at the height of the holiday season. They needed to be watched. It seemed not to occur to anyone present that such objects of suspicion were already being scanned thoroughly by every pair of eyes, and ears, in their vicinity. The

134

discussion had started because the McSpake character had disappeared. Having strangers disappear before your eyes was a matter of serious concern.

'Fit div you think, Lachie? Fit the hell's he up tae? Fit are they aa up tae? Bird watchers? A dodderin fool and a wino! They're nae mair bird watchers than my granny. I wonder if the police ken aboot them.' Billy polished a glass furiously.

'I'm not really sure,' said Lachie. 'Binoculars on the shore could mean they're really watching for boats or, I've been thinking, for folk that spend time on the shore.'

'Aye, Lachie. Ye'll be meanin the witchie wifies. That's a strong possibility; a near certainty. Fit think you, Andra?'

'Dammit, Billie, I saw the mannie wi the battleship binoculars ower at the dunes twenty minutes ago. It's gey hard observin birds at nicht. He must've been watchin the witchies. I suppose he micht even be a newspaper reporter. I wonder fit the hags hae been gettin involved in.'

The barman nodded and shook his head simultaneously. 'And fit aboot the mannies in the Yankee motor. I think you ken a bit mair than you're tellin, Lachie. Come on. We'll promise tae keep it secret. Right lads?'

The lads nodded their agreement.

'Well, all right. They're hiding out in an old cottage on the Leithland Estate. I don't know what they're up to, but they've a lot of satellite-communication equipment. It seems that His Lordship knows about them and so does the Government. Now lads, they're operating under the Official Secrets Act and, if any of this gets out, they'll fry our balls for breakfast. So not a word to anybody. Right?'

Daniel, who'd just walked in, caught Lachie's confidential revelations. So Lord Leithland was working with the Americans and, it appeared, the British Government as well. He wondered if his own assignment was a diversionary scheme for something bigger. If so, what the hell was really going on? The Leithland Estate, eh? He'd follow that up tomorrow. The silent customers made way for him as he ordered a large malt whisky.

At that point, the other oddity, McSpake, entered and inquired if anyone had been asking for him. He meant it as a joke but the barman said that Maggie MacPhail had phoned earlier inviting him to tea.

'You better hurry, Mister McSpake. She said half past five an it's twenty past already She'll be gey anxious if you're late. Ye maun look your best, but mak sure she disnae get her claws inti yi.'

Archie rushed upstairs to wash and change. He had mixed feelings about the invitation but felt obliged to accept it. When he came down, he'd call her from the lobby phone and ask if she would hold back her tea preparations for fifteen minutes.

*

(Scarr Manse):

The minister had almost completed the preparations. Earlier, he'd locked the disciples' garments in the vestry and now he was making 'blood' in the manse kitchen. In his African days he had always used the blood of newly-slaughtered goats. Here, the problem of doing so without raising suspicion was insoluble. Carefully recorded experiments during the past ten days, however, had produced a fairly realistic substitute. It required precise quantities of the various constituents, and timing and temperatures were crucial to a successful outcome. The exact proportion of gelatine needed in the mixture had been solved early on, but the problem of getting smell and flavour right had seemed completely intractable. Juice extracted from lawn grass had given the closest approximation and he'd settled for that. He added the measured amount of food dye, stirred the liquid with a pencil and licked its end carefully. Yes, that was just as he wanted it. He carried the jug through to his study, checked the temperature inside the stationery cupboard and locked away the brew. That 'chalice' from Ibiza was quite impressive enough to fool the silly sods. The minister smiled in anticipation.

The sexy Tricia was coming early to have a private robe-fitting. That left only the problem of the missing disciple. He had worked out a strategy to solve that, but it would require speed and exact timing. He would bundle her into the kirk while the others were getting robed up in the vestry. He was so certain it would work that he avoided considering any alternative outcome. No reason why the information he'd obtained from the Meade woman shouldn't be reliable.

A car drove past the study window. Well, Tricia was on time. He hurried into his bedroom and was turning down the sheets when the doorbell rang.

*

(Birch Cottage):

The large, drab room upstairs had been transformed. The extra lights and old Christmas decorations Bob had installed, gave it a festive look that Marco hadn't expected. He was starting to relax, having shaken off sufficient shyness during the meal to begin talking to Margaret. And now they sat in adjacent chairs while Arc and Jimmy set up the C.D. player and argued over choice of discs. But that didn't concern Marco. They could play whatever they wanted so long as they kept the volume down. It was much more important that he and Margaret could hear each other. While their four companions danced with so much enthusiasm that Bessie came up to see if everything was all right, the two of them spent most of the evening discussing their families, schools, hopes, ambitions and hobbies.

'Hey, Marco, Alison interrupted. You said you might tell me about where you went off to in the summer and what happened after you came back. Go on. Give us the whole story. We won't tell anybody else, will we gang?'

So Marco told them about his trip to Karos, recounted some of his adventures there, and described the journey back to earth. But he hadn't been believed by his parents, by the police or by medical staff, he informed them indignantly. They'd accused him of making it up.

137

'Here's one of the communicators that the Karosians gave me so I could keep in touch with them. But it can't work on its own. You need two of them. The stupid Doctor at the hospital gave the other one to the military people. I think it's them that's trying to get their hands on this one too. Arc saw them running after me. Didn't you Arc? I've to keep looking for new hiding places so they won't find it.'

Marco passed round the metal cube for everybody to handle, until Bob came upstairs to tell guests it was time to go home.

The rain had stopped and breaks in the cloud promised frost later. The girls got into Bob's Skoda for the first journey. There wasn't enough space for five passengers so the boys were to wait for a second trip. Marco and Margaret looked at each other. He wanted to kiss her and he thought that she wanted him to. With Bessie watching from the kitchen window, however, shyness gripped him once more. The sight of Alison and Arc sharing a brief hug made him angry that he hadn't taken his chance. But it was too late. The girls were on their way home and the boys went back indoors to wait for Bob's return.

'Marco, you should come down to my house tomorrow,' said Arc. 'I could show you some of my gear and some of the places in Scarr that summer visitors never see. Ask them if they'll let you.'

'Well, my grandmother's going to hospital in Aberdeen tomorrow for a check-up. A consultant wants to see how her metal hip thing's doing. They're expecting me to go with them. I'm not supposed to be out of their sight. If I ask to stay, they'll just say no. But if your mother promised to keep an eye on me … . Nah! It probably wouldn't work. But it's the only thing I can think of. Get your mother to ask them, Arc. I don't want to go to Aberdeen. I've had enough of hospitals. Have you anywhere to hide this communicator? They wouldn't guess you had it and I've run out of ideas.'

Arc pocketed the cube and the two of them helped Jimmy to pack his gear. Soon Bob was back, turning the car round, ready to take Arc and Jimmy home. Marco went along for the ride, though he was secretly hoping someone would point out Margaret's house – if they passed it.

Jimmy got out at the corner of Scarr Brae and High Street. The others watched him unlock the door and carry his backpack into the house. His aunt waved at them as they drove off. Just past Scarr Kirk, they saw the Mitchells' car turning into their driveway. Al and Hetty were just returning, Bob said, from a function at the Portlach Arts Centre. When he'd dropped Alison off, she had said she was going to prepare tea and sandwiches for her parents who were due home any minute. She had given Bob a wave after she'd unlocked the side door and had then disappeared inside. He had waited for the light to go on in the hallway before driving off. Now, he turned the Skoda right onto Middlefields Road, then left into Harbour Lane and dropped Arc off at his house. Bob waited to see him go inside. But Arc had left the door key in his other trousers, so he knocked and waited. There was no reply and the house remained in darkness. He returned to the car, puzzled. The only thing he could think of was that his mother might have gone to something at the kirk. Arc wasn't sure what it was but she'd been 'waffling on' about it on her way home from the shop.

'Then we'll see if she's at the kirk. I didn't notice lights there when we came down the brae, but I was keeping my eyes on the road. Did either of you two notice anything?'

Neither boy had. Bob continued down Harbour Lane, turned left onto Shore Road and, from there, up Scarr Brae.

*

(Scarr Kirk):

The kirk was in darkness as they pulled up on the road outside. Bob shook his head and was about to drive off when Al and Hetty Mitchell appeared beside them, beating on the Skoda's side windows and demanding to know where Alison was. Bob began to tell them that she'd entered the house about fifteen or twenty minutes ago. Arc, reminding them that his mother was missing as well, got out of the car and approached the darkened kirk. Marco joined him in knocking at the heavy door but there was no reply. The boys ran along the front of the building and met the three adults who'd gone round the back. They all looked at the manse. Arc knew that the minister always spent every Thursday night in Portlach on some kind of secret business, but he raced across to the house anyway and started hammering on the front door. As soon as the others joined him, he ran round the corner and rained blows on the kitchen window. No sign of anyone. The minister must be away after all. But his mother had been talking about a 'Ceremony' at the *kirk*. He rushed back there pursued by Marco.

The boys had almost reached the main door of the kirk when it started to open. They dodged behind opposite sides of the porch and watched fearfully as a short, stocky figure in dark robe and hood stomped across the step. When he started to relieve himself against a laurel bush opposite, Marco signalled 'come on' to Arc and together they slipped into the building. It was dark inside, apart from a pool of light at the pulpit end. Down there was a group of people dressed in robes and hoods, just like the stocky figure outside. They could hear that one coming back so they dived between rows of pews and crouched, terrified, listening to the door being relocked. Heavy footsteps passed them and continued down to where things were happening.

Peering cautiously from their hiding places, the boys listened to high-pitched chanting, its words incomprehensible. Seven robed figures stood in a semi-circle facing a tall, heavily-built individual; clearly he was the one in charge. This leader held up a hand for silence and then struck a small gong that stood on a table beside him. The knocking at the outside door was barely audible.

'Kneel, disciples', boomed the leader. 'Kneel before the Grand Sorcerer, courtly attendant to the Great Lord of the Kingdom of Capricorn.' Seven figures knelt. The Grand Sorcerer raised a metal cup, like some kind of sporting trophy, and approached the first of the kneeling disciples. 'Drink, minion! Drink of the blood of the goat.' The minion stood up and, without removing its hood, did as the Grand Sorcerer had commanded.

'It's Slugpole', Arc whispered. 'I always knew he was a maniac. What the hell's this about? It must be the ceremony my mother was ... '. Arc stopped, frightened at what he was thinking. But his mother couldn't be so stupid. Could she? Yes! There was every chance that she could. He watched the disciples get up, one by one, and bend over the chalice of goat's blood. None of them looked like his mother. The only disciple he might make a guess at was the one who'd been outside having a piss. He had a strong feeling that it was that builder, Mason, from Portlach. One of his trucks had been parked in the school yard earlier.

'And now, here to join our blessed group is a young, eager novice. Pray welcome Alison into the bosom of our church.'

Marco struggled to restrain Arc as the minister removed the hood from the figure who'd been sitting, almost unnoticed, behind him. She was tied to a chair with some kind of decorative cord. The others chanted in unison and then exclaimed loudly, 'Welcome Alison to our blessed group. Drink from the blood of the Holy Goat. Drink to the glory of the Great Lord of the Kingdom of Capricorn.'

Marco looked back at the church door. He thought he could just make out a key in the lock. How could he reach it without being seen? Suddenly his friend provided a diversion. As Stackpoole pushed the chalice towards Alison's face, Arc shouted in as deep a voice as he could summon up, 'All right ya bums. Hands up! We got ya covered. Don't move!'

But they did move. They were struggling with each other to get through the bottleneck of the vestry door. Only Stackpoole stopped in his tracks and fought the tide of panicking disciples. He had detected the merest hint of falsetto in the intruder's voice. He started up the aisle.

'Hold him, Arc, till I open the door.'

It was a silly demand. But Alison needed help and Arc did his best. The minister brushed him aside and ran at Marco who had opened the door and thrown the heavy key as far as he could into the night. Bob met the minister just in time to save his grandson from a swinging fist. He, himself, landed on his back with the Grand Sorcerer's hands tightening round his throat. Marco ran towards the struggling men, jumped into the air and landed, feet first, on the enraged minister's back. That had no effect. As he prepared to repeat the attack, Al Mitchell came through the door and joined the battle. Although he was younger and stronger than Bob, the two of them couldn't restrain their maddened adversary. Stackpoole burst past Hetty on the doorstep and, pursued by the two men, sprinted down the churchyard. They saw him reach the high wall and thought him trapped. But he sprang onto a flattened gravestone and, from there, onto an upright one. A final leap carried him to the top of the wall and, with robe streaming theatrically behind, he vanished into the night.

**

CHAPTER ELEVEN

Friday Morning

(Herry Baxter's Lane, Portlach):

Stackpoole shivered and wrapped the robe more tightly round his upper body. Wind-driven sleet was whipping along the lane, clinging to his beard and eyebrows and melting through the lightweight black fabric to soak his chest and shoulders. He was thankful now that he'd resisted the temptation to scrap the telltale garment before entering the bus station. He would probably have got clean away if it hadn't been for his suitcase full of knickers.

While the furore at scar Kirk had been escalating to higher levels, he'd bolted round the manse wall in the darkness and slipped in through the garden gate to reach the kitchen door. Retrieval of the suitcase from its hiding place under the bed was vital. So too was collecting his passports and other personal documents. They could make all the difference between escape and capture. He had grabbed the case first and then hurried to find a suitable change of clothing. But he'd forgotten about the Meade woman tied-up in the wardrobe. Somehow she had managed to work the gag loose and, when he'd opened the door, she had started screaming. The racket must have been audible along a large part of Scarr Brae and in adjacent streets. Racing out to the yard with the suitcase, still wearing his robe, he had been confronted with Tricia's car. Good for her! She hadn't locked it and the keys were in the ignition switch. Neither Tricia nor her fellow disciples were to be seen. Well, they could bloody well take their own chances. Starting the Rover in haste, and leaving its lights off, Stackpoole had driven a few yards up the brae and swung sharply into Highfield Crescent. The Crescent ran round the edge of the village to meet Easter Road which opened in turn onto Shore Road on the east side of the village. At the junction, he had accelerated off in the direction of Portlach Town, fairly sure that no one had observed his escape route. However his stash of banknotes and personal documents were still in their hiding place beneath the floorboards in the entrance hall of the manse.

Now, he was scanning Herry Baxter's Lane in both directions. Unsurprisingly, no one was about at one o'clock on such a miserable morning. The minister turned, teeth chattering loudly, into Mason's yard. Ignoring the sudden glare of security lights and the screeching of an intruder alarm, he stumbled across irregular flagstones and between piles of building materials to hammer at the house door.

Lights went out; the alarm ceased abruptly and the door opened slowly. Jackie Mason seized him by the arm, dragged him inside and slid home heavy bolts.

'Christ, Solomon, I thought you'd be miles away by now. They'll be looking for you. I don't know if Lorna and I were recognised at the kirk but, if we were, there's bound to be a visit from the coppers. You can't stay here, but just sit down for a minute. You look knackered. How the hell did you get here? You didn't walk all the way from Scarr did you?'

'I need a large cup of tea, Jackie. I'm bloody desperate for something to drink. I could demolish a bacon sandwich – and a stack of eggs too, if you can spare them.'

'Come through to the kitchen. And keep your voice down. Lorna's in bed. She's on early shift tomorrow. She seems to think it was all a bit of a laugh. Here we are. Four eggs do you? And bacon to match? There's a bottle of brandy and glasses in that top cupboard. You definitely need a reviver.'

Mason put a frying pan on to the cooker and brought a pack of bacon and box of eggs from the refrigerator. The minister poured a large brandy and swallowed it neat. By the time he had savoured a second drink, the food was ready. Mason watched his weekend breakfasts vanish down the minister's gullet, pursued by several cups of tea and yet another brandy.

'Now then, what the hell are we going to do with you? You need to get as far from here as possible, and you need to do it fast. The longer you hang around, the more chance of being nicked – of us all being nicked. It's just possible that nobody else was recognised, but they're bound to have your name at the top of their suspects list. Have you got money? You need a plan.'

'I think I got away without being seen. I took Tricia's car – you know, that sexy friend of Marietta's – but the damned thing got bogged down on the old golf course. I came into Portlach by the railway cutting and hurried across to the bus station in good time to catch the last bus out. I dropped my case outside the ticket office for a few minutes to go for a piss and, when I came back, two people were directing passengers away from it. Looked like the manager and a bus inspector. I was going to grab it and tell them to fuck off when a policeman walked round the corner. I had to skedaddle down the back steps without the bloody thing. I expect the police will be swarming all over buses and passengers tomorrow. Probably suspect they're dealing with a bomb. That could be a useful diversion. Anyway, bus travel's out of the question. What I need's a car. I don't suppose you can see your way … ? I thought not. Maybe I can pinch another one somewhere. But you can let me have a bed for the night, though? It'll just be for one night – and I'll definitely go tomorrow. I'll make plans and be off at first light.'

'I don't like it Solomon. The cops could arrive at any time. If they do, you'll have to get out by the chapel exit as fast as you can – and without leaving signs.'

*

(The Meade House, Scarr):
It was two a.m. and Effie was refusing to go to bed, terrified

that the 'awfa beast' might break down the door to get at her again. Arc was sure she was exaggerating her terror, but he played along with it.

'It's safe, Mam. Alison's father saw him drive aff in a car. He'll be far awa by this time. A gang o folk are tryin to catch the divil. I bet he'll be sorry if that happens. Here's a cup o cocoa. Drink up an get some sleep. I'll sit in the corridor wi this chair leg and smack him across the lugs if he comes here. I'm sorry. Jist jokin. There's little chance he's within ten miles o Scarr.'

Effie, weeping as piteously as she thought the occasion demanded, agreed to go to bed but needed a biscuit with her cocoa. When she'd vanished up the stairs, Arc sat on the chair in the corridor. He'd wait until she had time to fall asleep and then he'd nip out to see what was happening. He was curious to discover if anybody had found a clue to Slugpole's whereabouts. He had a strong suspicion about where the minister would have gone and wanted to send the vigilantes in the right direction.

It was now after two and sleet whirling in from the sea was starting to build up in the corners of the windowpanes. Arc reached for the old-fashioned oilskin smock that had hung behind the door for as long as he could remember. It had been his grandfather's and was now stiff and cracked with age. By Christ, his grandfather would have flattened Slugpole up at the kirk, just as he was said to have flattened many aggressive boozers at the Lobster Creel on long-gone Saturday nights. Aye, the smock was the right garment but he'd need to watch that he didn't trip on the hem. He slipped out into the night, taking practice swings with the chair leg.

*

(The Mitchell House, Scarr):

'Right then, Mr. and Mrs. Mitchell, a C.I.D. team should get here from Aberdeen in about an hour and they'll do formal interviews. But I need information fast if this man's to be arrested before he gets too far, so help me please. Tell me what

146

you know about this incident at the church. If you've any suggestions about the whereabouts of the Reverend Stackpoole, tell me that too.' Police Sergeant Gregory opened his notebook and looked at each of the Mitchells in turn.

'My wife, Hetty, wasn't directly involved in the struggle but she'll tell you herself how the maniac nearly knocked her over on the steps. I got involved when Bob Smith's grandson opened the kirk door and Bob and I ran in to tackle the bastard; sorry, but that's the only way I can describe him. Minister? He's no minister! There's always been a question about where he came from. You should look into that. Anyway, he ran down the kirkyard and jumped over the wall. Hetty's sure he actually flew away into the night. And that's the last we saw of him. Mind you, just after Effie Meade started screaming in the manse, a car without lights went into Highfield Crescent. I don't know who was driving it, though I think it might have been Slug – ah – Stackpoole. But we were all concentrating on finding out where the screams were coming from. Well, yes. Come to think about it, it probably couldn't have been anyone other than Stackpoole.'

'Thanks, Al, I mean Mr. Mitchell. Now then, Alison, what can you tell me? Start at the beginning. The party? Yes, begin with what happened when you got back from the party.'

'I got out of Mr. Smith's car at our front gate and went to the side door. That's the one I've a key for. The outside light had been left on for me. When I got inside, I put the corridor light on too. Then I looked out and gave Mr. Smith and my two friends a wave to show them I was okay. I went into the kitchen to make some sandwiches for my parents, return. Then I heard a knock at the door and somebody shouted "Alison!" It sounded just like Mr. Smith. I thought maybe I'd left something in his car. So I opened the door and it was the minister and he was wearing a long black gown, a sort of cloak things with buttons. He pushed me against the wall and covered my head with a cloth. I hit him with my plaster-cast, but that was painful. I tried to shout but he told me to shut up. And then he carried me out of the house. Oh yes, and he said he was sorry but I had to go with him. I was frightened that he would – you know ... .' Alison paused, shaking. Her mother hugged her and looked anxiously at the sergeant.

'Nearly finished,' he said. 'And then he carried you into the kirk?'

'No. Not at first. He took me to the manse and put a robe thing round my shoulders. It had a hood. He tied my hands together and put a kind of gag in my mouth. I think it was a stocking. It tasted horrible and nearly made me sick. Then I had to walk over to the vestry and be tied in a chair. He opened the door into the kirk and dragged the chair through. There were voices. Some were women and some were men. They wanted to know who I was but he told them to be patient. I didn't know what was going on but they were all chanting words. I thought it could be some kind of spell, some witchcraft maybe. But I was so scared that I can't remember exactly what the words were. Then the minister said they all had to drink blood. He was just going to make me drink it too when Arc and Marco started shouting and they all ran away. Not the minister. He started swearing and then there was a fight. That's all I can tell you.'

'Arc and Marco. Who are they? And did you recognise the other people in the kirk?'

'Arc's a friend who goes to the village school. His name's really Raymond Meade. His mother has the hairdressing shop down there at the corner of Middlefields Road. Marco's from England. He's staying with Mr. and Mrs. Smith. They're his grandparents. It was his party we were at in Birch Cottage. I never got a look at the people in the kirk because the minister was trying to make me drink the blood. I think maybe I recognised a builder from Portlach. He's called Jackie Mason'.

'I'll get onto Detective Inspector Wardle about that,' said the Sergeant, 'and suggests that he visits Mason's place as soon as he can. The fugitive might go there to hide. Even if he doesn't, Mason needs to be brought in for questioning. Now, is there anything any of you can suggest to help us arrest this Stackpoole fiend? No? Well, I'm on my way to talk to the folk at Birch Cottage – if they haven't all gone to bed.'

(Mason the Builder's House, Portlach):

Solomon resurfaced from long ago with his face pressed into a tear-soaked pillowcase. He hadn't been Solomon back then; he'd been little Robbie Stockdale. Once again he was experiencing the feeling of devastation that had engulfed him when his mother died. He'd been six years old at the time. Although she was now just a shadowy impression, he was still unable to smile. He had learned to laugh eventually, but it was never spontaneous. He still shed tears sometimes when alone. Overnight, the tiny farm in County Sligo had changed from the sunniest spot in the whole world, to a miserable, grey place that Robbie would never again be part of.

Fergus Stockdale had little time to spend with his unhappy son as the farm teetered perpetually on the brink of failure, so it was left to the boy's sister, Rose, to mother him.

Ma had come from Glasgow. Her family, the Donaldsons, had been nominally protestant. Da, who didn't believe in any religion, had met young Betty Donaldson when he went to Scotland in nineteen forty to work as a labourer on airfield-construction projects. He'd been nineteen and she seventeen when they first got to know each other, and they had kept in touch throughout the war. They'd married in nineteen forty six, Betty's family having been assured that Fergus Stockdale wasn't a Catholic and, more importantly, not a supporter of Celtic football club.

Fergus took his new wife back to Ireland when a great aunt that he'd never heard of died, leaving him a crumbling house and a run-down piece of agricultural land. To Fergus, hard work was second nature, and he began to hack out a bare living from the farm.

Towards the end of their first year of marriage, Betty began to be drawn away from her lukewarm Protestant roots towards the Church of Rome. Fergus couldn't understand why his wife would consider changing one set of chains for another. He was adamant that no 'fools in frocks' would ever set foot on his property. When, in nineteen forty eight, the Stockdales' first child, Rose, was born, Fergus swore that his daughter would never have her mind warped by religion. It was another six years before the second child, Robert, came along.

When Betty died, twelve years old Rose took over the care of her little brother. Hiding her own grief when anyone else was present, she became the attentive mother-substitute that the boy needed. Secretly, Father Riley offered all the support that he could, but he had to beware of Fergus Stockdale's hostility. Everyone, except Rose, thought that young Robbie was 'going to be all right' and he made such good progress at school that one report spoke of future academic distinction. If Fergus was aware of the boy's restless, tearful nights, he never mentioned them. Rose would take Robbie into her bed and hug him back to sleep. He would cling to her until he was calm. His sister's bed became his place of refuge. She would often find him cuddled up there, clinging to her nightgown or other clothing. Eventually she had a lock fitted to her door, banishing him permanently to his own bed. Father Riley, who knew about these things, confirmed that her action had been right. One day when Robbie came home from school early, he had overheard Rose and the priest talking about him.

Now, Solomon was starting once more to feel something of his old anger at what happened that day. He remembered running down to the bottom of the field to tell Fergus that the priest was in the house with Rose. Da dealt with that by pinning Father Riley against the wall and threatening him with a battering if he ever came back. He also stilled Rose's protests by hitting her across the mouth and making her promise to avoid 'bloody parasites' in future. Robbie saw clear signs, however, that she was still meeting Riley secretly and he often followed her when she left the farm. One day he saw Rose and the priest lying together in the long grass behind the wood. He had known then that he must kill them.

A dull boom sounded in the distance. Solomon sat up suddenly, listening. A police car came wailing down the street. The abandoned suitcase! That had probably caused enough anxiety for the bastards to blow it up and, with it, all that remained of his prized knicker-collection. He snatched up his still-damp clothes and was heading for the stairs when the pitch of the siren altered. The vehicle had gone past this time, but there was a strong possibility that it might return. A change into dry gear was a matter of urgency in case he had to run for it. He went through to Mason's bedroom. There was nothing of his size in the wardrobe but he managed to squeeze into a pair of extra large, and extra uncomfortable, stretch underpants. He confronted himself in the mirror and shook his head. His old clothes promised a cold, miserable time but he'd have to put up with that until he could find better ones. And where the hell could he get those without alarming the very conservative inhabitants of Portlach? A clothes shop? Yes, perhaps. But it would have to be located in a quiet side street. A second-hand shop would be best. His lack of money wouldn't matter so much there. He could even grab what he wanted and run. Yes, he'd give that a try. He put on his wet trousers and tucked a pair of Lorna's knickers into the hip pocket. They'd been worn and he found that comforting.

*

(The Bay House Hotel):

McSpake and O'Donnel were having a very serious conversation about something, but in voices so low that Annie Moston couldn't make out a word. She approached their table for the third time with an offer of more coffee and hot rolls, but once again they declined. They had their bird books and binoculars with them but they'd given up any attempt to maintain their birdwatcher facades. McSpake had been demonstrating some kind of camera and the boozy one had concentrated on every word. But they'd both gone silent whenever Annie got near.

She was determined to get them talking to her, however, so she smiled and told them she was sure the minister would soon be caught. Their puzzlement was just what she'd been hoping for and she began to pass on her version of what had happened last night at the kirk. Archie, having met the man face to face when he arrived at the hotel, was less surprised than his companion. Daniel, his mind grappling with the possibility that the incident had been some kind of diversion mounted by the smugglers, wanted as many details as Annie could provide and suggested that she join them. She sat and answered most of Daniel's questions, but became guarded on the subject of the Americans in the Cadillac. Annie didn't know what the penalty was for passing on Official Secrets and would rather not find out. Clearly, nobody had told her that Daniel overheard the confidences which Lachie Tradwell shared with customers in the bar last night.

When she was called away to answer the telephone, the two men resumed their planning. Daniel had put in a session on the laptop yesterday – before his usual bedtime requirements drew him inexorably to the bar. The blank wall that he'd come up against, had pointed him towards his next move; one that could possibly secure vital information about the link between the Americans and the Leithland Estate. He'd avoided contacting Gurley back at the office because of suggestions about the Government's involvement with Lord Leithland. He mustn't risk being pulled off the case at this stage and he was sure the bastards would sideline him without hesitation if they thought he was getting close to something hush-hush. He had to safeguard his own interests at all costs.

Leithland Castle was open to day-visitors from Easter to the end of September. Daniel suggested that he and Mc.Spake arrive at the front door and proffer admission fees. A friend, they would declare, had visited the castle last July and had recommended it as the finest example of Scottish Baronial Style architecture in the district. They'd be surprised to find that it closed for visitors in the autumn and would turn away disappointed. Driving back through the estate Archie would drop Daniel off at a suitable location to scout around secretly for information. If he were to be caught, he'd be a birdwatcher who'd got lost. If not, Archie would pick him up again at five in the evening half a mile from the main gates.

'Right then,' said Archie. 'I'll meet you here in the bar in an hour's time. Don't forget your bird book and binoculars. I'll bring the camera. But I need to go and check on the Powell boy first. I mustn't forget my real mission here.' Archie picked up his equipment from the table and hurried out to the car.

*

(The Cardingtons' House, Portlach.):

From his study window, Jon Cardington saw that the vehicle on the old golf course hadn't moved from where he'd spotted it at first light. Nigh-time joy riders, no doubt, and it was probably stolen. He tried to read the registration plate through binoculars. No use; the bloody thing was at the wrong angle. Evidently, the car was bogged down in an extensive muddy hollow where snow-melt had collected during the night. Jon, always apt to take decisive action against anything that dared to be out of place, decided that the local police would deal firmly with this matter. But, before he reported it, he'd go down and make a note of the number plate. The police weren't what they'd been in his youth. Always prevaricating nowadays! Didn't seem to give a damn unless somebody was being murdered or driving too fast. He would ring the chief Constable with details and then tell the Sergeant in Portlach what he'd done. He'd demand removal of the offending vehicle today.

Dressed in heavy coat, Wellington boots and flat cap, Jon set off down the path. Marietta's Porsche, covered in mud, sat outside its garage. The careless woman was probably still drunk when she came home. Next time she was caught, he wouldn't pull any strings on her behalf. A quiet word in Anderson's ear and they'd throw the book at her. The bloody bitch!

The bogged down car was an old, medium-sized Rover that had been left with the ignition key still in place. Jon slipped the key into his pocket. No sense in offering anyone the temptation. The boot-lid was secure and the car had been fitted with locking wheel nuts. Good. Something on the floor behind the driving seat caught his eye; a watch, and a very good one at that. He recognised it almost at once. Platinum with diamond studded bezel and bracelet; the initials MC engraved on the back. She had insisted on that particular model on their very last trip to Paris all those years ago. It had cost an obscene price and she'd said she loved it. What the hell was it doing in this scrap-yard jalopy? The bitch would tell him – even if he had to freeze her funds for a month. Growling angrily, Cardington headed back towards the house.

*

(Leithland Castle, South East of Scarr):

Archie and Daniel, well scrubbed and wearing neckties, pulled up at the far end of the car park and walked round to the front door of the castle. The building wasn't at all what trickles of summer tourists had been led to expect by fading brochures in Visitor Information Centres. Certainly, it was recognisable. There, for example, was the 'Grand Entrance Door' set in the front of a square, two-storey structure. The walls were topped by battlements and, at the corners of the building, towers rose up an extra storey. On top of each tower, a turret with a pointed slate roof carried a limp pennon on a miniature flagpole. All over the front of the castle, set between the windows, were imitation arrow-slits which, on closer inspection, proved to be backed by black glass, – or maybe it was lacquered wood. The whole place looked like something from a low-budget film. Archie could remember when this building had been a single storey tuberculosis hospital. As a child he had scrambled over

154

the pile of stones marking the location of the original Leithland castle away over there beyond the trees. He peered more closely at the nearby wall. It appeared to consist of stone facings on brick. And then the door opened.

'Good day, gentlemen,' said the tall, stooping man who looked down on them from the top step. 'It is Mr. O'Donnel, isn't it? And Mr. McSpake, of course. What kept you?'

The two visitors, surprised, tried to regard the man impassively. Neither spoke.

'Commander Gurley said I should expect you on Thursday morning, O'Donnel, but a day late isn't bad. The severe weather has delayed many things. Why don't you come in? Time for morning coffee. I see you don't remember me, McSp-Spake. Think Moscow Embassy. I was an Honourable then, not an Earl. You were an up and coming agent and I'd been sent over by Harold to neg-neg – to arrange an agreement with the Soviets. Still top secret, I'm afraid. Yes, I see that you remember me now. You caught me in flagrante delicto. Took me a while to live it down. Still – under the bridge now. Through here, gentlemen. I'll ring for elevenses and then we can talk uninter-uninter-, um yes.'

Daniel and Archie followed the Earl indoors. Unlike the shabbiness of its exterior, Leithland Castle was comfortably furnished. It was obvious to Archie that the paintings and sculptures on display in the hallway had been assembled with much care and at great cost. The study was clad in exotic wood panelling and held a large collection of English watercolours. A heavy, glass-fronted cabinet contained exquisitely carved jade items that Archie would have been delighted to handle. But their host was in a hurry to get on with the discussion.

*

(Mason's House, Portlach):

Loud knocking on the front door made the minister leap out of his kitchen chair. He grabbed the road-map which had fallen to the floor and stuffed it down the waistband of his damp trousers. Pausing just long enough to snatch up his sandwich, he ran down the back stairs towards the concealed entrance to 'the Chapel'. His first intention was to hide there until the visitor had gone but that was altered by the sound of shouting and a loud crash. The bloody police – and they meant business! The outer escape hatch from the chapel opened into a narrow conduit between Mason's house and lorry-repair workshop. Stackpoole squeezed along the narrow passageway to reach the yard. The sound of a police siren coming along the lane stopped him with his hand on the gate. He slid home the security bolt and looked around.

That ladder was the solution. Quickly! He propped it against the high dividing wall between Mason's and Jenkins the plumber's yards. On top of the wall, he pulled up the ladder, threw it into the piles of plastic piping and metal plumbing attachments and jumped down after it. He couldn't risk staying this close to police activity so he continued on to the next yard, that of a motorcycle dealer. As he scrambled under a garage workbench, he heard the police breaking through Mason's back gate.

*

(The Meade House, Scarr):

'They werena ower keen on you dodgin the Aiberdeen appointment. It must've been the police promisin tae patrol the toon till Slugpole wis trapped that changed their minds. Will you pare the tatties?' Arc handed Marco the bowl of potatoes. 'There's a fine sharp knife in that drawer.'

'Actually it was the phone call from the doctor that did the trick along with your mother refusing to be left on her own. I tried to convince them I should stay and collect the medicine from the shop because you needed to keep an eye on her all the time. I didn't tell them that the Malcolms had said the order must be collected by an adult. I thought Lizzie Malcolm looked kind of strange when I asked her about it. She didn't seem to be listening at first and she was jumpy every time somebody came into the shop. Do you think she could've had something to do with the church business last night? Anyway, you're right. My grandparents weren't happy about me staying back. My grandmother said she'd cancel her appointment but the cops just laughed and said Slugpole was well away by this time. They've managed to follow his trail to Portlach and think he's probably heading for Aberdeen. They said they'll catch him some time today but that my grandfather shouldn't stop for any strange hitch-hikers on the road. These potatoes okay? Right! If you think the medicine'll be here by now, I'll run across and ask if somebody can deliver it. You can tell me when I come back about the plan you've got for this afternoon. I hope your mother's going to agree.'

'Nae problem Marco. I listened well t'the Doctor's instructions. My mither's pairt o the plan.'

**

CHAPTER TWELVE

Friday Afternoon

(Whitescar Cottage):

'Cup of tea for you, Victor. Would you like a biscuit?'

Victor shook his head. 'Thanks, Maggie, but no. I'm too screwed up to eat anything. I'll be like this till the delivery comes ashore. Radek confirms it's all set up for tomorrow but they're doing a test-run tonight to check that everything's in order. If the coast's clear they may even risk flying the actual route like they did two years ago. If there's any suspicion of inshore vessels, they'll make a diversionary flight somewhere else. I thought he seemed a bit jittery and he did admit that the risk could possibly be higher this trip. So stay alert Maggie and watch out for unusual activities at sea and ashore. What about this McSpake character? Is he nosing around our operation? What happened when he came over to scrounge supper?'

'I'm not absolutely certain what he's up to. He all but admitted that the bird watching was a front. I'm inclined to believe that he really *is* looking after the safety of the Smiths' grandson. The Americans are targeting the boy for some reason but he wouldn't say what that might be. When they chased the lad across this way from the beach, McSpake knocked one of them down – a very aggressive one. He got up and started shouting and swearing but Archie didn't bat an eyelid.'

'Archie, is it? Be careful Sis. You don't want to get involved until you're a hundred percent sure of him.'

'I won't take chances, Victor. You know I can't afford to. But when this business is wrapped up, I'll go out of my way to get involved. There's something very sexy about him. Don't you think so?'

Victor snorted, making it perfectly clear that he didn't think so.

'Right, Victor; let's go over things again. I'll collect the package after they drop it tomorrow night, only this time I won't deliver it to you at the Hall. I'll lock it in the lab until Sunday. You'll come over then to collect it. Is that when you're bringing the ones from your safe? And I'm to send those off to Bristol on Monday? It all seems more complicated than usual. Are you sure there isn't something more that you're not telling me? I'm going to be pushed to get things organized in time. Will you help me to get the crates ready?'

Maggie was puzzled when Victor agreed to her request. He'd never done that before without an argument. Her unease grew.

'By the way, Sis, have you any extra crates handy? Have them ready – just in case. No! Don't ask. See you tomorrow.'

Maggie's anxiety increased. But she recognised the old signs telling her that further questioning would make her brother clam up. She changed her ground slightly. 'Oh Victor, there's mother shouting for me to get her up after her nap. I don't suppose you want her to find you here. I'll phone tomorrow after the delivery – usual code.'

*

(Nikolai Rykov, North of Scarr):

The small, black stealth-aircraft stood in its hangar on three retractable legs. Cockpit gauges indicated that liquid-fuel supply and electrical-power storage were at maximum levels, thus ensuring that the disc was ready to take to the air at short notice. Its mat-surfaced bodywork came to within inches of the hangar's sides. The tiny flight deck, projecting blister-like from the upper-front area of the craft, emitted a faint green glow. Aft of the cockpit was a broad circle of dual-purpose air intake and exhaust output vents. Under the belly of the disc, the cargo-bay door was surrounded by a ring of jets. As intended by its re-designers, the aircraft had all the outward appearance of a science-fiction flying saucer.

A large part of the vehicle's interior was occupied by a vertical, tubular structure stretching from the cabin's low ceiling to the floor. This housed a squat turbine. Above the cabin ceiling was the craft's main gyroscope which could be powered up by the turbine as required. Three dome-shaped bumps on the floor surrounded the turbine tube at a distance. Each one of those housed its own small, independently-controllable gyroscope. Finally, beyond an insulating plastic wall that protected the cabin from high-tension electricity, a large-diameter metal ring was wound with miles of fine, copper wire. This was connected to the gyroscope and, when spinning in the earth's magnetic field, provided the craft with directional propulsion in level flight – at least that is what Yashin said.

To Yashin, who had once studied heavy electrical engineering on secondment to Imperial College, London, the disc's functioning was simple. He had tried to explain to the captain how the turbine, as well as topping up the power cells, could drive the large flywheel to very high speeds. Channelling the exhaust upwards, meanwhile, kept the disc firmly on the ground. To make it lift off, the exhaust was re-directed downwards and controlled through the underbelly nozzles. It took only a fraction of the turbine's power, he said, for the disc to lift off.

Radek, however, didn't try to understand the science involved. He found the electro-magnetic drive stuff especially incomprehensible. The fact that it all worked was what mattered. Looking at the sinister black craft always gave him a feeling of satisfaction. He didn't know anybody who actually liked Zhirkov, but he couldn't imagine that anyone would be unimpressed by the man's ability to get things done, and done thoroughly within strict time limits.

The bastard had acquired the stealth aircraft, along with three others, in the free-for-all that followed the demise of the old Soviet Union. Based on German World War Two technology that didn't work sufficiently well to satisfy military requirements, the craft had been redesigned by Zhirkov's engineers using more recent developments. Newer, lighter construction materials had reduced inertia, and its performance had been further improved by advanced electronic equipment from Japan and Taiwan. The computerised sound-frequency-cancellation system for the turbine was the final addition that turned each of the machines into a near-perfect transport for contraband cargo.

Their greatest success had been in smuggling diamonds from African, Asian and South American countries onto fishing-factory ships working outside territorial waters. But the Asian and South American parts of the operation were coming to an end with the imminent opening of Zhirkov's new mining concessions in Siberia. Offers from United States business interests to buy the 'saucers' had been rebuffed by Zhirkov. Why they should want the craft was a mystery. Perhaps someone had seen them as cheaper alternatives to their own existing underhand schemes – or even for law-enforcement use, perhaps in anti-drug-smuggling patrols over foreign territories. In any case, their interest gave Yashin the opportunity to do a deal that would secure him the new life he'd always hoped for. How long that would last, was problematic.

Captain Radek's own plan was unknown to his co-conspirator – a very necessary precaution. He went below to relax with a bottle of vodka.

*

(The Leithland Estate):
Lord Leithland drove his guests along the muddy track in an old Range Rover. The Communications Post was the property of her Majesty's Government but was being managed at present by his Lordship in conjunction with the Americans. When the two investigators had observed its functioning, they were duty bound to maintain secrecy about it under all circumstances. Daniel

remained highly suspicious of their aristocratic guide who was casting surreptitious glances at them in the rear-view mirror. He could see that Archie was aware of his Lordship's interest as well. Lord Leithland? He'd have to try running some more checks on him at the first opportunity and without Gurley's knowledge. The man had met Archie in Moscow! What was that really about? And why had Archie not recognised him? Daniel was beginning to have a strong resurgence of doubts about his co-investigator as well. Nothing about *him* on the internet and not very much about Leithland – other than as an organiser of tourist travel and accommodation.

From an elevated parking place they could see a near-derelict cottage close to the burn below. His Lordship changed his brogues for green Wellington boots and asked them to come this way. Daniel bent down behind the vehicle to fiddle with his bootlaces, took a couple of gulps from his hip flask, and did as he was asked. Archie said he would have to stay by the car since his arthritic joint would be overtaxed by the steepness of the slope. His hand was on the pocket in which he carried the camera. Daniel nodded at him and hurried to overtake their long-striding guide.

By the time his companions had reached the cottage, Archie had captured two shots of the scene. Limited by the restrictions of a 'two-times' zoom-lens, however, he knew that the communications mast among the trees opposite would occupy very few pixels of the memory card. He needed to get much closer. The others had vanished inside the building, so he hurried along the top of the ridge to reach a hawthorn hedge and slithered down the slope behind that to reach the burn. He splashed through the frigid water and peered up over the far bank. A slight alteration in position brought a gap in the vegetation into line with the communications mast that stood on the rise beyond. There was no time to lose. Three more shots and the camera was displaying the 'Card Full' signal. Must move quickly! When Leithland and O'Donnel came out of the cottage accompanied by the two Americans, Archie was standing by the

Range Rover, wheezing a bit, pretending to capture shots of rooks flying above the trees. He hoped they wouldn't notice his muddy trousers and soaking boots. He was fairly confident that they'd no idea of his real activities. They hadn't, of course, but a sharp-eyed watcher on the other side of the valley had not only observed his actions, but filmed them as well.

*

(The Meade House, Harbour Lane):
'Right Marco, she's fast asleep. The capsules did the trick. The Doctor said that twa o them should knock er oot for eight hours at least.'

'Are you sure you should have given her two? I could swear the instructions say one in the morning and two at night.'

'Well the Doctor telt me she could hae twa immediately if she wis agitated. When I mentioned Slugpole, she wis very agitated. So I gied er twa. I'll hae anither peek through her door tae mak sure she's fast asleep. Then you can help me wi my special scheme.'

'What's the scheme, Arc? You've been hinting at a scheme but not saying what it is. Is it about capturing Slugpole?'

'Nah. He's lang awa. It's aboot my new raft. I've got the bits in the shed. Be back in a minute.'

Arc went upstairs, making lots of noise on the way. He returned smiling. 'Oot like a light', he said. 'Come on.'

It looked like a building-site after an earthquake – and the Meades called it their back garden. At the end farthest from the house, close to the next-door neighbour's fence, a pile of bricks and slates marked the site of a collapsed outhouse. Drifts of bishop-weed partly covered pieces of wood, lengths of rope and scraps of torn fishing net that were scattered across the area. A cracked, lichen-covered birdbath leaned at an angle in one corner while, in another, assorted wheels and bicycle frames were piled against the side of a new shed. The origin of Arc's personal transport was obvious. Although Marco had never built a raft and had only a vague idea of what one looked like, he was sure that there was enough stuff here to build several.

Arc opened the shed door, moved his current bicycle aside and wrestled a handcart out into the yard. It consisted of a shallow box mounted on a long axle with a bicycle wheel at each end. A single shaft enabled the cart to be pushed, or pulled, along. Arc referred to it as his 'hurly'.

'Give us a hand Marco. You tak it ower to the gate an I'll get the rest o the gear.'

Loading the hurly was easy. Arc threw the items out of the shed and Marco piled them on, trying to make things balance. A heavy coil of blue rope was topped by several short lengths of thinner orange-coloured cord and a fish-filleting knife with a bright red handle. Four large plastic flagons were placed on top of the load and everything was covered with an old tablecloth. Arc returned to the back door to listen for any sounds coming from upstairs. Satisfied, he opened the garden gate and, with Marco's assistance, manoeuvred the hurly onto Harbour Lane. 'Watch for the mannies in the big car', he warned as they approached Shore Road. At the junction, they looked carefully in both directions and waited till the road was clear of traffic.

'Right, Marco. Let's go.' They wheeled the cart off towards Blackscar.

*

(Twenty Five Miles North West of Aberdeen):

Fog had been thickening along the A947 road ever since they'd cleared the city limits and the traffic had now slowed to a crawl. Bessie was urging Bob to fid a place to stop until things had cleared a bit. Bob believed there was little chance of that but was tempted to pull up at a pub in any case – if only to reduce his stress level. Then, if things did get worse, they could ask about a room for the night. At least they didn't have to worry about young Marc. Effie Meade was a reliable, if over-excitable, guardian. Her own son too was totally unflappable. He'd done well in last night's extraordinary fracas at the kirk. Yes, Marc was much safer with them than he'd be on this fogbound road. Thank goodness they'd left him in Scarr.

'I hope Mark isn't worrying about us being late, Bessie. If we do stop for a break we'll need to phone Effie and ask her to reassure him.'

*

(Grover's Motorcycle Shop, Portlach):

Roddy Grover let his cat, Sunbeam, out into the yard and returned to the comparative comfort of the back-shop. It had always been Roddy's habit to work outside when the weather was fine, and in the garage at the bottom of the yard when it wasn't. Today, however, he felt a cold coming on and had no inclination to work at all.

A specialist in rebuilding old motorcycles, Roddy's high-season for business had always been spring and early summer, but even the Easter period had been a washout this year. Nowadays, large city dealers stocked extensive selections of the very latest machines at 'special prices' and few local customers were interested in the old, and increasingly scarce, Manx Nortons from the nineteen fifties that Roddy loved. His all-time favourites, Vincent Black Shadows, were completely unobtainable. Since the beginning of May he had managed to acquire and restore a solitary bike. The Matchless G9 had emerged from an old garage in Strath Isla with only its delivery mileage recorded. Advertised in a national magazine, it had brought an interested customer all the way from Swindon. The Matchless had changed ownership in minutes – and for ready cash. Since then, business had consisted of repairs and servicing for a handful of owners who seemed unable to carry out the work themselves. It wasn't exciting employment for someone with his background.

Roddy couldn't kid himself any longer. His life was on the skids. One more year and he'd be out of business – probably bankrupt. He was regretting his recent attempt to get up to date.

He must have been mad to succumb to the impulse which made buy the modern Honda that gleamed in the front window. He had to admit to himself, however, that it *was* beautiful and that it had attracted a lot of hard-up young men, and some women, to gaze longingly at it through the glass. Less than two years off the assembly line and with only six thousand miles on the clock, it would have tempted him to break every speed-limit around; tempted, that is, if he hadn't shattered both legs in what had turned out to be his final road race.

He was comfortable now with the consequences. His left leg had been amputated above the knee and the right had healed badly. Roddy glanced at the stumps of two missing fingers. He'd long since stopped shaking and sweating when he replayed the accident in his mind. Unlike some crash survivors, he was aware of its every detail. He could still see his front wheel converging on the wooden telegraph pole and remembered how his mind clicked into hyper-drive. He had leaned slowly to the left, away from the line of the pole, releasing the grasp of his right hand on the throttle. A split second after the impact, as he began to rise from the saddle, he'd let go of the left hand grip. He had flown for what seemed ages, floating through two somersaults, controlling his posture so as not to land on his upper body. It must have looked to observers like the game of some insane acrobat. Roddy had landed feet first and, as his legs began to collapse under him, he'd rolled forward, head over heels in the muddy field. Some newspapers had said forty feet, some, fifty; he thought it more – but of little relevance after the event. The fingers didn't matter, but the leg problems had ended his ambition to win a string of famous victories on the Isle of Man. He had continued to lavish care on motorcycles as a business; it was all he knew. But he'd never driven another one. He didn't even consider car ownership.

Roddy decided he might as well close early today. If there was to be any business this week, it would be on Saturday. He locked the front door and changed the sign to 'Closed'. Oh shit! He'd forgotten about Sunbeam, still out in the yard. Drizzling rain was beginning to distort his view through window as he approached the back door.

*

Under a bench in the garage, wrapped in a tarpaulin, the minister was feeling cold and hungry. He'd heard voices from Mason's place and then the arrival of Mason himself under police supervision. Soon afterwards, they were being shown the concealed exit from The Chapel by Mason who was struggling to find a plausible explanation for why such an escape facility was necessary. They took him back out to a car in the lane and drove him away. Stackpoole was starting to wriggle from his hiding place, in the hope that the lane was now empty, when the arrival of another vehicle sent him back under cover. This time it was Lorna, thanking the Police Sergeant for having waited until her shift at the hospital was finished. She began insisting loudly that Mr. Mason and Mr. Stackpoole were to blame for everything and that she was an innocent dupe of their devilish schemes. Her voice was cut off by the closing of a door.

Pressure on the minister continued as the area of the police search was extended. Previously, they had searched the yards on either side of the Builder's one and they were now visiting other properties in the street. He heard voices in the motorcycle shop. The back door opened and he readied himself for a fight. Having got halfway down the yard, however, the policeman made a remark about 'fucking awful weather', and retreated towards the house. His warning about the need for vigilance was acknowledged by the small crippled man in dungarees as they went back inside.

Twenty minutes later, the minister was weighing up which of his two preferred escape strategies he should adopt when a cat mewed at his ear. He swatted the animal, sending it running towards the house. Yes. The decision had been made for him. He crawled from under the bench and pursued the animal. He could hear Lorna being escorted out to the police car in the lane just as he caught up with the cat. It jumped onto a window ledge and began pawing at the wet glass. Stackpoole pressed himself against the wall beside the door and waited. The car drove off. He was sure that Lorna would soon be facing formal questioning in an interview room. Pity! He'd had plans for Lorna. He fingered her knickers in his pocket. Just then, the door opened and a voice called, 'Sunbeam. Here, puss, puss.' As Sunbeam ran in at the door, the minister, barely a step behind her, pushed Roddy Grover back into the house.

*

(East Beach, Near Blackscar):

Assembling the raft didn't take the boys very long. Arc had previously transported the flotsam door from West Beach to Blackscar and now they pulled it from under its covering of seaweed and stones and dragged it down to the water's edge. Marco was surprised to see a decorative glass doorknob still attached. He examined the door itself more closely. About two dozen small metal rings were scattered over one of its faces. Arc explained that these were screw eyes that he'd fitted to allow the floats to be tied securely underneath the deck. He pointed to the orange cord and plastic flagons on the hurly. The rising tide was starting to lap at the raft by the time they got it ready. After giving the float bindings a final security check, Arc produced two crude paddles from a rock crevice above high-water mark. Finally they carried the heavy blue rope down the beach and loaded it aboard the raft. Marco tied one of its ends to the doorknob while Arc tied the other end to a long thin boulder – the anchor and anchor- rope. The plastic-handled filleting knife, which they'd used to trim the bindings, was stuck into the wood so it wouldn't fall overboard.

'Fine,' said Arc. 'Noo we jist sit and wait for the tide tae rise. We'll be afloat shortly.'

'How far will we go?' asked Marco nervously. 'Not out to sea? What if your mother wakes up? There's a police car outside the library. They'll be wild if they see us. Are you allowed to just go out on a raft without telling anybody? Don't the coastguards kick up a fuss?

'Everybody maks a fuss. My grandfather tell't me aboot the things they did awa back. If the copper caught them, he'd gie them a smack on the lug and mak them promise to stop whatever it was. So they just did something else instead. I'm fed up bein treated like an infant by adults that never try anythin interesting and then complain if somebody else does. Hey. We're liftin aff. Yahoo! Grab a paddle. We'll sail oot along the side o Blackscar, then back in time to tak things to bits again. I want to store it in the shed till next simmer. It'll be a great divin platform in the holidays. I'll anchor it ower the deep water at the end o the scar.'

Synchronising their paddling was very difficult, and made steering almost impossible. Marco believed they should have had a rudder but it would have required a third crew member for that to work. He doubted if the floats under the door would give sufficient flotation for more than two people. Luckily the sea was calm this afternoon. As they neared the outer extremity of Blackscar, however, small waves caused the raft to pitch and swing. There was a current here, flowing westward across the inner bay, pulling them away from the shelter of the rocks. Unable to halt their progress, Arc threw the anchor over the side but, in spite of the long rope to which it was attached, it didn't reach the bottom. The raft was speeding up as the current strength increased and they were beginning to get soaked by fine drizzle.

Arc expected to catch the attention of someone as they passed the harbour entrance but the very last angler on the pier had packed up and gone home. Shore road was too far away for anyone to hear their shouts and they didn't have anything to signal with.

'Don't worry, Marco,' said Arc, trying to sound cheerful. 'At this speed, we'll reach Whitescar in aboot twenty minutes.'

Marco wasn't taken in by his companion's mock optimism. He was worried by the approach of night and by the bank of fog moving in quickly from the north.

By the time they came close to Whitescar it was becoming

more and more obvious that they'd be swept past it if they couldn't change course. They paddled frantically until it seemed that shipwreck on Inch Greele was inevitable. Well, that was better than being swept along the miles of empty coast beyond. The raft stopped with a jolt and water washed across the deck. Far below, the anchor had caught on a snag. The boys were at a loss what to do. Waves were growing steeper and the rising tide was lifting one side of the raft. Its other side, now firmly attached to the rocky bottom, was gradually sinking farther and farther under the surface. Water swept up the sloping deck with increasing power. When one of the floats popped out from beneath the door, the tilt of the raft increased further and they were hanging on desperately.

'I'll cut the rope.' Arc reached for the knife embedded in the deck but, just as he was grasping it, the raft gave a lurch and the knife flew from his hand into the sea. The doorknob had given way and had disappeared into the depths along with the anchor rope. Freed from its restraint, the raft was tossed forward towards the islet.

'Get ready to jump when we hit the rocks. We'll be safer there.'

'Yes. Okay Arc. I'm ready.'

*

(Harbour Lane, Scarr):

Archie parked the Mini near the top of the lane and walked slowly down past the Meade house. It was in darkness; there appeared to be nobody at home. That was strange. Geordie Moston had told him the Smiths had driven off to Aberdeen before midday, leaving their grandson with the Meades. He went back along the side of the house and looked over the fence. The yard was dark too. Where could the occupants have gone? Knocking at the door wasn't an option. That would blow his cover. He walked along to the library and saw the police packing up their makeshift Incident Room. No members of the public were about, except for a solitary angler crossing the road from the harbour. Would the Meade boy have gone to his favourite location, the beach, and taken Marc Powell with him? If so, why go there at night? And where was the mother?

Archie walked back slowly to the Mini in Harbour Lane. He was in the act of opening the driver's door when the dark Cadillac turned into the street and slowed down. Then, as if its occupants had just become aware of his presence, it speeded up and turned right at the Shore Road junction. Archie got into the mini and followed, but when he reached the corner, there was no sign of the Cadillac. The agents, if that's what they were, appeared to be poking around everywhere that Marc Powell went. His Lordship's assurances were obviously not to be relied on. O'Donnel had met the Americans at the old cottage but, with an estate gamekeeper cadging a lift on the way back to Scarr, there hadn't been an opportunity to talk about what he'd seen and heard. Archie looked at his watch. By now, O'Donnel would be well into his evening booze-up. The discussion would have to be one of tomorrow's priorities.

It was time to get the Mini back to the hotel car park before that sea-fog rolled over the village. If it hadn't become too dense after supper, he would walk the entire length of Shore Road from Whitescar in the west to Blackscar in the east, and then on as far as the gates of Bolson Hall. Marc Powell must be somewhere out there. Locating him was becoming a matter of urgency. Visibility was reducing rapidly by the time Archie reached the car park. He entered the hotel by a side door and managed to slip into the small dining room without O'Donnel noticing him...

*

(Roddy Grover's Flat, Portlach):

The minister sat in the armchair fully alert. He had positioned it to give a clear line of sight into Grover's small kitchen. Now, slurping the liquid from his beer glass and sniffing at the cooking smells, he wiped saliva from his mouth with the back of his hand. He poured himself another glassful of the pale golden ale, impatient at the delay, becoming angry. Just as he was starting to rise from his seat, Roddy Grover entered the sitting room, cleared away some oily tools from his newspaper tablecloth and replaced them with items of greasy cutlery. Roddy went back to the kitchen and reappeared with a large plate containing slices of toast topped with minced beef and macaroni, and a smaller one loaded with over-fried eggs.

'The tea. I forgot to make the tea.' Roddy turned back towards the kitchen.

'Stop there! What the hell d'you think you're doing? I told you I would drink beer.' Stackpoole reached for another bottle. 'You wanted to get to the phone, didn't you? Go on then. Have a look. You'll see I've pulled the wires out. Right, you stay where I can watch you. But switch on the television first. You must be dying to see the local news; haw-haw! After that, we'll look at the scrapheap motorcycles downstairs. I hope there's one that's got a bit of grunt left. And I need clothes. You better have something in my size.'

The minister forked the last egg into his mouth and, still chewing, swung round to see a news item requesting information on a Reverend Solomon Stackpoole from Scarr who was 'not to be approached by members of the public under any circumstances'.

*

(The Islet of Inch Greele):

'I wonder if my mither's woken up. She'll do her nut when she finds me gone.'

'But you said she should sleep for eight hours. What's the time now? There must be a while before she comes round. I think my grandparents are the biggest problem. They said they'd leave Aberdeen early to beat the rush-hour traffic. But I don't know what that means. Could be three or half past. Her appointment was for two o'clock, but she said they kept her waiting last time. My grandfather told me yesterday that Aberdeen's about an hour and a half's journey away, so they could be back by five. That means they're probably here. They're bound to wake up your mother. Jeez, there's going to be some rumpus now.'

'Sh! Marco, can you hear a funny noise? No? Listen! Up there.'

Marco could tell from Arc's voice that he was standing, and he got up to join him. The fog was certainly a little less dense at this level, but he could only just make out the diffuse patches of yellow light where Scarr's streetlamps struggled to penetrate the curtain of fine water droplets. A stronger glow, appearing intermittently over to the left, would be the lighthouse. Its foghorn had long been silenced with the demise of the fishing fleet and the arrival of holiday-home owners demanding their due entitlement of rural tranquillity. The noise? Yes, he could hear it now. It was a sort of whining sound and he thought it was coming from high in the northern sky.

'What do you think it is Arc? It's too high up to be a boat. There's a strong wind starting – oh, look!'

The wind blowing down on them was joined by a powerful beam of intense white light. The two boys were stunned when a teardrop shaped flying vehicle descended and hovered ominously a short distance above their heads. At last Arc found his voice and said hoarsely, 'It's a flying saucer, isn't it? Bloody hell!'

'Well, its nothing like the one I went off in. Must be a different sort', Marco said with the air of an expert. There was nowhere to run to, so the boys had to watch anxiously as a figure in dark clothing and spherical helmet descended towards them.

Arc gaped and repeated, 'Bloody Hell'.

*

(Shore Road):

The low-level fog was starting to thin and to yield transitory openings, which enabled several people on Shore Road to catch glimpses of what became known in UFO circles as 'The Scarr Incident: Episode One'. This drew some attention from the media before a blanket was drawn over it. ('Episode Two' was hushed up completely by broadcasters and journalists. Only the recently re-launched Northern Trumpet covered the matter in the following week's edition, thereby becoming highly sought after by collectors of 'Ufological Lore and Artefacts' across the world). A fair number of dogged ufologists, members of the public, military personnel (and a few secret agents) saw the following evening's Episode Two. Larger turnouts on subsequent nights were unlikely to have seen anything, and an investigation by Jon Cardington's PAPS members found no evidence to back up any claims.

Those who witnessed part of Episode One, included Maggie MacPhail, Archie McSpake, Geordie Moston and Meggie Munro's great grandson, Sammy Gordon. Wullie Tate, leaving the hotel with a 'skinfu' was never sure what he'd seen. A stationary man, dressed in tweed coat and plus-fours and wearing an odd-looking watch, stood stoically on the forecourt of the derelict petrol station next to the library. He couldn't possibly have missed the event and would probably have submitted a detailed report to his employer. The occupants of the alien Cadillac had also taken note and would definitely have reported *their* observations in code to those who were paying for their snooping. McSpake had watched them from the shadows of Easter Road and knew exactly what they had seen.

At Portlach, Jon Cardington hadn't been available to view the episode in person but rumours persisted that his time-lapse photographic equipment had captured something. Only a very few interested parties would have been able to say what that was, or what happened to the images.

After the black, disc-shaped craft had swung away eastwards, before dropping down again into the sea-hugging layer of fog, only Archie and the Americans had been close enough to see it come in to land on the grassy area beyond Blackscar. They'd had had a clear view of Marc Powell and Arc Meade being helped down a short ladder by a man in a flying-suit and helmet. Having signalled the boys with a zip-across-the-mouth gesture, the man disappeared back into the craft which took off at once and disappeared into the night.

The boys came racing past Archie without seeing him, and turned into Harbour Lane. As the Cadillac turned to follow them, Archie stepped out on the road as if to block its path. It slowed down and then drove past. He looked up the lane and saw the boys disappear into the Meade house two minutes before the Smiths' Skoda pulled up at the kerb. They'd probably got away with whatever they'd been up to. And now they had first hand experience of what was clearly a small stealth-type flying disc.

Although the craft had been silent in level flight, he had heard the distinctive note of a turbine as it descended and again when it ascended. It had left behind the metallic smell of very hot electrics and his hair was standing on end from the static charge in the surrounding air. This vehicle seemed fairly basic in comparison with the latest generation of antigravity machines, but it worked quite well. Its outline looked surprisingly like that once sketched out by Henri Lagrange during a runaway wine-tasting session at the French Embassy in Moscow. Henri had been holding forth on his favourite topic – German experimental aircraft of the Second World War. He always asserted that the early flying-disc prototypes which were tested over the Baltic Sea, had not been destroyed as was widely believed, but that undercover Red Army engineers captured much of the planning and materials of the V-7 project. Those had disappeared eastward. Conclusive evidence as to their destination had been scarce at the time and Henri's Doctoral study had foundered, he said, in face of Soviet secrecy about the matter.

Archie had heard only a few words pass between the flyer that he'd seen and someone inside the craft, and those had been in Russian. This could be what O'Donnel was waiting for. He'd be sober enough tomorrow, perhaps, to take in the information.

At Whitescarr, Maggie, satisfied that the aircraft had been

working as well as ever when it dipped towards Inch Greele and then flew off to the east, unlocked her boat from its retaining chains. She'd float it off tomorrow night ready for rowing out to the island.

**

CHAPTER THIRTEEN

Saturday Morning

(Market Street, Portlach):

The silent Town Hall clock showed half past midnight and the last drunks had gone home. Stackpoole, more menacing than ever in his new, extra-extra-large motorcycle leathers and helmet, opened the shop door and looked along the street. The fog had cleared leaving glistening tarmac. Persistent cloud cover would prevent it freezing. A perfect night for a rapid getaway! He wheeled the big Honda onto the pavement, went back to lock the door and then lobbed the keys, along with Grover's prosthetic leg, into a rubbish skip in front of Mason's house. Somebody would find Grover eventually. For now, the man was chained to his central heating boiler in the locked airing cupboard, unable to raise the alarm. Under aggressive questioning, he had admitted that a cleaning lady came in on Monday mornings. The minister had left him with a large bottle of mineral water and a bucket. That would keep him going for a couple of days.

These bloody gloves were tight but they were the biggest the shop could provide. He fumbled a little as he started the bike then, anxious that the sound of the powerful engine would draw the attention of nosy people, selected first gear and let the clutch bite. By the time anyone could have reached a bedroom window, the Honda rider had vanished round the corner into South Street. Its sound, echoing between the silent houses, faded into the distance.

Solomon remembered his very first motorcycle. He had bought

it on easy terms when he started the job in the mental hospital. That was near the end of his stay with the Donaldsons in Glasgow. After Rose left Sligo 'to start a new job in England', young Robbie had become increasingly morose. While his Da carried on his struggle to make a living from the land, Robbie had grown more and more irritable, and sometimes he was downright abusive. He had chosen to go fishing most days rather than stay at home or go to school. When he caught a fish he would pull its head off and throw it back into the river. His school attendance was the worst ever known in the district. Then, one day, news came from England of Rose's sudden death. His Da couldn't tell him why it had happened, and said that she would be cremated privately in London. They wouldn't be going to the funeral. But Robbie had discovered the truth when a neighbour told him how sorry she was to hear about Rose and the baby. The fucking, fucking priest!

Unable to cope with his feelings, or with local gossip, Robbie's rage was taking control of his life. He became physically aggressive on the slightest provocation. Fergus had started drinking more heavily. People said that the farm was 'on the slide'. Realising at last that things had reached a tipping point, Fergus managed to persuade Robbie's uncle, Davy Donaldson and his childless wife, Dora, to take the boy to Glasgow to finish his education. Robbie left the farm a week after Father Riley's inexplicable drowning in the swollen river.

Robbie, closer to contentment than he would ever be again, settled into a trouble-free routine with his substitute parents. He did well at school and everybody assumed he would go on to university. At the age of eighteen, however, he gave up academic study to take a job as a Nursing Assistant in one of the large psychiatric hospitals which were strung out across the central belt of Scotland. Robbie enjoyed the work so much that he decided to train as a psychiatric nurse. But fate, the roll of the dice, random chance, dictated a very different course for him.

It happened on his first spell of night-duty. The night Charge Nurse on the ward had been receiving the changeover report from his day-duty equivalent, when he looked out of the office window and saw that the light above the mortuary door was visible through the trees.

'Hey, Stockdale! Go down and check the place out. Here's the key. McGonnagle says somebody died this afternoon in Block Nine. The post-mortem's tomorrow. They must've forgotten the light. Make sure everything's okay inside – just in case. A lot of funny bastards prowl around hospitals at night. Well then, get a fucking move on!'

Robbie was not unfamiliar with death after six months of work. Death was a frequent visitor to such large institutions. That night, however, he started to feel anxious on his approach to the mortuary. The sound of vehicles drifted down from the main driveway, telling of day staff heading off home – or wherever else their interests lay. In this corner of the grounds, there was no sign of any living being. Robbie pulled his shoulders back and marched quickly towards the squat, windowless, brick building. Well, there might be someone watching him from somewhere, and he thought he'd detected unspoken communication between the two Charge Nurses. Testing him? Very likely.

He found the mortuary door shut but unlocked. The Charge Nurse's concerns were justified. Robbie inserted the heavy key in preparation for a quick getaway and then pushed the door open. In the centre of the room, a figure draped in a sheet lay on a metal table underneath a fluorescent ceiling light. Below the table, a drainage channel led to a grating in the floor. On the right hand wall was an ancient ceramic sink with brass taps above it and a coiled hose beneath. A narrow table, carrying a variety of metal bowls and plastic containers, ran across the length of the far wall. A glass- fronted cabinet above it held an assortment of museum-appropriate surgical instruments. The light over the cabinet had been left switched on. Robbie forced himself to take in as much of the scene as he could. He felt his skin tighten with the chill of the place. He must get out quickly. That light down there had its own inbuilt switch. He'd put that off first and then, on his way out, extinguish the ceiling light from the control panel by the door.

179

The click of the wall-light going off was followed by a loud groan. Robbie spun round, his heart stopping painfully for a moment, his legs powerless, his anal sphincter unclenching spontaneously. The covered figure on the table was beginning to move slowly into a sitting position. A scream, which he barely recognised as his own, unfroze him and he bolted towards the door. Afterwards, he couldn't remember picking up the heavy metal bowl, but he never forgot the loud thud of it hitting the corpse's head. By the time someone was sent to look for Nursing Assistant Stockdale, his motorcycle was approaching Glasgow at a speed far in excess of the statutory limit.

Wrapped in the still-disturbing memory of that evening, Stackpoole urged the Honda towards Aberdeen. Even when travelling fast, a twist of the throttle made it leap forward with a surge of power. A near-collision with an oncoming taxi brought him back to present reality. He slowed down and forced himself to concentrate on refining his broad escape strategy.

He must convince those who'd be looking for him that he was headed for the city. When that had been established, a complete change of direction would enable him to give them the slip – at least for a time. Yet more alterations in course might get him away completely. He had no doubt about what his final destination should be. Ah! There, up ahead – a petrol filling station. The minister slowed down and swung the bike onto the forecourt.

*

(Bay House Hotel):

Archie was resigned to another long, sleepless night. His mind struggled to make sense of the mass of data with which it was confronted. He felt like a child trying to solve a jigsaw puzzle without the box-top picture. At the very least, he needed some fixed reference points around which the data could coalesce. He ran through his information again, looking for anything that might serve.

O'Donnel's diamond smugglers – if that's what they were;

Russians with a ship out there somewhere and a kind of stealth flying-disc; Maggie MacPhail who had a rowing boat at the top of the beach; Inch Greele – a possible transfer point for contraband; Lord Leithland and the American agents – if *they* were involved in smuggling – doubtful; The boy, Marc Powell – doubtful; O'Donnel himself – it was almost certain that he had more knowledge of things than he'd revealed; The British Government; Other governments.

The Leithland set up as well as the Powell boy, Archie thought, were tending to obscure the broader picture. Leave them out and a fairly straightforward smuggling business came into some degree of focus. Were there two separate operations? That certainly offered to clarify some things but, in the absence of more specific information, couldn't be relied on. He needed to have another talk with O'Donnel, tell him about the stealth aircraft and demand facts in return. No point in trying to waken him now. He'd had a longer session than usual in the bar, they said, and then went up to his room with a half-bottle of rum. Serious discussion would have to wait until morning. Archie knew he ought to forget the whole bloody mess and confine his concerns to the task that Fractal had set him. But mysteries had always drawn him irresistibly into their grasp and this was a very intriguing mystery. It would take a lot of determination, or Fractal's very skilful powers of persuasion, to wean him off it. He would telephone her tomorrow.

Christ, it was still only one thirty. Something to read? No. There was nothing but the bird book and the bloody poems. He was getting-pissed off with both. He rose to make a cup of tea and sat looking towards Scar Bay as the kettle drifted sluggishly towards boiling point.

*

(Derelict Cottage Communications Room):

Al had received the message for which they'd been waiting. As expected, the timing was approximate due to 'unquantifiable

181

variables'. He didn't waken his colleague who was snoring loudly in the armchair by the fire, but left a curt note stuck to the front of the computer monitor. Leithland could wait until the morning when he'd be given a false time and bogus chart reference. The British, (he'd been ordered not to call them Limeys), were confident that the flying disc would arrive at one of their secret R.A.F. workshops before Sunday night. But it would be well out of their reach by then. Once on board a U.S. Navy aircraft carrier, there wasn't a thing they could do about it. Al hoped to be at his girlfriend's place in Miami by Monday night.

*

(Bolson Hall):

Victor twirled a tumbler of Glenscarr absentmindedly, watching the facetted crystal distort the light from his dressing table lamp. He war interrupted by a clatter from the next room, followed by muffled laughter. The pair of them had been at it on and off for nearly two hours. Well, let them make the most of it. Tomorrow night he'd be rid of them both. He had told them he was going off to a conference in Manchester and they'd swallowed it. Now, the tape recorder on the bookshelf had given him the evidence he'd wanted – Tradwell arranging to dispose of the cache of Glenscarr in his absence. That would keep the awkward bastard out of the way. Should Victor tip off the police before he disappeared? Better not. Tradwell would certainly respond by telling them about the diamond racket when trapped, and Victor wanted as big a head-start as possible.

Radek's remaining metal boxes still nestled in their stout suitcase in the safe. His and Maggie's own stones were in his blue leather briefcase. Putting a suitcase and a briefcase into the Bentley before a business trip was something they'd seen him do before. He smiled as he imagined driving off with the loot right under their noses. Then there would be Radek's new delivery tomorrow to add to the pile. He must remember to give Maggie instructions for accessing her share in the offshore bank account

182

he'd opened for her. A twenty-eighty split would be about right. After all, he would be the one they'd be searching for.

A signal from his mobile phone returned him to the present. The message was short. 'Ruski one. Op minus two. Repeat. Minus two'.

Radek was in a hurry to get things moving. Instead of the drop at twenty two hundred hours today, he'd brought it forward by two hundred. 'Eight o'clock tonight instead of ten', Victor would tell Maggie. The brass clock above the bureau showed that it was just after four hundred hours, so there was no point in waking her now. He'd wait another three hours before passing on the amended schedule. He was almost tempted to forget about the new consignment, to decamp with what he had already. But it would be insane to walk away from so much extra wealth.

Before his disappearance, he had to keep up the semblance of a normal routine. That, unfortunately, involved taking two of the Austrian sportsmen on the sea-fishing trip that they'd booked for today. They would set out from the harbour mid-morning, sail to Portlach to refuel the cruiser and then troll around the point of Portlach Ness for pollack. On the way back to harbour in the late afternoon, they would fish the Whitescar mussel-beds for the chance of an early cod. The recent storm might have stirred up the feeding sufficiently to tempt a few good specimens inshore. The Austrians seemed happy with the timetable. Hard luck for the ones who'd booked a trip for Sunday. Victor would be gone by then.

*

(Rural Track in Aberdeenshire):

The minister was leaning on a farm gate in the darkness when he heard the sound of an aircraft away to the south east. It was clearly flying low since he couldn't see any navigation lights, but it was close enough to worry him. He listened for a few seconds. The faint, throbbing beat suggested a helicopter rather than a fixed-wing aeroplane. His mind turned to infra-red emissions and the urgent need to reduce his own.

When he had driven away from the filling station, giving the attendant a rude gesture in lieu of payment, his course southwards had been clearly established for the information of those who would be pursuing him. By now, of course, they'd be aware of his change of direction although there was a fair chance they wouldn't know what it was. Turning down a side-road with his lights off, just before two braying police cars rocketed past on the highway, had been a timely move. He had headed westward for several miles, towards the foothills of the high mountains, before taking another right turn onto this present track. So long as it was dark, he'd thought, he would be safe here from pursuers. But now, the possibility of observation by a police helicopter's infrared detection system had to be taken into account. His next move should be to dump the bike. Its emissions would be a beacon to hunters. A derelict house or barn could make a suitable hiding place, although subsequent discovery of the machine would be a clear pointer to his escape route. There was the river, of course. His present route lay alongside a narrow gorge from which the roar of a torrent rose, indicating a powerful flow of water from the mountains. That could possibly hide the bike just as well. Yes, that's what he'd do; heave it into the gorge. That bridge he'd ridden across half a mile back might be a good location. The minister finished his last sandwich and can of beer, turned the Honda round and sought out the bridge.

He hoped that he'd made it in time. The aircraft seemed to be quartering the terrain, sometimes hovering for a minute or two, then recommencing its search pattern. It was getting closer. This was a big bike and he struggled to get it off the track. He had imagined heaving it over the low parapet but, in the event, found that impossible and succeeded only in splitting the seat of his 'leather' trousers. Finally, he pushed it round the end of the parapet where he thought there would be a clear drop. The bike plunged away into the darkness. The bloody biker's suit would have to go too, of course, but he'd need to find something to replace it first – something that would attract less attention in daylight. Meanwhile the protective helmet could go into the gorge as well.

Stackpoole headed northwards on foot, ears straining for aircraft noises. The gibbous moon, traversing high above the distant mountain peaks, gave sufficient light for him to set a fast pace. There had been a steep fall in temperature and rime was starting to crystallize on the trackside vegetation. The minister, however, soon began to feel warm and then to sweat until he was forced to unzip the top of his suit for ventilation. Only his posterior was feeling the sharp night chill.

The helicopter was back, coming closer. Where the hell could he hide? An infrared camera would pick him out clearly. No old buildings, no more bridges. That field of sheep! What if he got in there and lay down, curled into a ball to hide his outline? Would sensors be able to discriminate? No time to dither. As the moon floated away behind a solitary black cloud, Stackpoole stumbled over the piece of rusty wire bridging a gap in the dry-stone wall. Cursing as his trouser seat split wider, he flopped down behind the stones. The helicopter, flying low along the line of the road, passed nearly overhead. Animals stirred restlessly but the minister lay still. The throbbing of the engine faded slowly away to the south east. Give it ten minutes or so, just in case. He relaxed, stretched his body and growled.

A dog barked in the distance and then the night was quiet again – apart from movements of the sheep. The minister became aware of the sound of approaching footsteps. They seemed too heavy to be those of a sheep. Suddenly, alert once more, he looked in their direction. A large, moving bulk was obscuring the faint light of stars on the eastern horizon. From a horizontal position he cleared the wall in three seconds. Lying in the lane, winded, he listened for the bull to burst out of the field. The cloud passed away from the moon and the minister saw a shaggy mountain-pony regarding him across the wire. He doubted that ponies could smile but this cheeky bastard snorted and shook its head. He gave it a two fingered salute and resumed his march northwards at a much slower pace.

Half an hour later, when passing a wayside cottage, the minister saw an old bicycle in the front garden and lifted it over the gate. The saddle was loose and he had no tools to fix it so he could expect an uncomfortable seat. Still, it would be better than walking. His priority was to get as far away as possible before they widened their search. Perhaps he'd find some other transport opportunity ahead – if he remained vigilant. What a pity the clothes line was empty. However, something to cover his split trousers was bound to be waiting out there. The eastern horizon was hinting at the dawn's arrival and he pedalled off, trying to avoid the near-invisible ice patches.

*

(Shore Road, Scarr):

Archie slipped quietly from the hotel's side door. It felt good to be out in the open after another restless night. He found the chilly air invigorating, and a fast, twenty-minute walk took him well beyond the eastern boundary of the village. It wasn't very dark, the waning moon spreading its faint light across a peaceful land and near-motionless sea. He noticed, too, the pale streaks at the horizon – forerunners of dawn – and the distant pinpricks of streetlamps in Gardie Village strung sparsely along the base of Portlach Ness. There was no one about as he strode past Blackscar and on towards the river mouth.

The sea-pool was high, the recent storm having piled extra material onto the shingle bank that controlled its depth. Strong wind from a slightly different bearing could have swept the bank aside and turned the pool into a narrow stream. Archie remembered how heavy spates, following rapid spring thaws or torrential rain in the mountains, would also scour away the impermanent dam at the sea's edge – only for it to be rebuilt by the next strong northeaster.

He heard a faint splash out beyond the sea-pool, perhaps from a restless fish waiting for the top of the tide. And then the dark shape of a seal's head sent ripples out across the calm surface. He crossed the bridge and picked his way carefully down the river's right-hand bank to reach the top of the beach.

Sitting on the damp grass above the shingle, he relaxed his muscles slowly and recalled doing this very same thing many times before. That had to be nearly fifty years in the past.

It was over there that the old ship's timbers had emerged after a great storm. They must have been scoured from their ancient burial place in the sand. Blackscar had claimed many ships in the past, as had Whitescar. Most wrecks, however, were long forgotten; probably others had never been known about. Tenseness began to eat away at Archie's mood as he thought about men disappearing out there in raging seas; many men, across a time-span of hundreds, or even thousands, of years. Just like the Vikings in his poem. Here was the seed of a solution to the problem of that final verse! After the Maelstrom had swallowed the long-ship and its crew, the wreckage would be cast ashore in a storm many centuries later. Was that a bit far fetched? Well, not in a poem.

This morning he had a notebook and pen, even a torch. Five scribbling minutes later, it was beginning to turn colder and Archie was striding back towards the hotel, eager to knock the edges off his rough draft before it crumbled away of its own volition.

*

(Birch Cottage):

Bob Smith was washing his daughter's car in the grey dawn-light. Instead of flying into Aberdeen tomorrow as had been planned, she'd been travelling north overnight with some friends. A Miss. Mandelbrot and a Mr. Guy Oliphant were coming to Portlach to stay with Cardington, the retired banker, and they'd invited Jenny to accompany them on the journey. Jenny had told him on the phone last night about her change of plan and said she hoped to arrive at the cottage by breakfast time. Miss Mandelbrot worked at the hospital in Newton and had been helping Marc with his lost-memory problem. She was anxious to see how he'd been progressing.

Bob buffed up the car headlamps with satisfaction. He was sure Jenny would be pleased to find it looking so fresh. He had parked it in the big garage last Monday without cleaning it, believing there'd be plenty of time to take it to the supermarket car-wash later today. Jenny's change of plan had almost caught him out. There. It was finished. Bob wrung out the chamois leather, emptied the bucket of water down the drain and went to put on a clean shirt.

'Glad that job's done,' he told Bessie in the kitchen. 'Marc not down yet? I'll give him a shout. He'll be surprised about his mother coming this morning. He's fitted in very well here – and made some friends. She should be pleased about that. I bet he won't want to go back home. Do you think we could persuade Jenny to stay for a few more days? That tour she was talking about isn't a very sensible plan. The weather forecast's not good for next week.'

'I wish she'd stay, Bob. We've seen so little of her for years. It would do her a lot of good to relax, maybe meet some new people. When did she say she was starting her new job?'

'She wasn't sure when she phoned on Wednesday; said it could be before Christmas. But she didn't mention it last night. She'll be able to tell us in a few minutes. That sounds like a car stopping.' Bob buttoned up his shirt on his way to the gate.

Marco came downstairs rubbing his eyes, wondering why there were so many loud voices so early.

'I think your Mum's just arrived', Bessie told him. 'She phoned last night after you'd gone to bed. I believe there might be a Miss. Mandelbrot with her. Someone that you know, she says.' Bessie spread a cloth over the kitchen table and brought some of her fanciest crockery from the sideboard.

*

(Scarr Harbour):

While waiting for O'Donnel to resurface from his stupor, Archie had taken a stroll across to the harbour with his camera.

Among the assortment of yachts and motorised pleasure craft, there were only three small fishing boats. How Scarr had changed, he thought; his feeling of alienation was getting stronger every day. He became so engrossed in the activities of a crabber shooting creels along the line of the Girdle Reef, that he didn't notice an old Bentley draw up at the far end of the fish quay.

The sound of excited voices alerted him and he turned to watch three of the car's four occupants taking down heavy sea-fishing rods from a Heath Robinson roof-rack. They collected tackle-boxes, reels and large fishing-baskets from the boot and started to struggle into foul weather suits. The tallest of the men, who had a military bearing, was almost certainly Major Bolson. He approached a moored fishing-boat and was handed up a box – probably containing bait – by the on-board crewman. Eventually, all three men went off down the quay with much good natured shouting in German and English and boarded the motor cruiser, Cecil J Rhodes. The driver of the Bentley, meanwhile, turned the car round and drove off in the direction of Bolson Hall.

Just like the pseudo-mountaineers in the Lake District, those anglers were dressed first-and-foremost to impress observers but they were missing the mark just as widely, and in the same manner. Archie watched as the cruiser headed off eastwards. He smiled as he played back the images he'd taken of the performance then turned to see if there was any sign yet of O'Donnel. Yes, here was, coming down the hotel steps.

Archie took a couple of extra pictures of the Cecil J Rhodes' progress towards Portlach, and then turned to speak to O'Donnel. But O'Donnel had disappeared. He was probably on his way to the bar for booze. Archie hurried across to intercept him.

*

(A narrow track across a high moor):
The minister's trousers split further as he stooped to slake

189

his thirst at a runnel of peaty water. Christ, he could do with a cup or two of Tatey's coffee and a plate of biscuits. He was fucking starving. And that bicycle was a bastard. His sore arse and weary legs couldn't cope any more with its wayward steering and flat rear tyre. The buckling of the front wheel had provided him with a welcome release. No chance of fixing things out here in the wilds even if he wanted to. No more pedalling, he decided; motorised transport was the only sane option. He snarled at the disintegrating machine and hurled it into a stagnant pool. Motor transport? Apart from the helicopter, there'd been no sign of an engine since he'd dumped the Honda. Maybe he should have hung on to that and taken his chances with pursuers. He could probably have reached his destination before dawn. Instead, here he was, plodding down this miserable track.

With his watch now indicating nine forty, he scanned the bleak moor pessimistically. He had little hope of finding anything here to ease his problems. And then he saw a ribbon of smoke rising from beyond a ridge.

*

(Stag Lodge, Craglea Moor):

Sandy Bray could hear the sound of Maureen's walking-frame approaching from the bathroom. He cracked the egg into the frying pan to join the rapidly crisping rasher of bacon; just the way she liked it, he lied to himself. The toast was keeping warm by the fireside and the kettle was on the boil. He picked up the teapot and looked around to make sure he hadn't forgotten anything.

Sandy had been up for hours, cleaning and doing the laundry. After hanging out the wash, he'd fed the chickens, collected the eggs and 'milkit the coo'. He wanted things to be nice for Maureen's birthday. He couldn't have afforded flowers for her – even if he'd wanted to give her that sort of present – but the sprigs of bonny, red rowan berries in the jam-jar on the mantelpiece would do fine. In the springtime, their grandson

Ronnie had promised, he would take them to the theatre in Aberdeen for their wedding anniversary, followed by a night in a fancy hotel. Sandy was sure he wouldn't like that but Maureen was looking forward to it.

'Ah, there ye are, meh dear. Happy birthday. Eighty sax the day! Eighty sax the day! Dum dumdy dumdy dum – eighty sax the day! Did ye enjoy yir lang lie-in? Come awa'n sit doon. Yir eggie's ready. The dam't bacon's geen kind o hard an the butter's meltit richt throuw the toast, but it'll be neen the waur o that. Wite an ah'll poor ye a cuppie o tay.'

'Ach Sandy, it's fine. It's a richt treat. Gie me a wee kissie afore ah start.'

'Na, Maureen. Tak it easy noo. Ye nivver ken far that micht lead. Heh, heh, heh. Dammit, there's a gey strange lookin chiel oot there. Ah wunner fit he could be deein. Ah dinna like the look o him.'

'We dinna want strange mannies hingin aroon the hoose. We micht get murder't in wir beds. Is the door lockit?'

'Lockit back an front. Onywye, we're nae in wir beds. Oh my God, Maureen, he's at the claes-line. He's grabbit yir best knickers. He's taen three pairs. Ah'll try'n stop the bliddy thief.'

Sandy picked up the double-barrelled shotgun he'd cleaned earlier in preparation for shooting next day's rabbit stew, and made for the back door.

'Noo, dinna sweer Sandy. An dinna ging oot. He micht be dangerous.'

'Ah'll gie'm dangerous. He's nae gan ti mess aboot wi Sandy Bray – or wi's wife's knickers.'

The sound of the key turning was followed by a loud crash and a howl of anguish. Maureen tried to get up from the table but her legs wouldn't support her.

'Sandy! Are ye aa richt? Sandy!'

As she reached for her walking-frame, Sandy re-entered the room backwards. A very large man followed, pushing Sandy so fast that he fell on his back. Maureen screamed and the man raised his left hand to point Sandy's shotgun at her. She screamed again, more feebly and he took a step in her direction.

'Shut up you old bat or I'll blow your fucking head off. And don't think I won't. It wouldn't be the first time.'

Maureen opened her mouth then closed it again.

'Dinna worry lass, it's nae loadit.' Sandy was hoisting himself to his feet.

'Keep back you old turd', roared the intruder. 'A smack over the head'll do the same thing. You too, you hag, if you interfere.' Stackpoole reversed the gun and swung it backwards and forwards by the barrels. 'I want cartridges. Now! Where are they?'

'We hinna got ony. Clean oot,' said Sandy. 'So if ye leave the gun fin ye gang awa, we'll say nae mair aboot it. An it wid be affa nice if ye left meh wife's underclaes.'

But Stackpoole had noticed Sandy's eyes glance towards the top of the dresser at the mention of cartridges. He pushed Sandy into a chair and felt along the shelf.

'So what's this then, you fucking liar?' he bellowed, taking down the box of ammunition. He slipped two cartridges into the gun and another two into a breast pocket. 'Right then. Trousers. I need trousers, old man. What have you got? Show me! Your wardrobe through here is it?'

Sandy, with the loaded gun pushed against his back, had no choice but to obey.

'Don't bother with the phone old woman. I tore out the line. Get some food ready. A lot of it. And it better be good. You'll eat some first to show me.'

*

Some forty minutes later, Stackpoole, bloated from a meal of ten scrambled eggs, half a wholemeal loaf and two full pots of tea, was striding along the track. What a pity, he thought, that the skinny little runt hadn't had any clothes to fit. The kilt had been the only option. It had belonged to some long-gone relative of more robust proportions and it fitted perfectly. However, never having worn such outlandish gear before, and worried about the effects of the cold upland air on his buttocks and adjacent structures, he had pulled the three pairs of knickers over his trousers before donning the heavy swathe of woven tartan. Fortunately the old woman's arse had been bigger than his own. Now then, no more delays. There was still a long way to go. What a pity the old codgers didn't have a car.

Sandy was in the kitchen loading his long-disused hunting rifle. Good job the intruder hadn't guessed about it and hadn't searched the metal cabinet in the pantry. The madman was going to get an almighty shock in a minute. Left elbow on the sink draining board, Sandy pointed the rifle through the open window and took aim. His vision had altered a bit since he'd last fired it and he fiddled with the telescopic sight until he realised the intruder would soon be out of range. Oh what the hell. He squeezed the trigger.

It had been Sandy's intention to send a bullet wide of the man's head, to give him a fright, but a combination of eyesight problems, a slippery draining-board and a shout from Maureen affected the outcome. He was appalled to see his quarry leap in the air with a hand on the side of his head and then fall to the ground Disaster! What explanation could he give the murder squad? No court of law these days would consider the punishment he'd meted out proportionate to the intruder's crime. He wondered for a minute if he should sharpen his old gralloching knife and disembowel the corpse. There was also the boning knife in the drawer and a hacksaw in the shed. Could he hide the joints in the bog without attracting crows or foxes? At last, however, the big man got to his feet, looked back and shook his fist in the direction of the house. He picked up the shotgun and then, as if afraid of a repeat bullet, hurried away across the moor.

**

CHAPTER FOURTEEN

Saturday Afternoon

(Bay House Hotel):

Archie made a third unsuccessful attempt to connect with Fractal's phone number. Perhaps she was out shopping or sleeping off the effects of a heavy week's work. He'd give it an hour and then try again. He returned to his room, laid the card showing her land-line number on the bureau and sat down. There, in front of him, were the notes for his storm poem – if it could be called a poem. Force Twelve would do for a title, though he'd had something much stronger than that in mind. The third verse that he'd roughed out had been working away on its own, fragments scuttling along cerebral neurones, hurdling synapses, since early morning. Perhaps it wasn't too soon to see what he could make of it. He picked up notebook and pen and began to write until, at last, the piece declared:

I surfaced in the greyness of the dawn,
still drenched, with briny tang upon my lips.
The very house was reeling as the storm
shrieked, unceasing, through the empty streets.
Salt-laden foam and fusillades of sand
struck the windows and were whirled away,
while thunderous cracks above the bulging ceiling
forewarned of roof slates being ripped asunder.
A chimneypot crashed down, a greenhouse vanished

in flying fragments, high above the moors.
Worm-riddled timbers stranded on the shore
Slipped away beneath the pall of night.

Archie forced himself to concentrate on the piece. He thought that the stranded timbers image was even more anti-climactic than he'd expected. Otherworldly undertones definitely needed to be stronger. He should attend to that later – much later. His skull was pressing him towards the floor – a growing problem these days. Half an hour in bed and then he'd go and have that serious talk with O'Donnel – if he could find him. It was unlike O'Donnel to go out so early and just disappear. Of course Archie had only known him for a few days so the man could perhaps be more unpredictable than he'd seemed. Where the hell could he be? Mustn't forget Fractal either; strange that she hadn't called him for a progress report. Could the people she thought were watching her have got in the way? Did they even exist? If they did, were they associated with those men in the Cadillac?

He rummaged vainly in his pockets for an analgesic tablet.

*

(West Brae, Scarr):
Daniel was determined to cut out the whisky. The trouble was that he enjoyed it too much. The Glenscarr stuff was pretty special, though not as special as its price suggested. The price really reflected its scarcity. Geordie Moston had told him it would become even scarcer. Recently, a robbery had emptied the bonded warehouse at the distillery and the thieves had got clean away. The only remaining source of Glenscarr that Geordie knew of was held by a distributor who had bought in some stocks for maturing in his own cellars. It was currently available under a licensed label but selling out quickly. He had advised Daniel to stock up on stuff as a good long-term investment. Of course, Daniel knew, he would have it all drunk before such an

investment bore fruit. In any case he was trying to cut down on booze by making a switch to rum which he'd never liked. He was now learning that, when the craving for a drink got strong enough, he liked rum just fine. His lie-in, assisted by a couple of cans of lager, had shifted the hangover a bit but it was starting to come back now, more debilitating than ever. He resisted the pull of the four cans in his bag and trained the binoculars on Whitescar Cottage below.

Clearly, the younger of the two MacPhail women was having a very busy day. He'd seen her return in that battered van and had watched her unload carrier bags of groceries; it was *probably* groceries, he corrected himself. Since then, she had taken her aged, pipe-smoking companion for a dodder along the path at the top of the beach and back again. After lowering the old lady into a chair in front of the prefabricated outbuilding which, McSpake had told him, was a laboratory, she had gone inside. Through its windows, he could see her carrying bottles and boxes back and forth. She was definitely in something of a rush. It looked as if the intelligence was spot on and that tonight would see the culmination of Operation Stonewall. Daniel opened a can of lager to help him concentrate on his own, very personal, project.

Lying prone behind a bramble thicket two hundred yards farther up the hillside, an immobile observer with a camera kept both Daniel O'Donnel and Whitescar Cottage under scrutiny. The man saw the motor-cruiser, Cecil J. Rhodes, with three anglers on board, approaching Scarr from across the bay. It sailed past the harbour, turned side-on to the breeze and stopped engines. The men got fishing-rods over the weather side and lowered large baits to the bottom. The watcher caught an action sequence.

And there was McSpake, walking along Shore Road towards the eastern edge of the village. It did look as if he was making half-hearted efforts to protect the Powell boy from the American Agents. Just as well. In addition to their main assignment, there was no doubt that they would be happy to acquire the boy's remaining specimen of the anomalous ceramic-metal cube. The 'mole' in the British MOD had discovered that their scientists had assigned it the label Xi329X. Lord Leithland was having his every move monitored. He had slipped away from the castle yesterday evening to make several phone calls from the Fiddlers Bow Tavern in what appeared to be a simplistic, (perhaps overly simplistic), attempt to avoid scrutiny. The recordings were being analysed for coded information, but no definite result had been passed on so far. It would be useful to know whether or not the old aristocrat was still onside and if his real intentions were the same as his stated ones.

The watcher punched in a fourteen figure code on his bogus mobile phone, holding the last number down while waiting for the appropriate return signal. He then pressed five more digits and listened to a brief summary of the operation's progress. At the same time he observed that the anglers, having completed a second drift past the island, had decided to call it a day. He captured a sequence of the cruiser turning into the harbour entrance and of the Bolson Bentley waiting at the quayside.

*

(Rural Byway, South of Scarr):

Lying in the cart, the minister tried to relax and get some sleep, but his earlobe still smarted too much from the crazy old man's pot-shot. The folded handkerchief over the injury had become hard, and the strip of knicker fabric that held it in place was making his head itch. Getting rid of the makeshift dressing would be one of his top priorities. He ran a proprietary hand over the electric guitar lying on the wooden boards beside him. The second-hand shop owner must have been in the lavatory or somewhere, completely unaware of the early morning customer's arrival. That was just as well, since the customer had only the few pounds nicked from Grover's till – a small fraction of the guitar's marked price. He had taken out the cartridges, wiped the gun to remove fingerprints and left it on the counter in part-exchange.

The tractor driver, in a rush to get home, pushed the ancient diesel engine hard. His girlfriend, Molly, would be unforgiving if he turned-up late again. She had only so much patience, she'd stressed, and if he couldn't treat her fairly, others certainly would. Actually, he was getting a bit pissed off with her dictatorial attitudes. If she wasn't so good in bed, he'd dump her. However, he looked forward to their sharing another Chinese takeaway tonight and listening to some rock-music favourites. They both preferred that to the lightweight offerings of posturing youngsters who believed they could sing. It was a pity that so many others of their generation, who'd been deprived of great music, shared their delusions.

Now, that old guy in the cart was a real musician. Fantastic get up. You could just see him strutting across the stage in his motorbike gear and kilt, nearly exploding your head with bass notes. A big bastard. The sort of guy that groupies showered with knickers with their phone numbers on and offers of anything else he wanted. Pity he didn't dare ask him home for a drink. He would sweep Molly off her feet the instant she saw him and there was no way of coping with that. It was a real mystery what women saw in such ugly gorillas, while good looking young chaps like him struggled for attention. Bloody women! Molly would appreciate the guy's autograph though. What did he say his name was? Slackpole, maybe? Was there something that he could get him to sign? Oh yeh! What a good idea! Molly would be chuffed to have a condom packet with name of a Rock Star in his own handwriting. She could show it to the girls at work and explain how she had participated in emptying it.

Nice guitar that. A Fender Precision! It was just what you'd expect a famous musician to play. They must have been impressed by him on his U.S. tour. Pity his wrist had been hurt in the accident, but he said it should be okay for tonight's gig. It must have been pretty severe for a rock-music hard man to spend a day in hospital. The eccentric head bandage *did* make him look like a pirate. It certainly wasn't hospital issue. Discharged this morning and in a hurry to catch up with the rest of his group, it was tempting to offer him a lift right into Portlach. But that sort of delay would surely kill off his relationship with Molly. He'd just drop him off at the end of the lane. A guy that fit would reach the bus station well before the Inverness coach pulled out.

In the cart, the minister, still tired, still unable to sleep, was thinking again about his mission in Scarr. He'd remain outside the village, under cover, until it was dark. Then he'd try – exactly how would have to be decided on the spot – to get into the manse to reclaim his stash of currencies and bank documents. And there were the false passports. Those were even more important since they could help the police to work out his name changes and his tracks across the United States, Venezuela, Jamaica and South Africa. He must also remember the incriminating letters that he'd obtained deviously, and by coercion, which had enabled him to secure clergyman posts in many churches – including Scarr Kirk. His testimonial from the paedophile minister in South Africa had been so outstanding that the job in Scarr was probably his even before the interview. He wondered if he should go to Australia or Hong Kong next.

He suspected that it might now be difficult in this country to get a genuine passport in an assumed name. It had been dead easy when his uncles got him on a boat out of Glasgow after he'd killed the young fool who'd been mucking about in the hospital mortuary. He felt that events were now forcing him to act much too quickly – before he'd been able to do the necessary planning.

Stackpoole didn't know why he retained so much incriminating material instead of destroying it. Could it possibly be about clinging to some thread of his original identity? Or maybe it was to do with the buzz he always got from walking along the extreme edge of experiences, tempting fate. Lately, however, he'd been starting to feel his age, wondering if he should have a go at sorting himself out. Well, if things went smoothly tonight, he'd be seeing the last of Scarr and becoming another new person with another new history. Then he would decide.

The tractor had stopped at the end of a farm track and here was the driver holding out a condom packet and a pencil.

(Factory Ship, Nikolai Rykov):

Captain Radek looked at the two different flight plans. The first, intended to confuse Zhirkov's henchmen, was meaningless. It contained as many elements of truth as possible without giving away crucial details, and it identified Sweden as the destination of tonight's flight. He crumpled the paper and dropped it behind the bin in the corner. They'd find it almost as soon as they started searching for evidence. The second plan, of which there were copies for himself and for Yashin, detailed his real scheme. No element of information from this would be left on the ship. He laid the two sheets on his bunk alongside the case of stones destined for Scarr, and collected his flying gear from the locker. As an afterthought, he ignored his own anti-firearms policy and added a loaded pistol and a pair of grenades to the pile. And now, a supply of money was all that he needed. Radek swept every last banknote from the safe into a holdall.

It hadn't occurred to Captain Radek that Yashin would have another, strictly personal, flight plan tucked away in his own flying suit.

Ivan Konev, the Second Mate, was on the bridge watching the aircraft being removed from its hangar. He looked at his watch and made surreptitious notes about the activity below. Zhirkov wanted details of everything. To Zhirkov, detail meant precision, total clarity. Radek and Yashin were clearly tense this evening so there had to be something exceptionally underhand on their schedule. Yesterday evening's flight had obviously been a prelude to whatever was about to take place tonight.

*

(Scarr Manse):

It was now quite dark. Few vehicles were travelling up or down Scarr Brae. Nevertheless, the minister approached the village cautiously by way of the fields. He cursed soundlessly on stumbling over another molehill. Passing behind Birch Cottage, he heard the voices of Bob and Bessie Smith and their odious grandson talking about supper at the hotel. Seconds later, a vehicle drove away. What a pity he was pushed for time. He'd have enjoyed wrecking the place and carrying off some of the woman's underwear. He might even have taken a shower there and tried some of it on. He'd certainly be glad to get his feet out of these boots for a bit. They hadn't been designed for walking the kind of distance he'd covered during, (how long was it?), damn near eighteen hours. The blisters needed to be treated promptly. He could attend to them much more effectively at the manse, together with his damaged ear.

He found both kirk and manse taped off by the police. They were certainly being preserved as a scene of crime. It took him the best part of twenty minutes' prowling to be confident that there wasn't a single officer anywhere near. Anyone inside? No; the buildings were deserted. He found the spare key for the kitchen door where Tatey always left it – under the white quartz rock at the edge of the lawn. Once inside, he fumbled about in the darkness, checking that all the individual light-switches were in the off position before daring to reconnect the mains supply. He removed a heavy torch from a kitchen drawer, switched on the kettle and searched for whatever food might have been left.

It was five minutes past seven by the time he'd eaten, showered, fixed his sores and put on a black suit and matching shirt. He sighed with pleasure when he pulled the comfortable, elastic-sided Chelsea boots over his bandaged feet. He put extra dressings and antiseptic cream into a flight-bag along with banknotes, incriminating documents and sandwiches. What else? Oh yes, the moorland woman's two remaining pairs of knickers. He stuffed them into a trouser pocket. Now, Scarr deserved to be taught a lesson before he vanished. A careful advance down the fields in the direction of Whitescar Cottage would be his opening gambit. And then he'd take things from there.

(The Cardington Residence, Portlach):

In his ground-floor office Jon Cardington was finishing a glass of 'Sparkling Springwater' when his guests were shown in. He shook hands warmly with Lord Leithland who, he still hoped, had the necessary contacts to swing him a Knighthood – or maybe something even more elevated. Many years ago it had been made crystal clear to Jon that his wife's undisciplined behaviour precluded any such recognition. His aristocratic guest had repeatedly confirmed that this veto still applied. It had now become crucially important that Marietta's arrest should be kept under wraps and that she be sent on her way, a 'free woman' and, unfortunately, one with a substantial slice of Jon's hard-won fortune in her portfolio. It would take time for the divorce, and the circumstances surrounding it, to fade from public consciousness and he was getting on in years. But he certainly wasn't going to give up the ambition to leave behind a commemorative plaque on the house and a marble tomb in St. Mary's churchyard proclaiming his importance: 'Sir Jonathan Cardington' or, even more impressively, 'Lord Jon Cardington'. He yearned for the lasting mark on history that such a memorial would secure for him. Jon stepped forward and shook hands with the stranger, introduced by Leithland as 'Mr. Fu, a – em – business associate of mine from Beijing'.

The panelled dining room along the corridor was set impressively for dinner, and the very expensive celebrity chef was going berserk over the deficiencies of his grovelling staff in the kitchen below. It hadn't been easy for Jon to find the sort of chef he wanted at short notice. He had come to realise long ago that, in general, their tempestuous behaviour ran in direct proportion to their culinary genius. He'd had to settle in the end for the only one prepared to 'prostitute' his skills for 'a fucking suburban tea party' and Jon was praying that he would stay put in the kitchen.

It had seemed evident to Jon that discussions with his guests would be more relaxed over a meal at home than they would be in a hotel, and that good food and fine wines could make them more profitable as well.

'Dinner will be ready in thirty minutes, gentlemen. What would you like to drink now? There's just time for me to show you my observatory upstairs. Being on the edge of the sea, I suppose it's a marine observation post as well. I often think that it feels like the bridge of a ship. If you bring your drinks this way, we'll go up in the lift. I had it installed last year. Ageing limbs, I'm afraid.'

Lord Leithland, looking relieved at the mention of a lift, accompanied Jon into the corridor. The Chinese entrepreneur, looking at everything around him with interest, followed more slowly.

Up in the bridge, Leithland sat in his host's favourite chair with an air of boredom. But his Lordship was surreptitiously noting the plainly-framed seascape paintings on the walls and dong mental calculations on their value. Mr. Fu, intrigued by the array of optical equipment, especially the cameras, asked questions in excellent English with little trace of an accent. He watched the time-lapse exposures being taken of Inch Greele while Jon tried to answer his query about how well-exposed night-time photographs could be taken which allowed for changing light levels. Jon gave a summary of various techniques, but he suspected that the questioner knew the answers already. The intercom interrupted them with the news that dinner would be served in five minutes.

*

(Whitescar Cottage):

Earlier, Maggie had manoeuvred the glass fibre rowing boat down the strip of portable rollers and anchored it where it would be lifted by the rising tide. Emmeline had objected to going to bed this early, and Maggie had locked the doors in case the old lady succeeded in getting outside. The boat was nearly afloat. Maggie's watch said it was time she got a move on so she waded out to put the oars on board. The entire retrieval operation should take less than forty minutes – if the Russian's message to Victor proved to be accurate. What then? Victor had said he'd bring the Bentley along past the hotel and park it near the end of the track. Maggie should take the delivery straight over there in her van. And then what? She was becoming increasingly uneasy at Victor's secretiveness. Thoughtfully, she baited her hand-line with a cocktail of lugworms and mussels, binding these roughly to the hooks with strands of wool. Time to start moving! Maggie dipped the oars.

*

(West Brae, Scarr):

Daniel, working carefully under the faint illumination of a shaded penlight, made entries in his official notebook, followed by a brief scribble on a scrap of paper from his inside pocket. Only then did he reach for his portable phone to confirm a first move by the smugglers. It was twenty-two minutes past seven. He raised his binoculars once more, supporting them on a strong piece of gorse branch, a substitute for the tripod that circumstances required, and tried to focus through the gloom on the rower.

*

Farther up the brae, a figure dressed all in black, and with his head covered by a light-weight balaclava, also watched the rower, and *he* did so much more successfully through the latest Chinese night-vision camera. All the likely participants in the operation had been photographed doing whatever the agent believed was of relevance to his mission. Each image bore an imprint of the date and time when it had been taken. Whenever convenient, an audio recording of the agent's voice justified his selection of shots.

The man below him, trying to watch events on makeshift

equipment, was undoubtedly a British agent of some kind and would probably be in possession of secret information. So he shouldn't dismiss him as incompetent – well not yet. Those British were very inscrutable. They had a habit of wandering into messy situations and emerging from the other side calmly smoking their filthy tobacco pipes as if nothing had happened. But that one was less calm than most. He had been drinking heavily. The can that he'd just crushed and thrown away appeared to be his last. He had been getting more and more restless and would probably lose control of his actions soon. The Chinaman smiled as he waited for the Britisher to set off towards the hotel to get more alcohol. It would be possible to lie in wait for him and, if he returned to his lookout point, overpower him. No, he mustn't do that. Fu had given him very strict instructions to lie low and await further orders.

*

Even farther up the brae, another figure in black had been making his way carefully down towards the village. The minister had been unaware of anyone below him on the slope until a faint glimmer of light caused him to stop. He didn't know who had caused it but he couldn't take any chances. It would be prudent to stay here for a little while and see how things developed.

Bolson's cruiser was unlikely to be going anywhere. So long as he nicked it well before dawn, he could probably get away. He would go westwards along the coast and look for quiet inlets to moor in during the daytime. Each night he would get a bit farther from Scarr. He had no personal experience of navigation, but he could use a compass and read maps. Marine charts surely couldn't be much different and Bolson was bound to have plenty of those on board. Fuel, however, *was* a problem. There would have to be enough in the boat to get him well away and he would probably need to top-up the tanks during the journey. The bastards would expect him to go east and would most likely concentrate their hunt along that part of the coast. He, meanwhile, having reached the vicinity of Inverness, would turn northwards in the direction of Orkney. When he got there, he would identify his next objective.

Stackpookle wondered what it might be like in Norway or Denmark during the winter. His reverie, about working in a museum dressed as a Viking for the edification of summer visitors, was interrupted by the sound of a quiet voice almost beneath his feet. He stood absolutely still, listening. There seemed to be only one person at this point which was about two hundred yards above where the other one was moving noisily. It looked as if one observer was watching the other. The voice probably came from talk on a mobile phone or a radio.

The minister decided he couldn't hang around indefinitely on a miserable hill with people spying on each other. He needed space to operate. As he tried to devise a strategy to meet this latest problem, the farthest down watcher began to move. He saw O'Donnel silhouetted against the dim light of the streetlamps stumbling off down the slope. Having reached the sand dunes, he set off in the direction of the hotel. Very carefully Stackpoole readjusted the position of his flight bag. Gripping the torch tightly, he inched towards the nearby figure. The intended victim's quiet voice indicated his precise position.

*

(Bay House Hotel):

When Archie came downstairs, he wasn't at all surprised to find Fractal in the bar. The message she'd left with Geordie Moston had prepared him for that. What did surprise him was that she was part of a group that included Bob Smith, Marc Powell and an attractive looking woman that the boy addressed as 'Mum'. There was also a flashily-dressed man who Fractal called 'Guy' and who called her in return, 'Darling'. Just then, Bessie Smith, along with Effie Meade and her son Arc, joined the group. Archie turned down his hearing aid a fraction and watched them from the foot of the stairs. They appeared to be all in one party. That was confirmed when Annie Moston came out of the large dining room and told them their table was ready. Fractal said something in Annie's ear and Archie's location was pointed out to her. She came towards him with a smile. Guy paused for a second and then followed.

'Guy, this is my friend, Archie McSpake, the gentleman I told you about. Archie, meet Mr. Guy Oliphant.'

The two men nodded to each other, their hands remaining firmly by their sides.

'So you're the man hired by Fractal to watch young Marc Powell,' said Guy. 'She tells me you're an aspiring poet. I'm a down-to-earth prose man myself. My current W.I.P. is a film script. I'm expected in Hollywood next spring to give it substance. The Producer and Director Designate have high expectations of it. Fractal's going to be one of our psychological consultants. Isn't that right, Darling?' He put a proprietary hand on her shoulder.

'I'm sorry, Archie. I was going to tell you. When I phoned, they said you were resting in bed. That's understandable with such a demanding assignment. I had hoped you would have phoned me earlier in the week. The boy's clearly all right. He tells me your observation was so unobtrusive that he wasn't really bothered by it. I suppose that's experience in action. By the way, if you let me have your list of expenses, we can settle up tonight.'

Guy reached for his chequebook. 'I'll pay those', he said. 'No arguments. I insist. Have you got them to hand?'

'Forget it', Archie told him. 'I'm looking on this as a late holiday. It interests me to see how my home village has changed over the years, and I intend to spend a day or two looking up old haunts and trying to find one-time acquaintances. Have a nice meal.'

'But Archie, won't you join us? Jon, that's Jon Cardington the retired banker, is paying for the whole party and one extra guest is no problem for him. You can tell us about your week's work over dinner; and you could recite some of your verse for us. I've been telling Guy how talented you are.'

'She has. She has. You must join us.'

'Forgive me if I decline. I've eaten so much since I arrived here that I'm in need of a break. I'm just getting ready for my evening walk. I'll put all my mission details in a report for you Fractal – my treat. But you should know that there have definitely been people following Marc Powell and that they *are* trying to obtain something that he has in his possession. I suggest to you that that other boy, the one they call Arc, may be able to shed a little light on the matter. Then you should probably discuss it with the police. Now, I must get going. It seems like a nice evening out there. Bye.'

*

(Shore Road, Scarr):

The Reverend Stackpoole had approached Shore Road down the sloping pasture at the rear of the hotel. From the corner of the high wall, he could see Major Bolson's Bentley parked on the quayside almost directly opposite the library. O'Donnel re-emerged from the Bay House and turned in the direction of the minister who pulled back into the shadows to watch. Passing within a few feet of Stackpoole, O'Donnel continued to the end of the road where he spent some minutes under the last streetlamp making calls on his mobile phone. Then, he set off along the rutted track towards Whitescar Cottage and merged into the surrounding darkness. Looking round the corner again, the minister saw a van and a Land Rover, both with police markings, drive out of Scarr Brae and turn away in the direction of Blackscar. At last the road was deserted so he risked running across it to the beach.

He lay on the shingle, head resting on his flight bag, waiting for pulse and breathing to slow down. At last he felt able to make his way along the tide-rounded pebbles in the direction of the harbour. Raising his eyes cautiously above the level of the road, he could see that the hotel's lounge bar held a bigger crowd than was usual for a Saturday night. The large dining room at the far end of the building was full. Oh damn! McSpake had just come down the front steps and was crossing the road towards him. Stackpoole froze in the darkness with face pressed against the shingle and teeth gritted while the old bastard, muttering oaths, sprayed him with piss. Finally, the man zipped up and walked off towards the harbour swearing with a facility that even the minister found impressive. Stackpoole waited a few minutes and then resumed his long, cautious crawl until he found himself crouching behind the parapet of the 'Long Pier'. He looked around.

McSpake was just passing the far end of East Beach and would soon disappear into the darkness beyond. Much closer, the Major's Bentley hadn't moved from the place in which the minister had first spotted it. Although it was impossible to make out the identity of figure in the driving seat, it would most likely be Bolson himself. If so, he would certainly have the keys for the motor cruiser on him. Stackpoole stood up slowly to check the exact position of the vessel. Perfect! He ducked down again as another police Land Rover came down the brae. This one went off past the hotel towards Whitescar. Such activity was unknown in the village – at least during the minister's stay here. The bastards were obviously mounting a serious search for him. But that was strange. How the hell could they possibly know that he'd returned? He would need to be even more cautious than he'd anticipated.

*

Arc, tired of the inane adult chatter indoors, stood across the road from the hotel looking out to the north. He was hoping to see something more of the Russians who'd rescued him and Marco from Inch Greele. But there was no sign of them. There was, however, a fairly large ship out on the horizon. Its red port light showed it to be on a westerly course. Another, smaller, vessel was very much closer and the sight of both port and starboard lights told him it was sailing directly towards Scarr. Arc was always intrigued by unidentified ships and he headed for this one's likely destination – Scarr Harbour. Night arrivals, particularly at weekends, were almost unknown in the village and he was eager to get to the bottom of the mystery. Could it be the ship that the Russians had come from?

*

McSpake, having seen nothing of the American agents tonight, made a diversion up Harbour Lane on his way back to the hotel. It was possible that they could take advantage of the Meades' dinner outing to poke around. He would just check that things were okay. He realised that Birch Cottage, also, would be vulnerable to intrusion and thought he might give the Mini another outing later – if the Smiths remained too long at the hotel. Of course, it could be that the Americans had found the mysterious cube already. Maybe that was the reason for their disappearance. He spent several minutes looking at the Meades' house and was starting to open the gate to the yard, when he became aware of a neighbour watching him from behind net curtains. Shit! It's time to go Archie. That one would spot the Americans right away.

*

It was so comfortable in the car that the Major, in spite of imminent action, struggled to stay awake. The clock showed three minutes past eight. The diamond delivery was late. He reminded himself that the planned times were approximate and that there was no cause yet for concern. Maggie must be nervous, and very uncomfortable, out there by the island. He had a lot to thank Maggie for. He couldn't have got the undertaking off the ground without her. Maybe he'd up her share a bit. A twenty five / seventy five split would be about right. No sense in loading her down with too much financial responsibility.

Victor looked at the clock again. Radek's four delayed boxes of diamonds were in their case in the car boot ready for the addition of tonight's shipment of twenty four more. His and Maggie's six boxes were in the blue briefcase there on the front passenger seat awaiting the arrival of tonight's two bonus boxes – commission for their essential assistance. After snaffling Radek's delivery, he'd be heading off southwards, the possessor of thirty six boxes of quality, uncut diamonds. A stopover at his old crony Jenkins' place in Birmingham would give him a breather before Major Victor Bolson vanished forever from the face of the earth. He'd just get out of the car now to put his briefcase into the boot beside Radek's case. Then he'd stretch his legs before the action started.

It started instantly. He was half out of the door with the briefcase in his hand when he was seized and thrown to the ground. Something hard was pushed against the back of his neck. Victor had no doubt that it was a gun.

'Keep still, you bastard and listen. Not a sound or your head'll have two extra openings. Stand up slowly – don't look round – and reach into the car for the keys. Right, hold them out to the side. Which one's the ignition key for your boat? You sure? Okay, I'll take these, thank you. Now slowly, slowly, round the back of the car. Make a sound, make an unexpected move, and you're fucking dead. Head down, quickly!'

'For Christ's sake minister, you don't have to shoot me. I'll do whatever you want. Take the car. It's yours.'

'Shut up you ass. You better un-recognise me if you don't want to disappear. Here, take the keys and open the boot. Hurry up – then give them back. Right, climb in. That suitcase in there! Give me that first. Ta. In you go. Remember, one shout and I'll riddle the fucking car with you in it.'

Victor managed to slump into the boot at the second attempt and curled his arms round his head as the lid was slammed shut.

Arc, who had seen all that had happened – and heard most of it – headed towards the pier's end. Long before he got there, the motor cruiser was past him, heading towards the harbour

211

mouth and the open sea beyond. When he and an assortment of breathless hotel patrons reached the lighthouse, Stackpoole was steering, with increasing confidence, out into the bay. Someone suggested that the pirate should be pursued, but there wasn't a vessel in Scarr that had the speed to compete with the Cecil J. Rhodes. The unlit cruiser's position was now marked faintly against the dark sea only by its foaming wake, and that appeared to be converging with Inch Greele. All ears listened for the collision.

Arc remembered Major Bolson in the boot of the car but couldn't make his voice heard in the general hysteria. He ran up the pier again towards the Bentley. The police Land Rover that had been waiting at Whitescar pulled up as he approached it. He waved and shouted for help. The bogus birdwatcher, O'Donnel, got out and gave the policemen instructions with an air of authority. They drove off down the pier.

'Right then, young Whatsyourname, let's see to this business of the man in the car boot.' O'Donnel tried to open the lid but it resisted all his efforts. 'I wonder if the keys are still in the ignition.'

A search proved negative.

'Oh never mind! The officers will soon have it open. What's that you've got? And a very nice briefcase it is too. Evidence certainly. Now listen, young man,' (Daniel lowered his voice to a near whisper), 'I'm on a highly secret mission, working under cover. I'm impounding this evidence and directing you not to mention it to any other person. That means family, friends, even police. I must warn you that Secret Agents' lives could be at risk if the slightest hint got out. Here's my authority. Read what it says on the card. Now you must know a secure hiding place. You do? Good. Take this briefcase and hide it securely until I ask you to give it back to me. I'll do that when I've given the necessary instructions to the Security Services. Have you got that? All right, tell me slowly and carefully what I've just asked you to do.'

Archie McSpake, watching from the corner of the library yard, couldn't make out what was being said but had no doubt at all what the interaction signified. He smiled as the Meade boy, blue briefcase in hand, ran past on his way to Harbour Lane. But there wasn't time to think about it. Loud shouts and pointing fingers among the growing crowd of spectators drew his attention towards Inch Greele. A light had appeared over the island, illuminating its crest. Almost simultaneously, a blinding flesh came from somewhere behind the rocks, followed by the beam of a powerful searchlight from a vessel at sea. Another explosion followed and the police car at the end of the pier added a searchlight of its own. As the first pressure wave hit the spectators' ears, they saw a dark disc shape rising rapidly into the air above the islet. The sound of the second explosion rolled over the village. As the two searchlights fixed onto the craft, it moved rapidly to the right and then evaded the beams by diving at a steep angle to the left. The beams were unable to pick it out again.

Thus, 'The Scarr Incident: Episode Two' entered the annals of Ufology. Far more observers claimed subsequently to have seen it than could possibly have been present on the village foreshore that night. Wide variations in the accounts of eyewitnesses, together with denials by Military Spokespersons of any such incident, killed off the story for sensible people. Only those who believed in the existence of 'little green men' clung stubbornly to the story of a flying saucer. Reports of fighter aircraft travelling fast and low along the coast a little later in the evening were clearly unfounded as official records showed no aircraft to be flying at the time. Civilian radars, too, had nothing to report.

On the following evening, Jon Cardington was visited by anonymous men who removed film and digital images. He neither reported this to the Anomalous Phenomena Society nor made any notes in his private journal. He was, however, glad that he had passed fist-generation copies of the pictures to his usual contacts before the arrival of his interrogators.

**

CHAPTER FIFTEEN

Sunday

(Three hundred miles east of Peterhead):

It was well past midnight before Radek and Yashin dared direct their course towards the Nikolai Rykov. They'd been hard pressed to evade the persistent hunters who had forced them into constant changes of course over land and sea. Dodging into bays, around hills, and travelling dangerously-low up and down river valleys, had depleted their power supplies to a level that was beginning to cause them concern. And they still had the aborted Scarr diamond delivery on board. Radek realised that he'd have to take his chances with that in Norway – pending alternative disposal arrangements.

The big man they'd picked up clutching a suitcase, after they sank his boat, had turned out not to be Victor Bolson after all. An explanation was needed as to what the hell this stranger had been up to. In any case, Radek was sure that his decision to blow up the cruiser had been the correct one. The instantaneous responses from the shore and from vessels at sea, were clear evidence that a trap had been waiting. The hunting aircraft that appeared on the scene must have been ready in advance. Could Bolson's cover have been penetrated by the authorities? Had he confessed to his involvement?

And now this unexpected passenger was making things more complicated. The bastard was fully conscious now, lying there with his head propped up on his suitcase, making growling noises. Radek glared angrily and considered what to do with him. The options were: either take him with them to the ship and question him while Yashin was refuelling, or shoot him now and dump him in the sea. He pointed his pistol at the man and told him in English to 'Shut up!'

At the controls, Yashin was checking liquid fuel and electric power levels with increasing anxiety. He changed course three degrees to starboard and risked dropping to within a few metres of the waves. The faint glimmer of moonlight showed occasional flashes of foaming crests and Yashin knew that his concentration mustn't waver for a second. He continued to negotiate a fine line between discovery and ditching until the oilrigs were far enough astern for him to resume his former course.

Ivan Konev, the Second Mate, and his henchman, Mechnikov, would be waiting for them on the ship. Once there, they would start refuelling the aircraft in line with the captain's plan and under his supervision. Then, at Yashin's signal, Konev and Mechnikov would arrest Radek and lock him in the strong room with Zhirkov's diamond chest. The captain would be forced to face his employer's fury in Petersburg. Now, however, there was the aborted Scarr delivery on board. That would have to rejoin the rest of Zhirkov's hoard in the chest. Or maybe not! When the refuelling had been completed, Yashin would set his own scheme in motion. Supposing he could get away with the Scarr diamonds as well as the flying disc. He'd need luck on his side of course. And once he'd shown his hand, going back would be impossible.

The disc sank slowly into the pool of light on the landing pad. Yashin signalled 'Not yet!' to the waiting Konev and Mechnikov, then killed the engine. The tense observers saw a large, bedraggled man carrying a black suitcase, struggling to maintain his balance as he lowered himself to the deck at the point of Radek's gun.

'Mr Konev', the captain shouted, 'I need you to take this man and lock him in the strong room. But first, I want the large chest in there moved out of his reach. You better bring it up here on deck while I decide what to do with it. You, Mechnikov, start

215

refuelling the plane. There's a lot of naval activity out there tonight and we must be prepared for interference. Those bastards can ignore the law when it suits them. Our employer doesn't want his flying disc examined by incompetent NATO fools.' He glared at Mechnikov and gestured toward the aircraft. The man eyed the captain's gun and hurried to obey his orders.

Ivan Konev was beginning to realise that his plan would need perfect timing but that, for the moment, Radek still had control of the situation. Compliance with his demands, while waiting for the opportunity to strike, was his only option. He caught the keys that the captain threw to him and went below to collect the heavy, locked chest. It must be worth millions of American dollars – and all from a two year voyage to the West African coast. No wonder it was said that Yevegeny Zhirkov was the third- most-wealthy man in Russia. Radek's intention was almost certainly to send all of them below decks and carry off as much of the wealth as he could load onto the flying disc. Thank God Yashin was cooperating with himself and Mechnikov. Wait and watch and be ready to act instantly, he told himself.

Once below decks, Konev felt the gun in his own pocket. He started to drag the heavy chest on its aluminium trolley out of the strong room. He now regretted having ordered the crew to stay in their quarters under all circumstances. He even began to question the wisdom of having tied up the First Mate in the sickbay straitjacket. It was a matter of urgency for him to take control of the situation.

Refuelling completed, Mechnikov moved warily across to the position that the captain was indicating. He eyed the gun, alert for any chance to turn the situation round. Meanwhile, the minister, although he didn't understand Russian, had been observing the interactions taking place and was starting to consider points of vulnerability that he might exploit to his own advantage. When Konev reappeared with a large ornate metal chest on a trolley, all eyes turned in that direction. All eyes, that is, except the minister's. He tightened his grip on the handle of the black suitcase and felled Captain Radek with a swipe to the side of the head. As his victim lay on the deck, he kicked the gun towards Mechnikov. Radek got to his feet unsteadily, to find himself in the line of both Konev's and Mechnikov's gunsights. He raised his hands wearily. Radek and the minister were forced at gunpoint to return chest and contents to the ship's strong-room where they too were locked inside.

Zhirkov's agents returned hastily to the deck in response to the disc taking off. Helplessly, they watched its dark form melt into the night. Then the sound of the turboprop engine fell silent as Yashin engaged the SC System. Later, in the ship's strong-room, the minister brought an abrupt end to Radek's angry tirade. The captain slumped in a corner pressing a hand to the eye that would be swollen and discoloured tomorrow. He daren't look any farther ahead than that.

*

(The Meade House):

Effie listened to Arc coming in through the back door. Where had he been at this hour of the morning? He did what he wanted these days, no matter what she said. He really needed a father. She hoped he hadn't been doing anything illegal out there, especially with police all over the village. Effie had been relieved that, after checking all the names and identifications, they had interviewed those who'd been accompanied by children and sent them home. Other local residents had been allowed to go as well but with instructions to attend the library at specific times tomorrow to give statements about what they'd seen. When leaving the hotel, Effie had seen news reporters and those strange Ufologists being ushered into the hotel's large dining room to receive official instructions from that lovely black man, Mr. O'Donnel. He was certainly very important and even the most-senior police officer showed him respect. Effie wondered if he carried a gun in a shoulder-holster in the way that Secret Agents were supposed to do. She shivered with delight as she recalled the feel of his hand on her arm when he'd helped her towards the

217

cloakroom. He hadn't been wearing a ring. Tomorrow she would drop in at the hotel to see if the Mostons could use some extra help with their unexpected guests. Effie sighed happily. She just knew that she was going to dream about Mr. O'Donnel.

She was walking down Scarr Brae in a short dress with a bunch of flowers in her hand. The high summer-sun was warm on her back and the gentlest of sea breezes played with her hair. She felt young, happy, relaxed. She approached Scarr Kirk and her mood began to darken. She hesitated. The sunlight had gone and the kirk, brooding and evil, towered over her. She knew that the minister was waiting there. He drifted out through the gateway, a great menacing hulk in a black robe. She screamed as he came towards her, but heard no sound. She tried to run but her legs were powerless. When he stretched out a great, hairy claw, she realised that this was the Devil himself and that she was on the road to Hell. And then Mr. O'Donnel was by her side, a protective arm round her shoulder. With his other hand he drew a pistol from his pocket and pointed it, dark, shiny and powerful at the Devil. She found herself reaching across to push what she just knew was a silencer onto the weapon. The gun fired! - and again! - and again! ...   ... and again. The Devil disappeared.

Effie woke up leaning her head towards Mr. O'Donnel. The warm, relaxed feeling remained with her and she sighed happily. Although he wasn't by her side now, she knew that that is where he belonged. Tomorrow, she wouldn't allow her natural shyness to stand in the way of achieving that goal.

*

(Birch Cottage):

Jenny Powell sat in the kitchen with her parents. No one felt particularly sleepy after the recent excitement on the shore. Bob told them that he'd seen Maggie MacPhail being driven off in a police car. It was strange, he thought, that they had taken her somewhere else. Marc had been told by his friend Arc that

Major Bolson also had been taken away, probably to Portlach – or even Aberdeen. The Major was a strange man. He could very well be guilty of something, although they might just want to talk to him about his stolen motorboat.

Upstairs, Marco lay in bed grasping the metal cube that he'd got back from Arc. He knew that the military people would never return the one they'd confiscated and that there was only one way to end the snoopers' interest in him. He had to get rid of this one as well and then make sure they knew what he'd done. He could tell Doctor Ross but give him a false location. Let him pass that on to the Air Force or whoever was involved. He was certainly not going to hand over what really didn't belong to them. Later this morning, he would ask Arc about a safe disposal place.

He had been keyed-up last evening with hopes of seeing Margaret again, but Arc said she'd gone off with her parents to visit a relative somewhere. If his mother could be persuaded to stay spend a few more days at Birch Cottage, Margaret might be back before he had to return to Newton.

*

(Secret Location on Speyside):

Some forty miles from Scarr, Lachlan Tradwell, with Davina Bolson by his side, turned the Land Rover on to a cinder track and followed the lorry's taillights towards a group of derelict buildings. As they reached the complex, a man dressed in dark coloured tweeds and carrying a shotgun stepped in front of the vehicles and signalled them to stop. After talking to the lorry driver briefly, he came towards Lachie and Davina and shone a powerful torch through the vehicle's windows. He inspected the two of them for a full minute.

'Lachie Tradwell? And the lady is -?'

'Yes. I'm Lachlan Tradwell and this is my fiancée, Davina Bolson. You must be the gentleman I talked to on the phone. Mr. MacConnachie is it? Where do you want the delivery?'

'Not here. Let me get in and I'll show you where. I've told the lorry driver to follow us. Right then, go through between those buildings, take the first turn on the left and drive up the hill. I'll tell you where to go when we get to the top. There'll be just enough room for the lorry.'

Twenty slow-and-bumpy minutes later, MacConnachie directed them to wait near a large stone-built barn. He got out of the Land Rover, unlocked a pair of heavy metal gates and signalled the lorry driver to turn into the entrance. A tall, skinny man in a warehouse coat joined MacConnachie and said something in Gaelic.

'I'll have to make sure you've brought what you promised.' MacConnachie told Tradwell. 'Eric here will test it for strength, quantity and authenticity. Do you want to wait or would you prefer me to send a cheque through the post? Yes, I know we agreed cash. So you'll be waiting then. Come inside and I'll rustle up some tea.'

*

(Bay House Hotel):

After having escaped the crowd downstairs, Archie had gone to bed right away. But he'd been kept awake for hours by the noise. Vehicles coming and going on the road outside had indicated undiminished police activity. Evidently someone at a very high level had considered this investigation more important than escalating overtime costs. At sea too, the crew of a brightly lit naval tender had been doing something close to Inch Greele; probably searching for Stackpoole's body. Lights farther offshore had showed where a large warship lay at anchor.

Archie had put his hearing aid aside and stuffed screwed up paper tissue in his ears to block out noise, but had still been startled by someone stumbling, cursing, along the corridor. Whoever it was had tried the knob and then hammered on the door before clomping away. One of the press pack most likely. He was surprised that the police had allowed Geordie to sell them drinks in large quantities in the middle of an investigation. Perhaps there was a reason for turning a blind eye.

He got up and went to the window. There were still two men with cameras sitting on the bench across the road, obviously prevented from getting closer to the explosion site by a police car blocking the approaches to Whitescar. He wasn't sure if the two watchers were pressmen or Ufologists. They appeared to be sober which would clearly suggest the latter. He saw O'Donnel, on his way back from the dunes, stopping to talk to a uniformed policeman and a woman in nurse's uniform going in the opposite direction. Of Course! The old woman, Emmeline, would need somebody to keep an eye on her. Archie switched on the kettle and dropped a teabag into the mug on his tray. A silent ambulance with a blue flashing light passed the window.

Later this morning, he would wander up Scarr Brae to revisit the woods where he used regularly to metamorphose into Tarzan fifty years ago. Of course, that depended on whether or not the police wanted to keep him here to answer questions. They had said two o'clock at the library but that the timescale was flexible. Archie made his tea, unwrapped a biscuit and yawned. Then, too weary to waste time on either, dropped one into the sink and poured the other into the waste bin.

Lying on his bed once more, he was barely aware of two sets of blue lights going past the hotel again – but in the reverse direction.

*

(West Brae, Scarr):

Sammy Gordon stepped carefully on his way down the dark hillside but he had no worries about losing his footing. He had been using this shortcut since he was a young child and knew its contours perfectly. He was, however, conscious that the official cordon below sought to exclude unauthorised sightseers and pressmen from the vicinity of Whitescar. Keeping close to the fence which marked the field boundary, he made his way towards

221

the small, nearly-level area on which he intended to set up the sturdy tripod. Tonight he had opted for a fully manual camera and a six-hundred- millimetre catadioptric lens. From this distance, on a near infinity setting, that should fill the frame with Inch Greele and the naval search activities. He swung his camera bag round to the front and felt for the light meter which was already set to the film's ISO sensitivity. A spot reading from the hull of the naval vessel should give a perfect exposure.

His great grandmother had urged him to shoot a whole film, concentrating on securing a picture-story. Anything sensational would be a valuable commodity and Meggie Munro wasn't one to miss out on a profit. She had once been Scarr correspondent for the Caledonian Bugle, forerunner of the present Northern Trumpet, but had fallen out with them over their savage editing of her copy. Now, her target was invariably the national tabloids which paid very high rates and could syndicate material worldwide. Over the last twenty five years, she'd sold only six pieces – but they'd all been very profitable ones. However, every scrap of local news was recorded for posterity in her extensive diaries.

Sammy had acquired all of his journalistic knowledge from his great grandmother but was beginning to feel the need to strike out on his own. Here he was, doing all the legwork, taking all the risks to secure shots of the most interesting events that had ever taken place in Scarr, and there she was, snoring her head off at home, expecting to take all the credit. No chance! This was *his* story. It would make his reputation – and several thousand quid at the very least. Some wreckage was being winched aboard the vessel so he hurriedly locked his camera to the tripod. And then Sammy was presented with a quandary.

The wire fence at his elbow began to emit twanging noises. He would have assumed that some farm-animal was to blame had it not been for the accompanying muffled sounds of a human voice. A short, carefully-shielded beam from his pocket torch picked out a struggling form nearby. Sammy moved closer. It was a man dressed in black. He was tied to a fence post and gagged with a broad strip of pink cloth. Damn it! Just when he was all set to get some irreplaceable shots. The captive was turning his eyes away from the light and, Sammy guessed, would not be able to identify him again. So he did what any professional news photographer of note would do – got some shots. He took five or six exposures of the work down below and then, with a police van pulling up at the bottom of the field, fitted a flashgun to the camera and shot several more frames of the captive. Two uniformed policemen were stumbling and slipping on their way up the muddy slope. Sammy pulled up the hood of his anorak then stooped and removed the captive's gag to show his face. He shot a frame of that. Finally, pointing the camera at the toiling policemen he fired the flashgun once more. Shoulder bag in one hand, tripod in the other, Sammy had melted into the wood at the top of the field before the officers reached the captive.

*

(Police Car on the A96 Southbound):

Daniel told the Detective Sergeant that he'd have a nap on the journey so he'd be refreshed and fit to question the detainees. However, his craving for alcohol was so overwhelming now that he sat, red eyed and shivering all the way, not daring to produce the half full hip-flask from his pocket. The D.S., fully aware of his passenger's stress, said nothing. After all, he'd been through the same torment many years ago. Then the car's radio interrupted them with the news of Mrs. Emmeline Borges' sudden death.

*

(Stealth Flying Disc, North Sea):

Now, there was enough pale dawn-light for Yashin to discriminate between the container ship he sought and others in its vicinity. It was important to be right on target as he was under a communications blackout. The vessel's position was almost exactly two hundred and fifty kilometres due east of the port of Grimsby as had been specified. He approached it at near zero altitude, checking, noting its outline against the eastern horizon, and then lifted over the deck to look at the arrangement of stacked cargo containers. There was no doubt whatever that this was the right vessel. They had been ready for him and were giving the correct visual identification signal. Yashin hovered and began to move closer to the ship. Near the bows, crew members were stripping away flimsy pieces of imitation cargo-containers to reveal the promised landing area. Afterwards, they would be replaced with stronger, semi-permanent imitations for the long voyage to the South Atlantic and across the Indian Ocean. Yashin edged the hovering craft ever closer, following direction signals from a man in a white coat, and let it settle gently. He had fulfilled his contract and looked forward to the voyage to China. Once clear of the North Sea and the so-called English Channel, there would be no chance of interception. He caressed the case of diamonds, Radek's aborted Scarr delivery, and realised that his future in the Orient was going to be special. In the meantime, the case would be passed off as personal luggage, of no interest to anyone but himself. He'd make certain that nobody else handled it.

'Please come this way Mr. Yashin. Captain will speak with you on bridge.'

*

(Various Locations):

This morning, some people were unhappy at the course of recent events in and around Scarr; others felt as if some benevolent entity had stacked things in their favour. However, most people remained ignorant of what had happened and many of those wouldn't have wanted to listen if offered details.

In the first category, were a United States Admiral, somewhere between the Faroes and Shetland, and a British Air Marshall at a secret base in the Outer Hebrides. Both of these important men realised by daybreak that the flying disc each had expected to take possession of, wasn't going to appear.

Radek's associate in Norway feared, rightly, for the captain's safety.

Commander Gurley's four Special Agents, (in North East Scotland, Northern Germany, South East England and on board a Fisheries Protection vessel in the northern North Sea), all waited in vain for confirmation that operation Stonewall had been a resounding success. The Commander, who, for the first time ever, had spent a long restless night in his office, was becoming resigned to the inevitable closure of his department in the next Government efficiency drive.

Emmeline Borges, (née Hill), who suffered a massive stroke late on Saturday evening, died in an ambulance on her way to hospital. Her granddaughter, Maggie MacPhail was helping police with their enquiries at the time.

Victor Bolson, (formerly Victor MacPhail), having been robbed of the diamonds with which he'd intended to abscond, was also being questioned. The likelihood of prosecution was high – though he harboured a slight hope that the Procurator Fiscal would be unable to obtain sufficient evidence to bring smuggling charges against him. The matters of deception and identity theft, however, seemed inescapable.

Victor's sister, Maggie, who hadn't yet heard of their grandmother's death, was optimistic about her chances. The presence in her boat of several fat cod that she'd caught close to Inch Greele bore out the reasons she gave for having been in the vicinity of the island on a dark night. An extra source for optimism for Maggie was that Archie McSpake would probably be in Scarr for another day and she was sure the police would let her go home soon. She wanted to see Archie before he left. She'd enjoy sharing with him what she knew of eider ducks. Maybe the sharing shouldn't stop there. For the time being, Maggie was certainly in the second category.

As the police car travelled rapidly through relatively quiet city streets, the Detective Sergeant turned a blind eye as his passenger finally cracked and drained a hip-flask. Daniel thought about the blue briefcase which, he was certain, contained uncut diamonds. That was his when he wanted it. He would contact deWet after a reasonable interval to obtain expert advice on the most profitable means of disposal. He also wanted to see Ephegenia Meade as soon as possible. There was no doubt they were on a common communications wavelength and he was sure that she would want to see him too. It would be worth going through the torture of drying-out in order to secure his future life with her.

Raymond Charles Meade, better known as Arc, was also in the optimistic category. He had been aware of the unspoken messages passing between his mother and Agent O'Donnel and was certain something would arise from that. She needed someone to lead her into a more common-sense existence. He was relieved that Slugpole had been blown-up in Bolson's motorboat.

The Moston's at the hotel were delighted with the inevitable increase in trade. There would be a lot of curious people coming in today for drinks and gossip when the police relocated their Incident Room to the library for the second time in a week. Geordie was determined to find a way to tap into the information-flow between groups of flying saucer hunters so that he could push Scarr's pre-eminence as a UFO hotspot. Maybe a letter to a magazine would start things off. However, a website would be the way forward if he could obtain advice from someone who knew how to set one up. His musing was interrupted by his wife demanding to know why he was standing there rubbing his hands together while there was work to be done.

Lord Leithland and Mr. Fu were delighted that their scheme to 'screw' the British and American military establishments looked well on the way to success. Once the stealth disc had been transported into international waters, they'd make a lot of money.

Jon Cardington, encouraged by His Lordship's good humour,

raised once more the matter of his overdue elevation to a position of rank. His Lordship would see what could be done.

Archie McSpake was quite laid back about the ill-informed speculation surrounding recent events in the village. He was interested, even now, in manipulating raw fragments into a definitive poem on his early impressions of Scarr. He had wanted to surprise and impress Fractal with it, but that hadn't worked out. The Oliphant man was the focus of her attention now. It was becoming more and more evident that she'd been using him. Oh well, he told himself, he really didn't care. On his way back from the woods later, he might call at Birch Cottage to have a chat with Marc Powell. He would try, merely as a matter of interest, to find out if the boy had any more information about the two Americans who seemed to have vanished once more – that is if the boy's mother would allow such a discussion. She'd come across as a rather blinkered and controlling person during the short time he'd observed her last night.

If Fractal *was* there, he might just give her a chance to glance at his poem – and maybe voice an opinion on it. However, what she thought was irrelevant. He would write what he wanted in the way that he wanted to. He was certain that, in the future, when people were laughing at the idiocies of Twentieth Century 'contemporary verse', someone would point out that quality hadn't really been absent – it had just gone out of fashion for a time. He still regretted his own partial surrender to current dogma.

He went downstairs for a beer, hoping the overnight guests had left some.

*

(Woodland South of Scarr):

Like Scarr itself, 'The Woods' had shrunk. The magical clearing of Archie's memory, where girls used to spread tablecloths for summer picnics and where boys built secret dens overlooking miniature mantraps, was now an overgrown wilderness little bigger than a tennis-court. A gusting southerly wind drove fine rain through the treetops and shook it in larger drops from withering leaves to drench the long grass below. Soaked to the knees, Archie turned back towards Scarr Brae, sure that he would never see this place again. He was almost overwhelmed by the sadness of time seeping away into oblivion.

Regaining the road, he pulled up the collar of his fishing jacket and set off towards where a very wet Birch Cottage looked down gloomily upon the village. A taxi emerged from the open gates, turned in his direction and, tyres hissing on the tarmac, swept past. Either she didn't see him or pretended she didn't. He lowered his hand and shoved it back in his pocket. His fingers touched the folded sheet of paper. Oh well, she wouldn't have wanted to read it. In the increasingly-heavy rain, it tore readily into tiny, clinging fragments which he fed away into the wind. The fucking sea could have it!

Bob Smith, closing the gates to the yard, stopped and waited for McSpake to approach.

'Not a nice day,' he remarked. 'I'm sure you could use a warm drink. Fancy a cup of tea? My wife's preparing supper if you're hungry. She would like to meet you properly. Our grandson has told us about your fight with the men stalking him. He and his mother are inside. I believe you know Miss Mandelbrot from Newton as well, though I'm sorry that you've just missed her.'

'Thanks for the offer Mr. Smith, but I need to get into dry clothes and do some packing. I'm going home on Tuesday. Give my good wishes to your family. That grandson of yours has great strength of character. He's a well-balanced young man who should do well in the future. Goodbye.'

Archie paused on the crest of the brae to look down upon the village for what he believed would be the last time. It was different in nearly every respect from the place he had known in his childhood. The geology seemed relatively constant, though he doubted if even that would resist man's destructiveness in the future. The ever-changing sea itself would surely outlast everything. Oh well. Perhaps his gloom would lift with a hot shower and a double whisky. Then what? Perhaps he should make a last search for the elusive Whitescar eider ducks. If there were any about, he might have an opportunity to take a few photographs from the rocks. And, if Maggie MacPhail had returned home, he could offer commiserations on the loss of her grandmother. It would be wise to phone first. He could ask her back to the hotel for afternoon tea and a face-to-face chat. He wouldn't ask about her future plans, but hoped she might share some of them with him.

The stiffening wind urged him down the brae. He found himself beginning to relax for the first time in months and realised that his mental stresses had gone with the scraps of verse.

SCARR 1942

The ridge runs roughly west to east
and, northward, stumbles down
to houses crouching on the edge,
stone gable-ends towards the sea,
- an often stormy sea-
where great, grey, plunging ships-of-war
butt through sleet-laden squalls
to secret destinations.
Up here, an ancient-woodland clings,
chamfered by scything winter blasts,
- a virtual extension of the brae itself.
There is a clearing in the wood:
sought out on clement summer days,

redolent of broom, of raspberries,
and earthiness of mouldering leaves
in damp hollows.
Beyond the wood: the bomber base.

**

CHAPTER SIXTEEN

Ten Years Later

(The Residence of A. McSpake and M. MacPhail, Norfolk):
Archie turned the Saab through the gate into the yard and looked around with his usual caution. No signs of intruders? Of course there weren't! Maggie's insistence on reduced security was entirely justified. He should have anticipated her refusal to stay in a house wired up to 'all those silly gadgets'. Luckily, she'd never guessed about the nine millimetre pistol in the concealed compartment behind the hallstand. A retired spy was entitled to a bit of extra security. However, the heavily-armoured front door had been scrapped to make way for a flimsy mock-Victorian one with flimsy mock-Victorian 'Letter Flap and Door Knocker Assembly'. He parked the car carefully in the space Maggie had marked out for him close, (but not too close), to her herb garden. He paused. Better take a look round the back before going in.

Having dropped Maggie at the railway station, Archie intended to force himself to write non-stop until she returned in the afternoon. She was off to give a lecture to a class of students on 'Health from the Hedgerows', part of a course arranged by some ass she'd known since her student days.

In the study, he brought a folder from one of the filing-cabinets and placed it beside the vacuum flask on his desk. Now then, coffee and concentration!

He had turned down the commission from Northern Trumpet Publishing to edit Meggie Munro's Diaries but hadn't yet told

Maggie. She'd be angry at losing possible income from the book and guaranteed income from the associated newspaper articles. In the meantime, it was essential that Archie push his alternative book-planning to an advanced stage before revealing his intentions. That might mollify her a little, though he could imagine objections continuing for a long time. He was often surprised at how Maggie, with her adventurous background, had become so opposed to his own birds-in-the-bush instincts. Perhaps the diamond racket had been more traumatic for her than she ever let on.

She just didn't talk about it. What Archie did know about the smuggling business came from his experiences during those extraordinary days In Scarr ten years ago, together with what O'Donnel had told him later. Maggie had also kept a strict silence about where her brother might have gone after jumping bail. Having stood surety for him, she'd had to sell Whitescar Cottage as a result of his action. However, Archie had no doubt that Maggie did know of Victor's whereabouts. The postcard from Goa that landed behind the door last Thursday morning had carried what was certainly a contrived message about sun, sea and sand, and bore the signature: 'An Old Friend!!!' After reading it he'd replaced it on the mat. It disappeared when Maggie came home and she hadn't mentioned it.

Archie opened his folder of notes about people who'd recently lived in, or been associated with, Scarr. These, rigorously edited for legal reasons, had been assembled to form a postscript to 'Meggie Munro's Diaries'. However, he now intended them to be integral to his own book. He shuffled the contents of the folder thoughtfully.

The village would require a new name of course. Then he should mix imaginary and real features with all sorts of details from similar villages in similar areas. People should have personal data treated in a similar way and be provided with aliases. With sufficient creative additions there could very well be enough material for a novel. He thought that he should incorporate some verse in it – to impress an ultra-perceptive publisher. His poetry might never be unveiled to an astounded public otherwise. An appropriate title for the book should emerge from the story. Might it be something about diamonds – or rocks? Leaning back in his chair, Archie tried to immerse himself in his fantasy village.

He didn't really need the 'People' folder because the folk in it were so deeply embedded in his memory:

Daniel O'Donnel and Effie Meade had married within months of meeting and rented a house in Portlach's upmarket west-end. Archie had met Daniel when he and Maggie went to Scarr for a holiday two summers later. By then Daniel had undergone treatment for his alcohol addiction – successfully, he'd claimed – and was hoping to move to Devon with Effie and her son. They'd gone to view a house in Plymouth and had just received news that their offer for the property had been accepted. He had seemed very optimistic at the time. And then, last month, a letter from Effie told Maggie that Daniel had died following a second liver transplant. Her son Raymond, who'd been so pleased when she remarried, had been badly affected by his stepfather's death. Raymond, or Arc as his school friends used to call him, was now a marine biologist working on a research vessel in the North Sea. He was totally teetotal. Poor Daniel! However, the ill-gotten diamonds had probably given him a few extra years and had, no doubt, paid for his stepson's education.

Effie intends to continue running her hairdressing business in Devon and has no plans to return north.

The Mostons' hotel business has done exceptionally well over the years as flying-saucer watchers and others have been drawn to Scarr. Demand for accommodation became so strong that they bought a house in Harbour Lane and offered it for let on a fortnightly basis. The return on their investment was excellent and they subsequently acquired two more cottages. Annie now runs Scarr Holiday Homes assisted by her daughter Polly.

Maggie has arranged that she and Archie will travel north later this month to spend two weeks in one of the cottages, and then fly south in January to join a Southern Ocean cruise ship. Emmeline's ashes are to go with them on a one-way journey to South Georgia.

Five years ago the Smiths sold their market garden. The Northern Trumpet's Business Supplement spoke in glowing terms of the fine reputation of Birch Cottage Organic Produce and of the development work that had been carried out by Bob and Bessie Smith who had turned a small plot of land into a viable business in the face of often inclement weather. The farmer, who had originally sold the Smiths some extra land, bought the business when they retired and demand for Birch Cottage produce increases year by year. The Smiths moved off to somewhere in the sun but if anyone knows their present location, they aren't telling.

Meggie Munro lived long enough to see her great grandson, Sammy Gordon, appointed editor of the Trumpet, then died three years ago aged ninety five.

The Powells probably never returned to Scarr. Archie hasn't met anyone who has seen them. O'Donnel told him on that last meeting eight years ago that the boy, Marco, had telephoned his stepson, Arc, to say that his parents had been reconciled and that the family was considering a permanent move to Australia.

Lord Leithland bought the repossessed Blackscar Distillery, along with the Hall and its sporting estate. Advised by Sir Jon Cardington, he is bringing prosperity back to the business. A Japanese distiller is now part-owner of the Glenscarr brand which is expected to make a considerable impact on the malt whisky market in that country – when the fifteen-year maturation period of the first distillation has been completed. His lordship freely admits that he's unlikely to see that day. He is cheered up, however, by thoughts of his heirs squabbling over the business when he has gone. A nasty surprise has been prepared for them.

The Leithland and Blackscar Estates are now amalgamated into one large sporting enterprise and the former Leithland residence has been refurbished as the Leithland Castle Luxury Hotel. The Bolson Hall name has gone – changed back to the original Blackscar House. Victor MacPhail's old study there suits his Lordship just fine as his rarely-used office. It is conveniently situated for fishing the River Scarr's Sea Pool below the old bridge and he sometimes lays aside his expensive fly-fishing gear – when he thinks nobody is watching – to trot a bunch of lobworms down the edge of the current at the turn of the tide – just as he used to do when he was a ragged schoolboy farther back than anyone would believe.

In Hollywood, Fractal P. Mandelbrot had worked on a film script with Guy Oliphant, only to find backing for the enterprise withdrawn. Their appearance on a minor television talk show, however, saw Guy being offered alternative scriptwriting opportunities. Between these and a number of Alien Abduction books, he is moderately successful. Fractal assisted in researching the first of those books, (later published under the title: 'The Abduction of Solomon Stackpoole'). She then found a profitable line in advising abduction victims. This led her, she'd told Archie in her only letter, to the more interesting occupation of counselling people suffering from various forms of sexual dysfunction. She took great pride in being 'a highly regarded sex therapist to some of the top stars in the movie industry'. Archie is sceptical about her claims. The sex therapist role, he doesn't believe. Sexual therapist? Yes – much more likely. She'd do that very well.

The Reverend Stackpoole's body parts were never found. Indeed, the rapidity with which the Navy's diving team completed their search, suggested that secret information had come to their attention, probably showing the minister to have survived the explosion and to have escaped the scene. Most people now believe that scenario. Others, especially Ufologists, declare that the man was certainly abducted by extraterrestrial entities. The 'blown to bits' hypothesis is still popular with some, however, and various sub-aqua clubs have continued to explore the sea around Inch Greele in fine weather, searching for material evidence.

Someone, at some time, leaked information about diamonds

having been lost in the wreck of the Cecil J. Rhodes. Now, visitors to Scarr can watch through high-powered binoculars from the front of the Bay House hotel, or from the hillside above, as divers emerge from the waves with small bags of tide-worn white stones which they rub against something-or-other and then discard. Inch Greele has become littered with worn quartz pebbles. Initially, scraps of window glass were used by treasure seekers to test the hardness of their finds, but Mr. Moston always pointed out that such glass is susceptible to scratching by quartz. He currently markets a special De Luxe Gemstone Tester which consists of a small plaque of synthetic sapphire set in a faux-mahogany base. This has become an indispensable piece of equipment for the serious diamond diver and is available on easy terms, subject to status. Should you just want to observe the divers but lack high-power binoculars, these may be hired from the hotel at very reasonable rates. The demand for equipment remains high and is boosted each time there is a new diamond find. News of these spreads rapidly between enthusiasts. However, no one ever reveals the name of the lucky treasure hunter.

Recently, there have been rumours in media circles about the disappearance of the Russian multi-billionaire, Yevegeny Zhirkov. Maggie, having heard of the mystery on a radio news program, and looking for more information about the man, came upon a photograph of him on an internet web-site. The shot had been snatched hurriedly as Zhirkov left a hotel in Moscow. In the foreground, out of focus and over-lit by photoflash, a powerfully-built minder is trying to fend off the photographer. The man would probably resemble the Reverend Stackpoole in a sharper image. Archie's one remaining contact at the Foreign Office believes that the minder shown is the one known by the pseudonym 'Rasputin'. Allowing for elapsed time, descriptions of the man do not rule out the possibility of his actually being *the* Solomon Stackpoole, aka the Mad Minister of Scarr. The Foreign Office, and even covert agencies, could be investigating matters at present – though ordinary citizens aren't allowed to know anything about that. Archie, however, imagines the sensation that the story will cause when he mentions it casually in the saloon bar at the Bay House Hotel.

He's brought back to present reality by the sound of the alarm clock. Damn! Just enough time to grab a bite before going to meet Maggie's train. He won't tell her yet about his plans for the novel but he *will* make one last attempt to talk her out of the Scarr visit. He has always hated the place in winter.

**

LIST OF PARTICIPANTS

BOLSON, Davina: Wife of Major Victor Bolson.

BOLSON, Victor; (formerly Victor MacPhail): owner of Bolson Hall.

BUSTER and OLLIE: Covert American military agents.

BORGES, Emmeline: Grandmother of Maggie MacPhail.

CARDINGTON, Jonathan: Wealthy retired banker.

CARDINGTON, Marietta: retired film star; wife of Jonathan.

deWET, Pieter: Shady South African diamond dealer.

FU KONG: Chinese diplomat and businessman.

GORDON, Sammy: Photographer; Great grandson of Meggie Munro.

LEITHLAND, Lord Eustace: Owner of the Leithland Estate.

MacPHAIL, Maggie: Self-employed biochemist; sister of Victor Bolson.

MANDELBROT, Fractal: Psychological Counsellor.

McSPAKE, Archibald ('Archie'): Retired spy and would-be poet.

MEADE, Ephegenia ('Effie'): Hairdresser; widow; mother of Raymond Meade.

MEADE, Raymond C. ('Arc'): schoolboy son of Effie.

MITCHELL, Albert ('Al'): Village butcher.

MITCHELL, Alison: Schoolgirl daughter of Al and Hetty.

MITCHELL, Henrietta ('Hetty'): Wife of Al.

MOSTON, Annie and Geordie: Owners of the Bay House Hotel.

MUNRO, Meggie: Veteran journalist and amateur historian.

O'DONNEL, Daniel: Undercover customs investigator.

OLIPHANT, Guy: Professional writer.

POWELL, Jenny: Mother of Marco.

POWELL, Marc ('Marco'): Schoolboy son of Jenny.

RADEK, Vladimir: Sea captain.

SMITH, Bob and Bessie: Market gardeners; Grandparents of Marco.

STACKPOOLE, Solomon (formerly Robert Stockdale): Church Minister.

TATE, Bella ('Tatey'): Part-time daily help.

TATE, William ('Wullie'): Unemployed husband of Zena.

TRADWELL, Lachlan ('Lachie'): Gillie on the Bolson Estate.

YASHIN, Leonid: Aircraft engineer and pilot.

ZHIRKOV, Yevegeny: Wealthy Russian industrialist.

READING LIST

ALEXANDER, M. (1973):   BEOWULF: a Verse Translation, (2001 Ed), Penguin Books, London.

ANSON, P. F. (1930):   Fishing Boats and Fisher Folk on the East Coast Of Scotland, (1974 Ed) J. M. Dent, London.

BATCHELOR, J. and
WALTER, J. (1988)   Handgun: Matchlock to Laser-sighted Weapon; Talos Books, David and Charles, Newton Abbot; ISBN 0-7153-9172-0

BUCHAN, P. (1992) Ed.:   Collected Poems and Short Stories. © The Executors of Peter Buchan; Gordon Wright Publishing, Edinburgh. ISBN 0-903065-77-0

CLOVER, C. (2004):   The end of the Line; Ebury Press, Random House, London. ISBN 13579108642

FISH, M. and
McCASKILL, I. (2007):   Storm Force: Britain's Wildest Weather; Great Northern Books, Ilkley. ISBN 978 1 905080 32 8

GOOD, T. (1998):   Alien Base; Century Random House U.K. Ltd., London. ISBN 0 7126 7812 3

HARLOW, G. (Ed) (1998):   The Nature of Diamonds; (© American Museum of Natural History). Pub. Cambridge Univ. Press, Cambridge, U.K. ISBN 0 521 62935 7

HEANEY, S. (1999): Beuwulf: A Translation; (2000 paperback ed.); Faber & Faber, London. ISBN 0-571-20376-0

HERBERT, I. (1972): The Diamond Diggers; Compton Press, Salisbury. ISBN – 0 85468 151 5

HUDSON, D. (1988): Highland Deer Stalking; Crowood Press, Marlborough, Wilts. ISBN – 1 85223 193 9

JACKSON, G. (1978): The British Whaling Trade; A. & C. Black, London. ISBN 0-7136-1840-X

McKIE, R. (2006): Face of Britain; Simon & Schuster, London. ISBN – 10: 0743295293

MORGAN, E. (1952): Beowulf: A Verse Translation into Modern English; Hand and Flower Press, Ashford.

PALSSON, E. and
EDWARDS, P. (1978): Orkneyinga Saga: The History of the Earls of Orkney, Translation from the Icelandic. Hogarth, London. ISBN 0-7012-0431-1

SMITH, Wilbur (1971): The Diamond Hunters, (a novel), Pan Books; (1998 Ed.). Pan MacMillan, London.

SPECIAL THANKS

In researching aspects of The Rocks Of Scarr, my stony path was frequently smoothed over by members of staff at Newton Aycliffe Library. Thank you.

After losing too many battles with an aged desktop computer, I was forced to switch to a new one mid-script. It seemed more intractable than its predecessor until help and advice from Rob Howarth of Aycliffe Computers taught me that the infernal machine didn't always have to win. Thank you.

When I asked Matador to help me self-publish The Rocks of Scarr, I found the company helpful and efficient and very particular about the quality of material they accepted. My book passed scrutiny and was added to their forward list. Subsequently, regular exchanges of information with staff at Troubador Publishing kept me informed with progress towards printing. They replied to my often-asinine queries and inane suggestions with patience and good humour. My choice of publisher has proved fortuitous. Thank you Terence and Jeremy.